CLOSER TO PARADISE

SCOTT LEIGH

Chiselbury

Published by Chiselbury Publishing, a division of Woodstock Leasor Limited, 14 Devonia Road, London N1 8JH

www.chiselbury.com

ISBN: 978-1-916556-31-7

Cover design by Indra Murugiah

Convoy element of cover photograph provided by Neil Oscarson, LtCol (Retired, US Army). Former Commander of the 1864th Transportation Company Kuwait/Iraq Operation Iraqi Freedom 2004-06

For MAD

AUTHOR'S NOTE

The events and characters in this book are wholly fictitious. Any resemblance, however remote or tenuous, to any person, alive or dead, is in the mind of the reader. All the characters have come from my imagination. Even if you think you recognise names or features, you are mistaken. The one exception has given permission to be included and everything he says and does is both imaginary and fictitious. All speech, both direct and indirect, is fictitious and any opinions or views that they may describe or portray are those of a fictitious character and do not represent the views or opinions of either the author or anybody connected with the writing of this book. The behaviour of the characters does not necessarily reflect a true view of either the British, American, Polish or Iraqi military and police. There is no intention to impugn the real reputation of regiments, units or indeed nations.

However, the background events to these five days in April 2004 did take place. The Abu Graib convoy ambush outside BIAP, the Blackwater murders in Fallujah, the demolition of the bridges on Good Friday and all the other incidents did occur at this time. Nobody that speaks in this book is real, as already mentioned, but the historical figures described in it are real. As are the place names and geographical features.

None of the military tactics, methods and weapons, both American and British, are confidential and all can be found from others' accounts of combat on the world wide web. I have tried to describe the military equipment, jargon and situations as accurately as possible. If there are small details that appear to be wrong, my apologies.

It is worth mentioning that the differences in British and American spelling are intentional and are used depending on the situation. Similarly, the slightly differing British and American acronyms and ranks are also used where appropriate in the narrative. A glossary of terms can be found at the back of the book.

My heartfelt thanks to PEC and GCM for all their initial help and encouragement and to Kathryn Hall for her diligence and enthusiastic hard work and David Roy for the important final touches.

Most importantly, my thanks to Stuart Leasor, and Chiselbury Publishing for daring to take the risk.

PROLOGUE

Christmas Eve 1993
Tekućica
12 miles SE of Doboj, Bosnia Herzegovina
0800 Local

At any other time in recent history, the village, really a small town, would have been ridiculously pretty. Pretty enough for a Disney film or a Christmas jigsaw. Nestled in the wooded hills of eastern Bosnia, it was situated on a bend in the river, and now the rising sun was creeping its golden light up the valley and onto the white houses. There had been a sprinkling of snow overnight and the sparkling meadows reflected a dazzling whiteness into his eyes. But everything had changed in the last year. He flipped the sight magnification to eight times and slowly traversed the gun. The houses on the eastern edge of the village had been heavily damaged by shell fire and a grey pall of smoke still hung in the air. Everything was still. Moving the turret right and upwards, he began to scan the meadows leading up to the edge of the pine forest. He could detect no movement and the snow was undisturbed. Yet, he had a feeling that there were eyes upon him, hidden up there in the woods.

'See anything, Sarn't Tree?' he spoke softly into the helmet mike.

'No, sir,' came the reply into his left ear from the vehicle behind him.

'Move forward then Jefferson.'

The vehicle rocked as it clunked into gear. Then the diesel engine whined and the tracks clattered as it moved down the icy road. They passed a maroon Lada stuck in a ditch and he saw the driver was still inside, sprawled across the front seat. A dark patch of blood stained the orange vinyl. The windscreen was latticed with shrapnel holes. He noticed the dead man's green-grey pallor, he had probably been dead for a few days. It was not the first body they had passed that morning. Further back they had come across the bodies of two dead women at the side of the road and they had swerved to avoid running over the corpses.

After two hundred metres, he commanded the driver to stop once again. He knew the village was on the front line. Three days ago, the Bosnian militia had folded against the might of a Croat onslaught a few miles to the east and now the remnants of its shattered volunteer battalions were pouring back. As part of the United Nations Protection Force, he had strict orders not to engage with any armed forces in the area, on either side. But this did not prevent them firing at his vehicles and he knew the Croats were bringing up heavy armour and artillery. Well armoured as it was, he did not fancy his Warrior taking a direct hit from a T62 tank or a Sagger anti-tank missile.

'Sir, sir,' it was Jefferson and he had seen something. 'There's movement on the crest. 11 o'clock from our front, up on the false ridge. Looks like infantry.' The gunner was already traversing the turret to search the area. He took out his binos and scanned the undulating fields and trees. He caught sight of a flicker of movement about two kilometres away.

Sergeant Tree's voice appeared again in his left ear. 'They've got at least one BMP up there. See the prominent boulder? Four fingers to the left you can see a cloud of exhaust.' He followed the directions and now could see the shimmer of hot gases in the cold air. They would be working along out of sight in the dead ground, possibly in the build-up to an assault on the town. And BMPs meant anti-tank missiles.

The first shell detonated between two of the burned-out houses on the eastern forward edge of the village with a whump. Black smoke billowed into the air and in the distance a few seconds later came the thump of the gun that had fired it. Two more followed in quick succession both hitting the forward edge of the houses, throwing mud, brick and timbers high in the air. There was a crackle of machine gun fire nearby from inside the village and he observed the almost lazy progress of the red tracer bullets as they flew into the tree line. Shells now began hitting the village regularly and he was reluctant to send his vehicles any further forward. It occurred to him that this was his first experience of shellfire and the realisation triggered an adrenaline surge. He felt his heart pound and his mouth was dry. For now, he would sit tight and wait.

As it happened, he didn't have to wait very long. Heading towards them on the road that followed the snaking river up to the village was a Land Rover being driven at speed. Although it was painted white, it was so covered in dirt and mud that it appeared dark against the snow. This must be what they were waiting for. His orders were to escort it back to the British base at Gornji Vakuf.

'Fuck me, here they come,' he murmured to himself and then over the radio 'friendly forces approaching in front, move forward Jefferson.' He sank back into his turret and closed the hatch and drove straight into the centre of the village amongst the crashing shells. The shelling had forced a few of the remaining population to take their chances and evacuate. Two old babushkas appeared on the road in front of his vehicle, doing an almost comical waddle as they tried to run. Another darted out of a door. She had two small children, each holding a hand. He could see the terror in their eyes. As they approached the front of the vehicle, the woman screamed accusingly at it. He couldn't hear her but he knew what she was shouting. 'Why do you always do nothing to protect us?'

He heard Sergeant Tree's urgent voice in his headphones. 'Three BMPs moving down the hill.' He looked through the gun sight and saw that the Croats were making a frontal assault. Each of the armoured vehicles had about a dozen men sitting on the top and as they bounced down the slope, they raked the village with machine gun fire.

Two more women made a dash for safety as a mortar round landed nearby and both fell. He looked dumbfounded at the bodies. A numbness was creeping into his whole being. He felt a morbid fascination and he traversed the gun to check for signs of life. Both were still. He flicked to magnification and recoiled in horror at the sight of the gaping hole in a skull. Another first. Witnessing the death of a human.

'Reckon they are both dead Sir' said the gunner quietly. It brought him back from his trance and he forced himself to concentrate on what was going on around him.

'Do not engage, I say again, do not engage.' It was Sergeant Tree in his ear again. He had probably seen the gun traversing. He squinted through his optics as the Warrior moved down the main street. There was a small square with a mosque on one side and what, in happier times, would have been cafés and shops on the other. It was now ostensibly deserted although he knew there would be defenders in the houses and in the roughly dug trenches out in front.

'Pull up in the shelter of that building on the left, Jefferson.' He commanded. The Warrior manoeuvred on its tracks and shuffled next to a wall. He checked rearwards and Sergeant Tree had pulled in behind. A shell landed close by and he heard the spatter of hot shrapnel on the outside of the armoured hull. He could still see the fields where the attack was unfolding but he had orders to wait in the town centre until he had met up with his targets. He became aware that his eyelid was twitching. He wondered if it was noticeable.

'Here are the Sneaky Beakies now, sir.' He saw the Land Rover skid round a corner on two flat tyres. It had been peppered by fire and one of the side windows had been shattered. It screeched to a halt behind his vehicle and he opened the hatch. Shouting at the men over the din of his engines and the crash of the shells was futile, so he gesticulated that they should get in the back of his Warrior. He dipped back down into the turret and looked behind to see the heavy armoured door swing open.

The first man in was handcuffed with cable ties and had a black hessian hood over his head. He was bundled in unceremoniously by a large soldier wearing an arctic camouflage para smock and a mottled green Arab headdress that covered everything except his eyes. He climbed in after the prisoner and dragged him by the scruff of his jacket to the front of the compartment and bellowed 'ne mrdaj'. The soldier moved back towards the rear door and began heaving in bergens and weapons. White paint dappled rifles, ammunition, a machine gun and what looked like a Milan anti-tank launcher and two missiles were all loaded in. The equipment was followed by three further soldiers, all in winter camouflage, none of it British Army issue.

'All in?' he shouted at the men.

'This the taxi for Hereford train station?' The man wore a black beanie woollen hat and had an impressive walrus moustache. Outside, the final man heaved a jerrycan onto the windowsill of the Land Rover and began sloshing fuel on to the passenger seat. He chucked the jerrycan in through the window and pulled the pin from a grenade, lobbed it through after it and gave him a thumbs up as he jumped into the Warrior and closed the rear door.

'Hurry up Cookie. Nobody's interested in your radio anyway, the fucking thing doesn't work.'

'SOPs, John...' The rest was muffled by the exploding grenade.

As he watched this all unfold, their calm demeanour had a settling effect. Who would wear a beanie in an artillery barrage? Of course, he had heard the stories but this was his first encounter. It was turning out to be a day of firsts.

<Zero tango three zero?>

<Zero send over>
<Tango three zero, candy stripe complete. Returning to base>
<Roger. Out>

'Jefferson, do a neutral and let's go back home.' The driver clunked the vehicle into gear and using one track to go forward and the other to reverse, spun the vehicle on its axis. The turret remained facing forward as the hull spun round under it, knocking aside the burning Land Rover. He was now looking out over the back decks as the they began to drive out the way they had come. He was glad to be moving out of the battle. He watched the Croat attack falter and the BMPs carrying the infantry turned around and drove up the hill, leaving behind half a dozen dead bodies in the snow. Three soldiers had been left behind and were now running after the lumbering vehicles. One by one, they were picked off by the defenders and lay still where they fell in the snow.

'Get a brew on then, O'Hanlon,' he said to the gunner, trying to mimic the iciness of his passengers.

'Already have, sir,' came the reply.

He looked below his feet at the troop compartment and saw that the large soldier had removed his headscarf. He had piercing blue eyes and a large ginger beard. He was staring intently at him, a quizzical not unamused look on his face.

'You chaps got mugs?'

'Youse what?' said Ginger Beard in a broad Scottish brogue.

'Mugs. Black plastic mugs. For tea. Never mind. Use mine.' He passed his mug of strong white tea down.

'Scouse,' said Ginger Beard. 'The baby cavalry Rupert has got us a crap hat brew. How the other half live, eh?' He stared open eyed at his companion, one white eyebrow slightly raised. Scouse gave a little 'don't ask me' shrug.

'So, we've been tasked to take you back to base with us. Should be about an hour and a half.'

'Change of plan. We'll let you know when you can drop us off' said Scouse.

'Sorry, brigade want me to take...'

'Listen Rupert, not to be too rude but we'll tell you when you can drop us off.' The finality of that sentence made him change the subject.

'Who's the prisoner?'

'Nobody you would know. Can I stick my swede out of this tank and see where we are going?'

'It's not really a tank but, sure, squeeze up here next to me.'

'Ginge, you got a smoke?'

'Aye.'

'Colour?'

'Orange.'

'Got the TacBe?' Ginge passed him a small handheld radio.

Scouse clambered up into the turret next to the gunner. He then turned and said 'how do you open this hatch?'

'Um, just pull the lever there.'

'Ta,' He opened the hatch and stuck his head out. He flicked a switch on the radio and spoke into it. He placed it next to his ear to hear the response. Then he said 'See that field up on the right? Just pull in there for us will you?'

He ordered Jefferson to pull into the side. Once the vehicle had stopped, the soldiers in the back opened the rear door and began off-loading their equipment. Finally, they pulled the prisoner out and pushed him to his knees. He had a sudden fear they were going to execute the prisoner in front of him. But Ginge walked a few metres into the field and popped an orange smoke grenade.

He heard the distant thump of a Chinook, its twin rotors unmistakable. It came in low over the tree line and landed heavily in the meadow. The orange smoke billowed and swirled.

'Thanks for the ride, Boss,' shouted Scouse.

'Don't mention it,' he shouted back, pleased not to have been called Rupert. Actually, he was chuffed to have been called 'Boss'.

The rear door of the chopper was already down and two more troops ran out at a crouch, pulled the prisoner to his feet and ran him into the back of the aircraft. He decided to climb out of his turret, more out of curiosity than anything else. As they loaded the equipment into the back of the Chinook, he felt almost envious.

He walked up to Scouse. 'Good luck with whatever it is you are up to.'

'Cheers, Boss.'

'Where are you off to then?'

'Need to know, Boss. If you need to ask, you don't need to know. If you would like to not need to ask, do Selection. If you are good enough, we're looking for Ruperts like you. Ginge doesn't know one end of a tank from the other. Trouble is, you are probably not good enough. Ta for the brew and merry fucking Christmas. By the way, you did pretty well today, Boss but you might want to, you know...' and his finger made a little circle in front of his eyes. With that, he turned on his heel and ambled into the back of the helicopter. The plane took off even before the back door closed and disappeared over the tree line the way it had come in an icy blast of snow.

He climbed back on to the turret. 'O'Hanlon, is there anything wrong with my face?'

'No sir.'

'Are my eyes ok? Can you see them twitching?'

'No sir.'

'Weird' he said as he climbed back into the Warrior.

1

Today was meant to be a good day. It was her daughter's fourth birthday and, in an odd reversal of tradition, she had received a homemade card in the post a few days back which was now tucked safely into the back pocket of her sand-coloured cargo trousers. She hoped it would bring her luck for this flight and this mission. She had been asked by the deputy Chief of Defence Intelligence to go down to the Divisional Temporary Detention facility at Shaibah, near the port of Basra, and had hitched the lift on the RAF Puma helicopter that was now coming in to land.

The Puma touched ground and the rotors began their wind down. The loadmaster kept everybody back until they came to a complete stop before allowing the passengers to jump off one at a time. She undid the safety harness that kept her secure in the red webbing seats and stood up, shuffled to the open door and, rather inelegantly, sat down and slid out of the helicopter on her bum. An RAF ground crew was marshalling the dozen or so passengers forward and away from the aircraft, so that the pilots could see them and there was no danger from the rear rotor. All standard stuff she had done dozens of times before.

An RAF corporal was there to greet her.

'Morning, ma'am... If you would like to follow me.'

She got into the Land Rover and was driven a short hop to a separate walled compound overlooked by guard towers. The corporal drove the Rover into the main vehicular air lock and out again the other side. In front of her was another internal chain link fence behind which was a row of low, shabby, flat-roofed single-storey brick buildings that was home to the ISG Headquarters. She entered the left-hand building, which was the Operations and Reception Area.

'Morning, Barbara,' said a senior NCO manning the front desk.

'Morning, Mel. All well? See what I did there?' She smiled.

'As well as could be, thank you, and, er, yes, I did, ma'am. Presumably you're here to see the JFIT? I'll let them know you're here.'

Barbara waited whilst Mel went to find her contact at the Joint Forward Interrogation Team. A few minutes later, a dapper lieutenant in immaculately ironed desert combats arrived and shook her by the hand.

'You must be Ms Bishop?' He smiled broadly and then said, 'Follow me,' without introducing himself.

He led her outside again and over to a new compound, also behind a chain link fence. They then went through a door marked *OC Joint Forward Interrogation Team.*

A major was behind a desk that was nothing more than a wooden trestle table on which sat two telephones, a computer, and a large stack of files. 'What have we got?' she asked the man she recognised as the Intelligence Corps OC.

'Hello, Barbara. Morning. Interesting one for you today. Thank you for coming down. Before we get down to the details, can I get you something? Coffee? Tea?'

'No, thank you, Will. Well, actually, a bottle of water would be nice. Can you give me an update?'

The major pushed a tan-coloured file towards her. 'The transcript is in there. But basically, we picked him up on the northern limit of our TAOR two days ago. The patrol was pretty clear that he wanted to be brought in and, indeed, when he was, he claimed he could help us.'

'Help us how?' asked Barbara.

'Well, I think we should go and ask him. He's in Interrogation Room 4.' The major stood up and Barbara followed him out of the office to another compound also behind its own security fencing. They entered one of the flat-roofed buildings.

The detainee was sitting at another wooden trestle table and an RMP stood in a corner. The room was totally bare other than the table and a pair of plastic stackable chairs. Barbara and the major sat down and she began reading the transcripts. The detainee started to talk but she held up her hand to silence him without taking her eyes off the papers. After a few minutes she looked up and smiled broadly. She saw a smallish man, about mid-thirties in age. He was dressed typically for an Iraqi, with scruffy, light brown trousers and a stained white shirt. He had a large moustache and a few days' worth of heavy stubble. That detail told her immediately that he was not strict Shia Muslim. In an early sign of what was to come, already some barbers had been threatened for shaving their customers.

'So, you are working for the Iranians but you want to work for us?'

'Yes. I have good contacts. I give you everything. You give me passport and asylum. Me and my family.'

'And if we do that, how will you help us? You can't help us from a house in Croydon now, can you?'

'I work for you six months. Then passport and asylum.'

'Well, I can't make that decision. But this is what I can do for you. I can pay you money for information and if, and only if, you are proving useful, we can maybe think about the asylum.'

'How much money?'

'Oh, that depends on the quality of what you tell us.'

'I am an honourable man. I will tell you everything. I tell you about Iranians' special military in Iraq.'

'We will get onto all that in a moment. We can give you a hundred US dollars and a mobile sim card. The sim has one pre-programmed number. You use that to call us and only us. Tell us something useful and we might give you another hundred dollars.'

'If they catch me, they kill everyone.'

'Well... don't get caught.' Barbara smiled broadly again. 'Tell me, why do you want to do this. Apart from getting out of here?'

'The Iranians killed my brother in the war. He is burning to death in a tank.'

'The war with Iran? I'm sorry to hear that and I am sorry for your loss. If you can get us some good information, we will maybe rehouse your family.'

'I want to go to US.'

'Oh, I'm sorry, you are talking to the wrong people, I'm afraid. But stick with us. We know the Americans very well and we can probably get you over there. If what you tell us is good. Now, let me see...you will be known to us as Clocktower. You know that word?'

The man repeated: 'Clocktower...yes, yes. Tower with clocks, no?'

'Exactly. Now, that is what we will call you and that is what you will use when you call us. Understand so far?'

'Yes, yes. Me Mr Clocktower. I get you very good information about Iranians.'

'Just to be absolutely clear on this, you don't actually use the name Clocktower. We never speak about who you are or your code-name in public, only on the phone that we will give to you.' She paused and looked him in the eyes to make sure he understood. 'Now, let's go through your details. Let's start with your name, address, and date of birth, shall we, and take it from there?'

. . .

THE FIRST DEBRIEFING of Clocktower took about an hour before Barbara called a break. The man stayed in the room and was brought some water and some tea.

Barbara left the room and went back to the JFIT block. 'I want to send a flash secret message back to London please, Staff.'

'Certainly, ma'am. The signallers are in the HQ building across the way.'

Barbara stepped outside into the heat of the day, crossed the road and went into the prefabricated building using her pass. She made her way to the signals section.

'I'd like to send something to London please. "Secret. UK Eyes Only".'

She composed a message to her superiors at Vauxhall Cross and copied in the top analyst at DIS. She had known Eric Scott-Douglas for a number of years. There was nobody who knew more about the tribal, religious and sectarian factions of Iraq. He received and interpreted all the various strands of intelligence that were gathered and his insights into the ever-changing alliances and feuds between the tribal and clan factions was legendary. Even the Americans asked his opinion. He had currently proposed that the Iranians were actively fomenting trouble against the Allies. He was certain that the Iranian Quds brigade were infiltrating into Iraq, providing both lethal military technology and funding for the insurgency. If Clocktower was to be believed, he might provide eyes and ears right at the heart of the Shi'ite South.

2

Maundy Thursday, 8 April 2004
Somewhere between Convoy Support Centre Scania and Logistics
Support Area Bushmaster South of Baghdad
1130 Local

Some lessons get ingrained quickly and permanently and one of those is to check the eyepieces of your binoculars. An old trick played on new officers in a tank regiment was to smear the rims with oily grease from the rear exhausts of a Challenger tank. This would leave two black rings around the eyes resembling a panda, until someone had the heart to inform the young officer. This could take several days if the crew and the troop were particularly brutal. But it only happened to you once.

A quick glance confirmed to him that this particular type of juvenile jape wasn't practised in the Special Air Service. Not that they were averse to elaborate and well-planned jokes, especially on officers. Just not that one yet, and anyway, never on Ops. Special Forces didn't recruit too many tank officers and certainly didn't come across many tanks. It was an alien world to them – big, noisy, dirty, unreliable beasts best left to the cavalry who, if they were being candid, only just qualified as soldiers and were officered by entitled chinless toffs who wore red trousers and lived in large houses with suits of armour on the wall. "Crap Hats" in their vernacular. If you ain't airborne, you ain't...yadda yadda.

'Two types of people in this world, Boss.'

'Here we go...'

'Soldiers and civvies.'

'And I'm...?'

'Cav. So essentially you're a civvy.'

He scanned the road 450 metres to the front through the heat haze. It was a vista he was well used to. There had been little traffic about and to the east it rose on pillars above the marshy ground. He observed the dust plume that had first caught his attention and then the battered red Hilux as it made its way down the raised section of the blacktop. Two in the cab and five in the back. No uniforms visible and he couldn't see any weapons, but that number of young men in one vehicle was noteworthy. Once the vehicle had passed, a quick SITREP would be sent to the Signals Section – the Scaleybacks.

Date/time/location/description/activity. Nothing too verbose.

He put the binos down, slumped below the berm, and reached for his water bottle and took a swig. The purification tabs made it taste like warm, orange-flavoured swimming pool water. But he was fine with that as the last thing you needed was heat exhaustion. Everyone carried sachets of rehydrating powders, normally sold to anxious mothers of young children with the shits. Them and plenty of water were the best defence against heat exhaustion.

He replaced his water bottle and shimmied up to have another look. Across the scrubland to his front, about half a click away, was the main road between Najaf to the west and Diwaniyah to the east. It was lined by a row of double-storey houses, each in a compound accessed through iron gates. A scabrous hound with a big dose of mange caught his eye as it got up from its place in the shade of a tree and wandered over to the side of the road. It cocked its leg and then, with the immediate relief, hunched into a squat and carefully coiled a thixotropic walnut whip of faeces onto the dust. Pleased with itself, it kicked a few times with its hind legs before returning to its sleep in the shade. He'd watched the hound perform this same ritual every day for nearly a week.

'Boss…' He dipped his head below the parapet and looked around to see the swarthy, bearded face of Stan, the patrol medic. The sun had turned him a dark shade of brown.

'What?'

'What does "capricious" mean?'

'Whimsical'

'Boss…'

'Yes?'

'What does whimsical mean?'

Stan was reading a John Le Carre novel. The radio was at his feet and a headphone covered one ear. His rifle, painted a dappled brownish yellow, was cradled in one arm.

'It means that you can suddenly change your mind for no apparent reason.'

'Would that make the OC capricious? He's always fucking changing his mind.'

'Um…he probably has good reasons but just hasn't shared them with you.'

'Doesn't share them with anybody, as far as I can see.'

'Hold on a sec…' The distant slamming of a door prompted him to resume his vigil away to his front.

The Hilux was coming back the other way, this time empty of its passengers. He noted the offside door was white. The driver stopped. He shouted at the nearest house – a breeze block square two-storey building with a flat roof built around a small compound. It had a green iron gate which now opened, and a second man came out.

The driver got out of his vehicle and, of course, trod in the dog turd. He didn't notice. The Boss let out a silent chuckle, not taking his eyes from the binos.

There was an animated conversation between the two Iraqis with much arm waving, which, to an uninformed western observer, may have appeared confrontational but was just the way they communicated in this part of the world. The other man returned through the iron gate and then came out again. The driver passed him a plastic shopping bag, which was evidently heavy. As he handed it over, the other man instinctively put his hand on the underside. He lit a cigarette and got in the car. Then he immediately got out again and began vigorously wiping his foot in the dust before once again getting in and driving off.

'Oh dear, unlucky, mate.' Staff Sergeant John Barnes, a veteran with nearly twenty years in the armed forces, most of it with the SAS, slid in silently beside him, also observing through binoculars. His walrus moustache twitched as he scanned to his front and mumbled to himself, 'Those pointy heads are fucking up to something.'

He concentrated on the two Iraqis for a while before lowering his binos. 'But it's not whatsisface.'

'Maybe it's a bag of WMDs then,' said the Boss.

'Stan...' the troop sergeant hissed back down the small bluff, 'get everybody stood-to.'

'Roger that, John,' Stan whispered back.

The three others of the five-man patrol were ready to move anyway but they all made sure their bergens were packed to go and that loose kit was stowed away. A quick double tug on the comms wire signalled to the men in the backstop to come in from the rear of the patrol base bringing with them the Minimi machine gun. The two Australian-issue ponchos that had been rigged up to provide some shade, were the only kit left out. If required, they could be stowed in a matter of seconds, or, if absolutely necessary, left behind.

'Right...' The troop sergeant had raised his rifle and was observing through his optical sights. 'What the fuck are these muppets up to?'

The road remained empty, the black tar shimmering in the heat. On the slight summit of the raised section there was the apparition of a line of silver water – a commonplace mirage. Through the binos, the heat haze distorted everything. He scanned eastwards up the road as it climbed on concrete pillars of the overpass. Below was the marshy ground and an oily polluted canal.

The Boss observed a fly land on his troop sergeant's moustache to glean any moisture that might be there. The sergeant blew a quick jet out of the side of his mouth and the fly circled around and landed again. Another twitch of the moustache and it went airborne, circled round and then landed again.

'For fuck's sake, will you fuck off, you twat.' The staff sergeant, without removing the sights from his eyes, reached down into a pouch and extracted a small plastic bottle of mosquito repellent. Finally, he put the weapon down, squirted some repellent onto his fingers and wiped his face. The fly flew off for easier meat.

'Boss, you got the cheat sheet?'

The Boss reached into the map pocket of his desert cams and pulled out his notebook. Wedged into the hard plastic cover were a couple of folded A4-sized photos.

'He definitely isn't the six of diamonds,' said the Boss as he scanned the photos. 'Not sure he's any of them, actually.'

'Give us a butchers,' said the troop sergeant, reaching out his hand whilst still looking through his binos. 'Definitely not Sabawi.'

'Definitely up to no good,' said the Boss.

'Definitely,' agreed the troop sergeant.

'Moving WMDs? It's not exactly the specialist mobile weapons platform they were talking about in the briefings we were given,' said the Boss.

'Dunno, Boss, but unlikely, I agree. Personally, these fucking WMDs would appear to be wholly in the imagination of that clown in Downing Street.'

'Agree. There aren't any, are there?' the Boss observed.

'If there were any to start with, they would have been shifted out by now. Probably moved out to Syria before the start of ground ops last year.'

'So you think Saddam would have got rid of them and not told the Yanks? Why would he do that?'

'Maybe he was bluffing all along. What a total fuck up. Get your country destroyed because you can't admit to not having something.'

'To be fair, he did deny it all along,' said the Boss. 'But I agree, the place is rapidly imploding now that his authority's gone.'

'Civil war is always the worst. Saw that in Bosnia. Fucking brutal.'

'It's hard now to think of this place as the original "Garden of Eden,"' said the Boss. 'Cradle of Civilisation. God's Paradise on Earth.'

'Yeah, it's a complete shithole now. The only things that have done well are the snakes,' said Barnes, without taking his eyes from the binos. 'There aren't even any apple trees.'

'And the flies.'

He moved back out of sight of the road where some of the others were laid up. Though out of sight, they was not totally out of the sun and the two cam ponchos did little to dissipate the heat.

'Ron, take over from John in half an hour, will you?' the Boss said to Ron 'Rocket' Stevenson, one of the men lying in the shade.

'Sure. He up there now?' Ron replied, picking up his rifle and his belt kit. 'I'll go and keep him company. Not as if I'm doing anything here that can't wait.'

The Boss took out his poncho and laid it at his feet, and then reached into one of his pouches and pulled out his rifle cleaning kit. He stripped down his rifle and gave it a dry clean. In these conditions, with the fine grit of the desert, any oil would attract the dust and possibly cause a stoppage. And stoppages could mean death, either to him or one of his closely-knit patrol.

In the heat under the poncho, he began to sweat again and the flies that had plagued them since the start of the OP began to buzz around his face. A squirt of mosquito repellent kept them at bay but their constant buzzing tested his patience. He glared at the bottle on which the Ministry of Defence, or whoever decides these things, had printed a skull and crossbones. He reassembled his rifle and silently operated the cocking handle before slotting in the magazine. He wondered if he could be arsed to read but instead opted to close his eyes.

'It's about this time you'd normally be having boiled egg and soldiers in the mess, isn't it, Boss?'

'Stan, can you just...'

'Well, I was just wondering if you would like me to rustle you up a couple? White or brown bread? I can cut the bread into a nice troop of Hussars, should you want. You must be missing your orderly.'

It was an old rolling joke.

'Thank you, Stan. Can you make sure the eggs are brown? I can't be doing with white eggs. So...so "Sergeants' Mess".'

'Pack up tomorrow and fuck off home, do you think, Boss?' asked Stan, the joke being rehoused for another time.

'Should get the nod to return to Basra. Probably leave at last light tomorrow,' the Boss confirmed, 'unless something kicks off. But there's not much sign of that.'

The troop sergeant slid back down the gully and told the patrol to stand down. As the sun went down, people rummaged in their bergens and pulled out tins of rations or boil-in-the-bag meals. These they ate cold and soundlessly with wooden spoons.

'Barnie?' Ron murmured.

'What?' replied the staff sergeant.

'I'm going to crimp one out, if that's ok.'

'This time, do you mind moving away more than three fucking feet from the rest of us?'

Rocket Ron Stevenson, was so called because he was the erstwhile under 18 Welsh cross-country champion from Abergavenny, Monmouthshire. Tall and skinny, he'd found that his natural ability at running had provided him respite from an unremittingly depressing childhood. His father had been unemployed since before his birth and took out his frustrations on his mother and her children. Running for the school had bought him a small sense of achievement and allowed him to travel around Wales for the races. Whilst on one such trip he found himself outside the Army Recruitment Office in Aberystwyth. In the window was a recruitment poster depicting runners and he signed up on the spot. He now moved about five metres from the rest of them behind a rocky outcrop that served as the patrol latrine area, dropped his combat trousers to his knees and, much like the dog, squatted down. All evidence of the activity was quickly scooped into a black bag and also stowed. It was a fundamental principle of manning an OP that nothing was left behind. This included human waste. Each one of them was carrying around six days' worth of black bags.

At that point, the thunderous sound of a jet engine shattered the still evening. Everybody grabbed their weapon and kit whilst simultaneously looking up, fearing the worst. The overly-large tail fin was a welcome sight.

'Tornado,' the staff sergeant said, scanning the sky. 'Crab Air, relax, everyone.'

'Here comes his mate.' A second thunderous boom washed over the patrol. The two planes, fast and low, were soon out of sight.

The Americans didn't fly Tornados, but had it been a US plane, there would have been a panicked struggle to get to the orange air marker panels and a Union Jack or Stars and Stripes, which would have been laid out on the ground. Not that it made much difference to some of the US pilots. In the first Gulf War, a patrol had been engaged by two Air National Guard F16s and were lucky to survive. Lucky as in the pilots clearly couldn't hit a cow's arse with a banjo. The sergeants' mess at Hereford still had the maverick missile tail fin mounted on a plinth lurking somewhere.

'Boss...'

'Yes, Stan?'

'Why are Yank fighter pilots called Rocky and Maverick when ours are called Julian and Sebastian?'

'I don't think their mothers actually christened them Maverick, Stan. And Julian and Sebastian are probably called Wazzer or Knobber in the mess. They just don't stencil it on the side of their planes.'

'Must be Wednesday, Boss.'

'Fuck knows, Stan. Is it?'

'Must be...' said the staff sergeant. 'Crab Air only fly on Wednesday's to avoid ruining both weekends.'

'Must be doing overtime. It's Thursday,' said Harry Wolfson. Known as "The Wolf" or "Wolfie", he was officially the patrol demolitions expert, but there had been little call for his skills on this current operation. Another orphan from society, he had found himself in front of a magistrate for arson after burning down his school's sports pavilion and had been offered the choice between borstal and the army. At the time, the right choice wasn't obvious, but from the first day of basic training, he knew he would fit in. Like Ron, he had at last found a family.

'Those cunts will be poolside in a five-star hotel in Kuwait with a couple of birds and a beer on the go within the hour.'

'A Campari and a couple of blokes more like.'

The Boss slipped down to where he'd left his bergen, thinking it'd be a nice change not to have meatballs and biscuits AB. AB which was printed on the packet officially signified Alternative to Bread in the official menu but they were known to the boys as biscuits Anal Blockage. He'd thrown away half his daily rations, the soups and sugar and other sundry items, because he hadn't the space to carry it. At this stage in a patrol, food became a slight obsession, especially when not much was going on. Nevertheless, he needed to get the calories and vitamins inside him on a daily basis if he was to operate at maximum efficiency. He opened the packet, poured in the water, and ate the gloop with his wooden spoon. He then field stripped his weapon again, making sure he emptied out his magazines, wiped down the rounds and then reloaded. He carefully put a red tracer round in third from last, one up the spout, and the safety on. *Don't want the dead man's click,* he thought to himself.

He then got out his bivvy bag, undid his webbing to use as a pillow, and tried to go to sleep. Though exhausted, he found sleep difficult and when it did come, it was often accompanied by nightmares. He stared at the stars and the usual doubts and anxieties came into his head. He had begun to question whether he could continue. Maybe it was best to find a nice job in civvy street and call it a day.

· · ·

AFTER LAST LIGHT, the OP set up the image intensifier night telescope.

The patrol prepared to stag on all through the night, two on, three off. It was a still, cool, cloudless evening, ideal for observation as the ambient light of the emerging stars enabled the night vision optics to work at their best. Soon after last light, the iron door to the house opened with a grinding squeak that carried over the still night to the OP. The sudden surge of light flared the image intensifier. Three men appeared, all smoking, the tips of their cigarettes also flaring the sights, leaving a little green retinal shadow. One of the men carried a shovel and the other two carried what appeared to be heavy cylindrical objects.

Stan and Wolf were watching.

'Wolf...what are they dicking about doing?'

'Either they're going for a crap or this, Stanley, is an IED party. They're going to mine the road, if you ask me. Get on the blower back to Squadron. Tell them it looks like they're putting out a command wire. Put out an initial warning. Wake Barnie and the Boss.'

Wolf continued watching. The man with a shovel was carefully digging a small pit in the dirt just to the side of the road in front of a wall, approximately 100 metres down from the house towards the raised section. He could make out the two objects were artillery shells, probably Soviet 122mm D-30 rounds. The man flicked his cigarette onto the road and ground it out with his heel. Once he had buried the artillery shells, he took a fist-sized white rock from his pocket and left it by the IED.

The IED would be simple enough. The two rounds would be detonated by a big lump of Semtex tamped into where the nose fuse would normally be and that, in turn, would be detonated by a command wire. The wall would channel the blast forward towards the road. Wolf watched as the shells were camouflaged. After a while, he saw the men walk backwards to the house with a reel of wire. They disappeared inside and re-emerged ten minutes later with palm leaves. They then proceeded to cover the wire with dust and to brush over their own footsteps. The firer would probably be on the roof of the compound.

Barnes had joined Stan on the lip of the OP.

'Stan, get on the blower to the lads. Get the wagons to the back-stop position and get the rest of the troop up here before first light, which gives them about three hours. Everyone else stood-to. Where's the Boss?'

'He's retired to the Ruperts' mess for a little shut eye,' said Stan.

'OK, leave him be for the moment. He needs his sleep otherwise he starts getting weird and wonderful ideas.'

The Iraqi bomb-laying team wandered back to the house and the soldiers could just make out their chatter in the still of the night. The sights flared again as they opened the door back into the house and then there was silence.

It seemed to the Boss he had only just managed to get to sleep when he was shaken awake by a series of distant, large detonations. He opened one eye and instinctively reached for his weapon. He must have been asleep for at least two hours as it was passed last light and there was a damp chill in the air.

'Rocket, what was that?'

'Fuck knows, Boss, but that was the third. You were gonking through the first two.'

'Airstrike?'

'Maybe. But I've heard a few airstrikes in my time and that was different. Maybe an IED.'

'No small arms fire. Maybe it was a bomb factory going up? '

'Fucking hope so. Do love an own goal, me.'

'Where's John?'

'On stag by the berm. By the sounds of it, there's been some tooling around up by the bridge. Barnie reckons they're going to assemble around here and then go out for a punch up with the Yanks on Tampa.'

The Boss donned his webbing, grabbed his rifle, and slid up to the berm just as Stan was wriggling down to get him.

'Morning, Boss,' said his troop sergeant. 'Enjoy your lie in?'

'What were those explosions?'

'Not sure, Boss. But it's been like bastard Piccadilly Circus here. They've been busy blocking the road.' He added that they'd seen the Iraqis laying an IED down the road.

He and the Boss scanned the road up to the raised section. A small whirlwind was whipping up sand and litter in a spiral as it moved along. The tarmac was covered in debris and the centre rail had been dismantled and placed in the road. There were a few lorry tyres and some big concrete blocks.

Just then, a flash below the horizon lit up the whole scene. Some childhood memory made him count the seconds until the sound of the blast washed over him.

'That was about twenty miles away to the east by my reckoning.'

'That would be on or near the Iraqi Expressway.'

'Tampa?'

'Yeah, on the map it's running about 35 clicks due east of here.'

'They're doing the bridges,' said the staff sergeant. He slipped down the berm and wriggled back to the radio where he found Corporal Cooke, the patrol signaller. Cooke didn't like people tooling with his equipment and so spent most of his time when not sleeping keeping a listening watch.

'Cookie, tell Zero we think they might have blown some of the bridges on Tampa in order to channel a convoy ambush into a killing zone on or near our location.'

'Wilco, John.'

'If that's the case,' Barnie said, more to himself than the Boss, 'then this is probably the backstop. Or maybe some sort of cut off.'

'Or maybe, they've ambushed a convoy on Tampa and this is the escape route out. All this shit is to slow the pursuit as they scoot.'

'Ginge, can you get up there and take over? Boss, let's have a butcher's at the map.'

They both crawled into a tiny, sheltered position between two over-hanging rocks and rigged up a small makeshift tent with an Aussie Poncho no more than two feet off the ground at the highest point. Once inside, they put on headtorches and turned on the red beams.

'We're here...' said the Boss, pointing to the map with a stalk of grass.

Pointing at the map with a finger was considered the crappiest of crap hat habits and, on SAS selection, would earn you a fine of a tenner into the Regimental Benevolence Fund.

'And over here is MSR Tampa. Which makes this high ground here and the built-up area here, the killing zones.'

'The trouble is,' said Barnie, 'we can't really get the vehicles to the killing zone, even if we wanted to, which we probably fucking don't, without going all the way around to the south.'

'So, what do you suggest?'

'Boss, you are the fucking Rupert. What do you suggest?'

'I suggest we stay here and if the backstop gets triggered, we hose them down with the GPMGs before fucking off in the pinkies.'

'Yeah...I like the way you're thinking.'

During the night, a two-man working party went back to the vehicle laager to get more link ammunition for the machine guns, some 40mm grenades for the M203s and several boxes of rifle ammunition.

At 0410, the Boss heard a whisper. The three soldiers of the backstop were coming up to the OP position and triggering the password. He put the binos back into his combat jacket and slipped down to meet them. They would set up an immediate counter ambush, tightly organised around the OP position.

The heavier weapons had been dismounted from the vehicles and they now had considerable fire power, including two general-purpose machine guns and the Minimi. On the first night, as they had set up the OP, the patrol had positioned two Claymore mines to their front in case there was an emergency withdrawal. Each member of the troop knew the Emergency RV and had rehearsed the drills of a withdrawal in contact numerous times. Get to the vehicles, head south and then south-east into the Ulu.

Just before first light, the Hilux reappeared, instantly recognisable by its door. It carried seven heavily armed men and, in the back, a DShK Soviet heavy machine gun mounted on a crudely welded pintle system. The men donned green headbands.

'Here they come,' whispered Wolf. 'Got a dushka, now.'

The vehicle drove behind the compound and out of sight. The seven men reappeared on foot and went into the house through the iron gate. Ten minutes later, a motorcycle drove out of the compound and up the road and out of sight over the incline.

'What do you reckon, John?' the Boss asked. 'Should we wait and see what happens? Or should we give them rooty-toot at first light. Nothing of ours will come down this road now that we've informed Zero.'

'I think we should ask Zero,' replied the staff sergeant.

'Stan, send a full sitrep to Zero and ask for acknowledgement on whether they want us to watch and wait or assault the position.'

3

Maundy Thursday, 8 April 2004
Camp Victory
Baghdad International Airport
1700 Local

Sergeant Major Javier Romaro, known by everybody except his wife as Yip, sat in the canvas fold-up chair and put his feet up on a wooden trestle table.

I'm way too old for this shit, he thought, not for the first time that day.

He surveyed the ever-growing pile of manifests on his desk. Twenty-one years in the US Army, first with a Ranger battalion and then with Delta Force, he was now seeing out the twilight of his career flying a desk as a quartermaster. The US military were shipping equipment to Iraq in prodigious quantities and it seemed, to him at least, that he was expected to account for all of it. Behind him, outside the makeshift office that used to be occupied by Saddam's immigration officials, forklift trucks were stacking pallets of equipment. Weapons, ammunition, rations, bottled water, medical supplies and batteries for the troops, plus ever more equipment for the quartermasters. Beds, sleeping bags, radios, generators, air conditioning units and a whole host of other shit that you couldn't even begin to envisage were coming in from all around the world on giant C-17 Globemasters, C-5A Galaxies, and even the old C-141 Starlifters that had probably taken his dad to Vietnam. Much of it was landing in Kuwait and was being transported up the main supply routes from depots such as Camp Virginia and Navistar in Northern Kuwait. Civilian contractors often drove the vehicles with armed protection from US Army Transportation units. This was the "Sustainer Push" – Donald Rumsfeld's determination to make army logistics mimic civilian operations and run *just-in-time* supplies. It meant there were continual convoys traversing the main supply routes up and down the country.

Likewise, Saddam International Airport, now renamed Baghdad International Airport or BIAP to those, like him, that lived there, had not functioned at full capacity since 1991 and the Allied-imposed no-fly policy. The Jordanians had been allowed some flights in after Desert Storm but it had been mainly non-sanctioned medicines and the like. It was now one of the busiest airports in the world along with the Theatre Distribution Centre at Arifjan in Kuwait. And it was all landing on Romaro's desk, or at least the paperwork was. It seemed to him that he was at the epicentre of all logistics for the invasion of Iraq and the subsequent suppression of an armed insurgency that was growing alarmingly by the week.

There were daily reports that the looting in downtown Baghdad had reached unforeseen levels. More worrying still was that the people of Iraq were not totally overjoyed at the idea of American liberation, or indeed, Western liberalism. There was no power, no fuel, not much food, and an increasing divide on religious grounds. The sporadic stone throwing of the early days had been replaced by shootings and IEDs. The previous June, two soldiers guarding an installation had been shot at, one killed, the other wounded. The disturbing thing being that the action was overwhelmingly popular amongst the bystanders that had crowded around the pools of drying blood. Now, shootings were commonplace and the grunts were shooting back. Or, if he was being honest, shooting first and asking questions later. There had been disconcerting stories of soldiers shooting up cars that had failed to stop at check points and then finding they'd killed a whole family including the children. This was turning into an ocean-going shit show, that was for sure. But perhaps the turning point was that a few days ago, some civilian security contractors from Blackwater had driven into downtown Fallujah for some reason, probably because they were lost, and were lynched by the mob. All he knew was that their charred remains now hung from a bridge and the US Army hadn't yet had the balls to go and get them.

'Yo... Yip.'

'Yo, Sergeant Major, I think you mean, Gubby.'

'Yo, Sergeant Your-Royal-Most-Highness-of-High-Things Major, I have a large consignment of flat screen TVs. They need to get on transport and sent to the Green Zone.'

'Gubby, you may think me old but I can still kick your fobbit ass. A convoy from the transportation company is due to go out tomorrow. Talk to the LT and see if you can find room on one of the M1078s.'

'Copy that, Sergeant Major. What time is the *Yip n Chip Show* tonight?'

'Gubby, if you are referring to the Battle Update Brief, then you will find that it's at the normal time of 1800. There's going to be a route briefing for the convoy, so you might want to swerve that. Oh...and Gubby?'

'Sir?'

'Make sure one of those TVs is left in here for combat assessment testing.'

As Gubby left the room, there was a tentative knock on the door and a head peered round. It belonged to a tallish lieutenant with blond hair and a smattering of boyish freckles.

'Might you be Sergeant Major Romaro?'

'That would, indeed, be me. How can I help you, Lieutenant?'

'1LT Eugene Cunningham from 751st Medium Truck Company, 105th Transportation Battalion.' The officer stuck out his hand, which Romaro shook.

'You are the dudes that arrived two days back from Anaconda?'

'Yes, sir, delivering POL to the Cavalry.' Petrol, Oil, Lubricant along with ammunition, was the lifeblood for any armoured unit and the insurgents were working out fast that the best way to disable an M1A2 Abrams tank was not to blow it up but starve it of fuel.

'How did you find the trip up, sir?'

'To be honest with you, Sergeant Major, disappointingly uneventful. We took small arms just north of Nasiriyah but otherwise quiet.'

Yip looked at the officer's clean, new boots.

'I detect, sir, that you have not been in-country too long. You from the OIF2 rotation?'

'Spent three months at Camp Virginia before moving up to Cedar a couple of weeks ago. Since then, we've been sitting on our asses as CENTCOM thought we weren't ready. This convoy was our first up the Iraqi Express.'

'Careful what you wish for... there was a total shit show in Nasiriyah exactly this time last year. 3 Forward Support and Maintenance Company were shot to shit there.'

'Yeah, they told us about that; they were the ones that took a wrong turning and ended up in the middle of the town where every Haji with an AK lined up for a turkey shoot. Sergeant Major, I need to get my M915 tractors back down to Cedar and then Navistar, and I'm hoping to leave tomorrow at first light. I was wondering if there was anything that you needed us to take down there? You know, might as well fill up the convoy if we're going that way anyway. I think your boys are providing the escort, too.'

'Mighty kind of you, sir. I will have a quick ask around to see what needs to go down. Have you been assigned the escort trucks yet?'

'Yes, two Humvee gun trucks and a five ton.'

'Do you know who's on the Rat Patrol?' asked Yip.

'No, I don't, Sergeant Major,' replied Cunningham.

'How many KBRs?'

'Probably five, I dunno, we had some mechanical failures on the way up to Anaconda and some of them only just made it here.' Cunningham was beginning to feel he wasn't really impressing the sergeant major too much.

'Lieutenant, make sure you double up on ammunition. I reckon you were luckier than a dog with two dicks on the way up. Which way are you going back?'

'Straight down Tampa.'

'Shit. Have your crews been through the anti-ambush drills?'

'Nope. To be honest, all we've done is some range work at Udari. Couple of mags each. 60 rounds, probably.'

'Holy fuck. You been through the rally point and boxing up drills?'

'Nope. I guess you'd better point me in the direction of the armory.'

'You're going to need the full house: 5.56, 7.62 and .50. If you're lucky, you might get an MK19 on the five ton. We've got a couple here somewhere modified with hillbilly armor by the Skunkwerks up at Anaconda.'

The Skunkwerks were getting a name for themselves: The 181st Transportation Battalion at Logistical Support Area (LSA) Anaconda that had started modifying some of the unarmored five tonners and Humvees so they were a little more protected. There were armored M1114 Humvees in the military capable of mounting weapons but there were not enough of them to go around and they'd all been nabbed by the teeth arm – frontline - units. Consequently, many of the escort duties had to make do with unarmored variants. Various wagons had sheet metal welded to the doors and cabs to protect drivers, and had gun rings cut into the roofs so that at least an M-249 SAW could be mounted, or, better still, the good old .50 calibre. Some of the five-ton tractors had armored boxes behind the cab, nick-named *dog houses*, on which various weapons could be mounted, including the MK19 automatic grenade launcher. Early in the conflict, the contracted civilian drivers from Kellog, Brown and Root, had refused to drive unless escorted by a gun truck. It was now standard operating procedure for all convoys to have a minimum of two gun trucks.

'LT, are you using contract drivers?'

'Yeah, we've got four or five right-seat left-seating it from KBR, but all have a regular with them.'

'Any TCNs?'

'Yup.' Cunningham rolled his eyes. Third Country Nationals often drove vehicles in military convoys but whilst many did so both professionally and on occasion, bravely, they weren't all totally reliable.

'Make sure they have M16s, body armor and plenty of ammo, too.'

'Sergeant Major, you are making me very freaking nervous. There's been very little activity on the main supply routes for almost a month. Why do you think this will be any different?'

'I dunno, sir. Just call it old soldier's intuition. The increase in insurgent activity in the towns will inevitably spill out onto the roads. You should know that Friday is not just Good Friday, it's the first anniversary of the fall of Baghdad.'

The officer caught sight of the special forces para badge on the older soldier's chest and wondered what an old lag like him was doing running paper work in a supply depot.

'Let's hope it is a "Good Friday". All day'.

1LT CUNNINGHAM WAS DIRECTED to the vehicle park and looked around for someone to tell him where the convoy briefing was to be held. Having ascertained the time and location, he went to the mess hall and found his sergeant, SGT Andersson, and his driver from the trip up eating pizza and watching MTV. The driver was an old hand and was shortly to deploy back to "the world", as the troops called home. Cunningham didn't really trust Andersson and felt that the sergeant had little or no respect for him in return. Nevertheless, an innate impulse made Cunningham want Andersson to like him.

'Round up the guys for a route briefing in the Ops hall across the way, will you please, sergeant,' he told Andersson, pointing to a single-story building across the gravel park. '1800, so get them there ten minutes early. Apparently, the CO gets bent out of shape about punctuality.'

He went back to the vehicle park and located his trucks. They were mainly M915 tractors that had pulled 5,000-gallon fuel bowsers up from Kuwait. He had a couple of bobtails and a recovery vehicle in case things went pear-shaped.

Parked a little way away were what he assumed the Skunkwerks gun trucks.

Hillbilly armor, holy moly, he thought.

There were some modified M915 tractors like his but rather than having a trailer to pull, they had sheet steel boxes welded to the back. Some had gun rings in the drivers' compartment roofs and iron mesh in front of the windscreens. The Humvees had either .50 calibre heavy machine guns or M60 medium machine guns behind armored shields. The grunts had been busy painting and naming them as well: *Alabama Rat Catcher, Rolling Thunder, Uncle Fumble, Bounty Hunter, Canned Death*, and so on. On the shield of one of the M60s was written in black masking tape: "7.62 All You Can Eat". There were several small-arms strike marks on the body works.

Cunningham felt both relieved and apprehensive. Back in Camp Virginia they'd heard various stories about convoy ambushes, but they seemed to be mainly amateur affairs with kill zones a few hundred yards long. The advice was "push the pedal to the metal and get through the ambush as quickly as possible". He'd heard other convoys being ambushed taking supplies to the teeth arms up near Fallujah where POL bowsers had caught fire and drivers being wounded or killed, but in his three months in country, he had not met anybody yet who had actually experienced anything more than sporadic small arms fire. He was strangely excited about the prospect of being in a fire fight, even if he was in a wagon. He imagined picking off insurgents with his M16 as the convoy sped through.

He wandered back to the briefing hall, where there were two blocks of folding chairs that could seat about 150 people, a projector screen and a plinth. The seats were about half occupied, with the front row left empty. He spotted his guys over to the left side, three and four rows back, close enough to be keen but, hopefully, not too close to get a random question. They filled both rows so he had to sit just behind them.

Standing at the dais was the sergeant major he had met in the terminal.

'Ladies and gentlemen...' the sergeant major began, just short of a shout. The room went quiet. At that point, a lieutenant colonel walked in from the side. He was holding a Styrofoam cup in one hand and a projector remote in the other.

'Good evening, people...' he started, in a lazy Southern drawl. 'I am the commanding officer of 6th Transportation Battalion Tactical Operations Centre, based here in Camp Victory. It is my job to get you people safely to wherever you are going so that you can drop your supplies and keep this show on the road. It is your job to listen carefully to what is said in this room during this Op Ord. Kindly give me your undivided attention.'

The lights dimmed and the projector beamed a map of Iraq on to the screen.

'Area of interest.' At that moment, he dolloped a globule of brown spittle into the foam cup and laid it on the floor, took out a laser marker from his pocket and pointed to the map with the little red dot. Cunningham thought the red dot shook around rather too much.

'As you know, you are currently here at Camp Victory, BIAP. Heading south out of here is route Tampa... here...' he pointed to the dot again '...which heads south all the way down to Kuwait. Note also, the west of MSR Tampa is ASR Cleveland and then ASR Miami. Note also, this route, running east-west joining the two routes, ASR Orlando. Gentlemen, I would draw your attention to this area here. This is where Tampa stops being a nice empty six-lane freeway and turns into a cross country track we call *Dirty Tampa*. If you came up that way, you probably know what I'm talking about. Also, note here, CSC Scania, which is your first objective and where you will RON.

'OK...Enemy Forces. We have a couple of developments regarding insurgents. First, a few days back, a dude calling himself Muqtada Al Sadr...' the colonel pronounced it *Mooktaddi ow Saddi*, 'has declared Jihad against all foreign forces.' He paused. 'That's us, folks, in fact, that's all foreign folks in the country. I want you to be under no illusion, this is a serious development. This means, people, that they have a God-given requirement to kill us, no questions asked, and they will get rewarded in heaven with a double ration of virgins. Believe you me, these people mean business. They've already ejected the Ukrainians out of Al Kut, probably not difficult, I grant you, and we believe Najaf on ASR Miami to be unsafe. The guys at Bushmaster are now under constant attack.

'Another development is that insurgents are beginning to distinguish themselves by wearing black fatigues, and green or sometimes yellow armbands and headbands. Right, listen in, this constitutes PID...I repeat, black fatigues, green or yellow armbands means positive identification of Mahdi Militia. You may open fire if you spot these people. In fact, you better believe me here, you *need* to open fire. Do not wait for a command or fire order... get the rounds down.

'We believe that insurgent ambush teams consist of five-to-seven enemy, often with RPG, AKs and sometimes heavier weaponry like RPKs and the like. Often, they use child spotters, but if you also notice a lack of LN activity, especially children, be on your guard. They also prefer built up areas so they can use cover to shoot and scoot.'

The colonel reached down for the cup and another dollop of brown liquid was deposited. The briefing hall was deathly quiet.

'Friendly forces...'

He pointed at the map and directed their attention to the various camps and bases along the route to Cedar, including the Logistics centres at Dogwood, Elm, Erin and Scania.

'We will be supplying you with three armed escort vehicles. They will travel at the front and rear of the convoy and there will be one roving Humvee that will patrol the length. Your job, people, is to keep moving until someone in one of those three vehicles tells you otherwise. Do not stop for any reason, and I mean that. I repeat: There is no reason for you to stop.

'You should also be aware that further south you may encounter the Brits. They have SF in this area but they won't release where or how many. These will be either Special Air Service or Special Boat Service – their equivalent of our SEALs. Do not fuck with these people. They have a habit of not wearing standard uniform and sometimes it's hard to distinguish them from LN. They will stay out of your way but if you put your stick in their hornet's nest, believe me, gentlemen, you will enter a whole new world of pain. They will fuck you up, I shit you not.

'Mission... Your mission is to deliver your convoy to Cedar 2, here.' The red dot landed in the south of Iraq. 'I repeat, to deliver your convoy here.'

'Execution... There has been a lot of enemy activity in the last few days. Since the call to Jihad on Monday, nearly all convoys in and around BIAP and Anaconda have been attacked in some form or other. Therefore, these routes here...' he pointed the little red dot onto the map, '...are now designated Black. People, do not use these roads. The convoy will deploy out of Entry Control Point 1, down Irish, here, then Vernon, here, and then south onto Tampa, here. Your escorts will block off traffic from the junctions.'

The colonel went on to brief the audience regarding Order of March, Actions on Casualties, the Communication network, including call signs and frequencies, codewords, and finally the passwords.

'Action on Ambush... To date, the majority of ambushes have been opportunistic and small. However, SigInt have released information that this is quickly evolving. We fear that the enemy now have the sophistication to execute larger and better planned operations against our convoys. Should you get hit, the SOP is the same...keep driving. Don't stop for nobody. You need to get through and out of the kill zone. That's why it's called the kill zone...it's the place where you die. The gun trucks will lead you out and sweep up the pieces. Once you are through the kill zone, box up into a laager. All personnel dismount and get into 360 fire positions.

'If your vehicle becomes non-operational, you should let Command know on the radio, take cover by the vehicle and wait for the escort sweep. They will come and get you. It is inadvisable, gentlemen, to try to escape into the urban area. Other than you will probably have your head chopped off and the video sent to the New York Times, we do not need US personnel in a hostage situation.

'Command and Control...'

Cunningham was disappointed to learn that his vehicles would only be carrying SINCGARS radios that could barely get from one end of a column to the other. The colonel, in his briefing, had been very adamant about convoy discipline, 100 metres between vehicles, no more and no less. However, even he knew this was impossible to maintain and that often convoys got strung out over several miles. Radio transmissions from the front to the back would have to be relayed through the middle vehicles. He made a note to have an experienced man at the midpoint. Anything else would have to go via text using the Qualcomm onboard computer that linked to a satellite.

'Any questions?' the colonel finished.

A hand went up...it was SPC Jamaal Chipunza.

Ugh, the Unit Clown, thought Cunningham.

'Sir, will there be, like, you know, Easter Bunnies at Cedar?' Chipunza looked around with a broad grin.

'Private, let's just get you there safely, shall we?' the colonel replied, slightly more seriously than Chipunza might have wanted. 'Finally, Sergeant Major Romaro will be in the roving Humvee, what we call the Rat Patrol. Do exactly as he says, if the shit hits the fan, he is the one most likely to keep you alive.

'Please now report to the Total Safety Task Instruction to be assigned convoy order but please come through Mr Romaro first.'

As the hall emptied, Sergeant Major Romaro asked all vehicle commanders up to the dais and handed them a CD Rom with all the maps and routes. Cunningham approached him.

'That was a bit down beat, Sergeant Major.'

'Sir, in the last twenty-four hours, things have gotten a whole lot worse. We are hearing that the whole country is erupting. You are too young to remember Tet in Nam. I think we're going to see the same here.'

'Should we delay? I mean, we could bunker down here for a few days until it's a bit calmer out there.'

'LT, and I mean this with the greatest of respect, war doesn't wait for nobody. Those bobtails and tractors are needed down south and down south is where you're going to take them, starting first light tomorrow. You'll be fine. Just stick to the route, keep the discipline, keep your ears and eyes peeled, and don't stop for nobody.'

'Copy that.'

'Have your team got themselves personal weapons and body armor?'

'They've all got helmets and armor and stuff but if we could get some ammunition, that would be great.'

'Get them over to the armory. And remember what I told you in my office, double issue of ammunition. Minimum of 440 rounds per person and as many magazines as possible. Seven minimum. Do you have a CLS?'

'Yeah, we got a couple in the convoy.'

'Make sure they carry the trauma kits, too. They can be drawn from the QM stores.'

Cunningham was beginning to think everybody was taking this very seriously indeed and decided he would brief the crews before they went out tomorrow. He was also beginning to feel there might be a slight disconnect between what *they* were expecting and what everybody he'd met *here* was expecting. And not in a good way.

LT Cunningham went off to find his platoon, which he duly did in the Morale, Welfare and Recreation Centre. They were sitting around in what looked like a shopping mall in any mid-western town, playing cards, drinking coffee and shooting the breeze. TVs were showing basketball and the speakers were playing country and western hits.

'Sergeant Andersson, get the guys in. I want to go through tomorrow and the order of march. Meet by the vehicles in fifteen.'

Cunningham had asked his sergeant to gather the crews so he could give his own briefing. He also felt he wanted to integrate himself as the platoon officer. He had a nagging feeling of being too remote from the other ranks, an outsider only nominally in charge because the army said you had to have an officer. Although everybody had attended the Op Order, it was also important that the smaller details were clear in everybody's mind. Whilst many of them had known each other for some time, they'd only assembled in Kuwait a month ago, although he had arrived on the advanced party before them. Prior to that, many had been part-time reservists in the North Dakota National Guard. On deployment, they'd received personnel from other units to make up the numbers and, as a unit, had not really been tested in a situation yet. Now, they had civilian drivers from KBR, who, in all fairness, were often ex-military or more mature drivers. Furthermore, KBR also employed Third Country Nationals, men from South East Asian countries like Bangladesh or Sri Lanka. He wasn't too sure about them. English wasn't their first language for a start and secondly, they were doing it for the money. A KBR driver could get $80,000 tax free a year. They had the right to quit at any time and he was hearing that after the increase in ambushes, a whole lot had already called it a day and gone home. He chuntered to himself that a PFC earning less than $20,000 was required to guard a civilian earning four times that amount or they wouldn't leave the compound.

Cunningham wandered out into the night air. It was cooling and he looked up and decided it might well rain. He could see no moon or stars. To the east was the glow of Baghdad. He could hear sporadic gunshots and occasionally, the faintest sound of automatic weapons being fired. He wondered what was going on out there, who was on patrol outside the safety of the compounds and whether anybody was in the process of dying as a result of the firing.

He walked past the scrap heap where there was a plethora of destroyed US vehicles. Trucks, Humvees, tractors, a forklift, more Humvees. Some had clearly been caught in ambushes or IEDs, the windows shot out and the hoods punctured with bullet holes. He noticed the star shaped impact mark of an RPG on the door of an M114, the armored variant of the Humvee that he had driven up in. He looked in through the shattered side window and saw the inside had been ripped to shreds by the blast. On the seats and in the footwell was the brown-black stain of blood, copious amounts of blood, and he wondered if the driver had bled out in the vehicle or had been medivacked to safety.

His heart was pounding and despite the cooling air, he felt hot. *Shoot,* he thought, *my Hummer isn't even armored.* Just the old REMF turtle shell. An RPG would blow the thing, and all in it, to kingdom come.

The mundane reality of war was just beginning to become apparent to him now that he found himself deployed. He had graduated last year but all through school he had been the odd one out. He had kept it quiet that he'd voted for the President because he felt none of his friends or fellow students had. When the twin towers had been hit he'd felt an urge to contribute something. Whilst his fellow students were organising peace marches and "not in our name" demos, he had joined the National Guard. His pop had been proud but his mom had begun to fret. When his unit had not been required to deploy for the invasion, he'd felt left behind. So, he had volunteered for the second rotation. And now, he was here, listening to live fire coming from Baghdad and looking at the blood-spattered wreckage of previous encounters with the enemy. He was no longer sure if he had it in him to do what was asked of him.

He suppressed the panic; he was about to address the troops. They couldn't see him having doubts and fears.

He came across his team standing by the vehicles. Some were smoking and they'd built a small fire in the sand shielded from the breeze by a rough cinder block hearth. Someone had a portable CD player linked up to some mini speakers and he could hear the familiar strains of Jimmy Buffet and Alan Jackson singing, *It's Five O'clock Somewhere.*

'Pour me something tall and strong...make it a hurricane before I go insane...'.

'Howdy, LT,' said the sergeant.

'Evening all.' He felt absurdly formal. They were in a combat zone and he was behaving like some preppy loser meeting his in-laws.

'I just want to go through tomorrow. I know the briefing went through it all, but word on the street from the old hands here is that the Hajis are going to use tomorrow as a day of rage against us.'

'Good Friday, LT, and the anniversary of us taking this shithole. Come and get your 72 virgins...' Chipunza's wide grin could not hide the obvious tension he was feeling since the briefing.

One of the army drivers, a rather attractive woman of about 23, reached below the door of one of the trucks, pulled a Coors out of the darkness, adeptly took the top off on a metal stud on the truck, and handed it to him.

Cunningham didn't really drink and didn't really approve of those that did. Alcohol was forbidden by the military and they had clearly stashed an illicit supply in their vehicles. By the book, he should report them. But this seemed different. He took the bottle and had a swig. It tasted remarkably good. More than that, by sharing their rule-breaking with him, he felt welcomed into the group as an insider for the first time since he had taken over command.

'Not tall and strong, sir. And definitely not a hurricane.' She had *Poklewski* embroidered on her name tag. He remembered her first name now. Alice.

'Thank you, Poklewski. Cheers.'

'You're welcome, sir... and cheers.' She smiled. A dazzling smile of straight, white, Hollywood teeth. He forced himself to snap out of the reverie and addressed the group.

'When we go out tomorrow, I want one of you to sit with each of the KBR drivers. I will be in the Turtle Shell behind the lead gun truck. Those driving our rigs to alternate between comfort breaks. Like on the way up, we will have ablution stops every few hours or so.

Get on the comms if you are desperate. Sergeant Andersson, will you detail vehicle numbers after this? It's a fairly straightforward route providing we don't get lost in Baghdad.'

'Irish, Vernon, Tampa,' interjected the sergeant. 'We've already plugged it into the MTS.'

Of course, he has, thought Cunningham, then said aloud, 'If we get hit, remember the drill is to drive through the kill zone. Don't stop. Identify targets out of the window and let them have it. But remember, single shots like we did on the ranges. We don't want to squirt off all the ammo in the first contact. It's an awful long way to Cedar with no ammo.'

The group laughed.

'What happens, sir, if the truck breaks down? We already know these rigs are always giving up.'

'If we are in the open and not in contact, we stop the convoy and dismount. We either repair the vehicle or we tow it behind a bobtail. Don't just sit around in the cabs. Get down on your bellies and look out for Hajis.'

'What about if we get stopped in a contact? What happens then?'

It was the killer question; what to do if your truck grinds to a halt in the middle of an ambush and all the others go rushing past.

'We've been through this in the Op Order briefing, Ciccarelli. You send a message on the MTS or the radio, you get out into cover and you wait for the escort Humvees to pick you up. We've got an M915 gun truck with a fucking big machine gun sweeping up the rear. You wait for them, make yourself known and they'll pick you up,' said SGT Andersson before Cunningham could answer.

'If they see you and stop and don't just go cadillacking on by,' quipped Chipunza.

'They'll speed up past you, Jamaal. Know why? Cos you're a shitbag.'

'Fuck you, Keszbom. LT, what about the truckers taken in Nasiriyah a year back?' continued Chipunza.

'Jessica Lynch? What about them? Her detachment got lost and then separated. Moral of the story there, Chipunza, is don't get separated from the main group. Keep your eyes both in front and behind.'

'She was the one that was rescued by the Seals, wasn't she, LT?' asked Poklewski.

'If you break down, we will see you,' interrupted Cunningham, wanting to avoid the conversation. 'Listen, we're probably going to have an uneventful trip down like we did on the way up and this time tomorrow you'll be chowing pizza and skyping home from the comfort of an air-conditioned billet.'

'Amen to that,' came a voice from the shadows.

'I've heard there ain't no air conditioning at Stankier. Nor pizza. Sweet fuck all.'

'Ok...thank you for that. Gather round for vehicle details,' said SGT Andersson.

He proceeded to list the drivers and escorts and then the order of march. First would be the armored Humvee of the escort and then there would be Cunningham, followed by alternating military trucks and KBR trucks. In the middle would be Andersson's roving Humvee ensuring convoy discipline and relaying any radio messages. Pulling up the rear would be the five-ton gun truck with the dog house and the .50. They had just been told that they were to take two, 5,000 gallon tankers of AvGas with them.

'Excuse me if I'm reading this wrong, Sarge, but didn't we just haul those mofos up here not two days ago?'

'We did.'

'So, not being too cynical, we are now going to haul them back down to Cedar?'

'That's what it says on the details...you know, "ours not to reason why, ours but to do and die"'.

'Sounds to me, LT, that maybe someone is making money each time we go anywhere.'

'That will be Uncle Dickie...' said a voice in the dark.

'OK... that's enough now,' Cunningham instructed with a laugh. 'We may be in a combat zone, but military discipline is still enforced.'

· · ·

MEANWHILE, Yip and his commanding officer, Major Chip McFadden, were in his office discussing the next day's detail.

'You didn't flinch when I detailed the rat patrol to you, Yip.'

'No, sir. But I wasn't expecting it.'

'There's a reason...a real good reason why you have to go.'

'Ok, sir, like to let me know what that real good reason might be?'

'Other than I think you need to get out, I need you to personally deliver a package to the Brits in Basra.'

'What sort of package, sir?'

'A goddam precious package. I need you to take it to the southern command in Basra. Basra is where the Brits are.'

'Yes, sir.' Yip made a conscious decision to prevent his eyes from rolling. He wondered if the commanding officer had been at the Southern Comfort. He had a reputation for hard drinking but those that worked most closely with him noticed it had gone from "hard" to "everyday".

Major McFadden squirted a jet of brown liquid into his Styrofoam cup.

'Goddamn Limeys are pissing everyone off up this way. Not pulling their weight.'

'To be fair, sir, they are very under-manned and, even worse, under-equipped they...'

'Yeah, yeah, I know, Yip, I know. They move about in unarmored SUVs, call 'em pussy cars or something...'

'Snatch Rovers, sir'

'Yeah, snatch cars, whatever. They're looking after an area that would tie down two US armored divisions with an under-strength brigade. They have about two operational helos and are constantly whining to us for air cover or FGA. Don't we know it, they never shut up about it.'

He paused, ruminating quietly and fiddling with a biro, spinning back and forth in his fingers.

'Don't misunderstand me, Yip, they are good soldiers. Man for man, some of the best.'

'I agree with you there, sir. Back in the day, I did some work with their SF. Special Air Service. Spent a year with them. Did a combat survival course in the hills in Wales and then three months in the jungle in Borneo. They have a very different approach to us.'

'Yeah...met some of them on Desert Storm. Fucking insane. I mean, literally mentally not all there.'

'They're a tight bunch, that's for sure. Maybe not so good at small talk with regular units but then again, nobody gets much out of a SEAL neither. Everybody in the Brit chain of command is both envious and irritated by their distance. Don't wear rank, don't salute. Nothing's formal. But that's just how they come across.'

'Maybe...skinny muthafuckers most of them I met. But with the dead look of a serial killer in their eyes. Goddam freaky. There's a bunch up at MSS Fernandez. Anyway, enough of those bastards. Come with me.'

He rose from his seat, picked up his cup, and walked out of the office past a defunct luggage carousel. Further down the long corridor, he turned out into a hangar in which there were hundreds of stacked pallets. Off to one side, there was a separate stack of ten pallets.

'I want you to take one of these puppies and stow it in your Humvee.' Major McFadden dug into his pocket and pulled out a transfer manifest, peeled off an orange sticker and adhered it on to one of the pallets.

'You can drive the Humvee into the hangar through the front. The MP detail will let you in. They know you're coming. You will then sign for the dough and be on your way.'

Yip thought, *They'd better let me in, they're my fucking MPs*, but instead said, 'Um...one of them pallets is not getting into the back of my Humvee, sir. No room with the gunner. How much is a pallet?'

'Sixty-four million bucks,' said the major.

'I meant, how much does a pallet weigh? Hold up, there, sir. Sixty-four million dollars? What's on those pallets?'

'Oh...you see these ones? The gold paper? These are hundred-dollar bills stacked into thousand note bundles. There are six hundred and forty bundles in a pallet. And they weigh fifteen hundred pounds, to answer your first question.'

'Shit...that makes a single pallet...'

'Sixty-four million US dollars, like I just said.'

'Does the US tax payer know about this?'

'Sergeant Major, there is no reason for the US taxpayer to know. These are not his dollars. They belong to the Iraqi people.'

'When I last looked, Benjamin Franklin was on the bills, not Saddam.'

'It's apparently oil revenue swapped for medical aid and the like. Fed reckons if it's theirs, they might want to spend it on rebuilding their shithole country.'

Yip stared at the pallets, unable to really believe what he was seeing.

'See these brown ones? They're fifties. And the blues, twenties.'

'Holy fucking moly, sir. Who is in charge of this?'

'Basel.'

'Basil? Basil fucking who?'

'Strange thing is, you know, Sergeant Major, I don't know his surname. I can tell you that I have it on the highest authority, General McChrystal no less, to let this Basel take this money to the Central Bank in the Green Zone. Once, this Basel guy picked up the moolah in a garbage truck. Can you believe that? Said it was less likely to get ambushed on Irish.' The Major spat into his cup. 'Mr Paul Bremer himself has requested these pallets, other than yours, to go to the CPA tomorrow. And you know what?'

'Tell me...'

'There's another load of pallets on the way. Airborne as we speak. Being flown out of Andrews in a C-17. Expecting it to land sometime early this morning.'

'Major, I'm not going to be able to put this in a Humvee. It will slow it down. We'll stow it in one of the tractors.'

'So you've said. Whatever you think, Sergeant Major. Just make sure it gets down south to the Brits. Once you get to Cedar, I'll text you the onward details on the MTS. If you're lucky, the Brits will come up to you and pick it up. They'll turn up in one of those SUVs that look like they were made out of scrap metal in the 1950s. Them pussy snatch things we were talking about.'

'Funnily enough, they're much better across rough terrain than our Hummers.'

'Sure they are,' said the major, spitting into his cup. 'Sure they are.'

4

Good Friday, 9 April 2004
Camp Victory, Baghdad International Airport
0430 Local

In the pre-dawn gloom, 1LT Cunningham took his personal equipment over to the M998. He looked at the vehicle and its add-on armor. His driver would be Poklewski, whom he had selected for all the wrong reasons. They had scrounged some extra body armor, including the SAPI plates, and these had been draped over the doors and door windows to give added protection. He stowed his equipment in the backseat footwells, including a slab of bottled water and about 1,000 rounds for him and Poklewski still in their cardboard containers. He also had seven magazines of 30 rounds.

Poklewski, Luckenbach and SGT Andersson's SAW gunner, SPC Wavebourne, approached the vehicle carrying their equipment. Wavebourne had already stowed the belted ammunition on the sergeant's Humvee the night before. His station would be behind an armored shield sitting above and behind the cab. He had 360-degree traverse on his machine gun and would be used as the quick reaction protection of the convoy.

Poklewski and Luckenbach were joshing about in a familiar manner that somehow disconcerted him. They were smiling and laughing as they walked along, banging shoulders.

'Nice morning for a road trip,' said Cunningham, rather more cheerily than he felt, intending to break up the horse play.

There had been a heavy dew overnight and the vehicles were covered in a film of water that was forming into rivulets and running down the bodywork and windows. He idly drew a target into the window in front of the driver but quickly scrubbed it into oblivion when he realised how inappropriate Poklewski might think it.

'Morning, LT,' both soldiers said. Wavebourne opened his breast pocket and flipped a Lucky Strike cigarette out of the pack. He rummaged in his pocket and pulled out a zippo, which he expertly lit one handed before offering the pack around.

SGT Andersson arrived with the rest of the drivers and shooters, a steaming mug of coffee in his hand making him look relaxed, competent and in charge. Cunningham felt a small pang of envy at the insouciance that he knew he failed to convey. He knew the troop would defer to Andersson despite him being nominally the LT. This was made worse when SGT Andersson gathered the troops around him for the final briefing without acknowledging Cunningham or even asking him to join. Cunningham found himself standing at the back of the circle, looking over everybody's heads.

As Andersson was going through the order of march for the convoy and the final routes, he saw Yip approaching.

'Kyle, I need to load a pallet on one of your tractors,' shouted the Sgt Major.

'Sure thing, Yip. What is it?'

'That's classified. Can you report to the hangar over behind the mess hall,' he said, pointing with his M16.

'You'll see an MP on the door and tell him I sent you...in fact, let me get in and I'll show you where to go.'

'Chen, can you take the sergeant major over and collect his cargo?'

Chen hoisted herself up into the cab. As the M915 spluttered into life with a black plume of diesel exhaust firing vertically into the air, Yip climbed into the passenger's seat. He felt the vulnerability of the cab. A wire mesh had been welded over the windshield but it had no ballistic glass.

At the hangar, Chen reversed the tractor, opened the back door, and a forklift, supervised by Yip, hoisted the pallet into the back of the container. Yip signed the manifest, closed the door and told Chen to re-join the other vehicles.

The convoy was now sorting itself out into the order of march, with an armored M1114 variant with an M60 gun ring over the cab at the front. Yip dropped out of the tractor cab and went over to his Humvee's passenger seat, then checked he had his personal weapon, body armor and helmet.

'Ready for this, Gubby?' he asked his driver.

'Ready as any Fobbit will ever be.' Gubby was grinning, but Yip could detect the anxiety beneath the calm exterior.

Cunningham was already mounted in his Humvee and was at the front of the convoy just behind Yip. Yip went over to him.

'Happy with the route, sir?'

'Sure...right out of the gate, and then Irish, Vernon, and then south on Tampa.'

'How about a quick comms check on the SINCGARS?'

'Um...yes...of course.' Cunningham cursed himself for having forgotten the basic drills in his excitement.

'LT?'

'Yes?'

'Relax...it will go fine. If we get into a situation, concentrate on the really small stuff. Weapon skills, radio procedure and the like. The training will kick in only if you keep your breathing regular and the heart rate down.'

'Right, yes...of course.'

Cunningham checked the comms and then slowly and deliber-

ately checked his MTS. He looked back down the convoy, the olive
green military tractors interspersed with the white articulated trucks
of the KBR drivers. Near the front were the two tankers and right at
the back was the M915 modified gun truck. He could see Zeller, the
gunner, up in his eyrie, the .50 calibre pointing forward. He sat there
looking straight ahead at the gate of the compound, the guard tower
looming above. There was a Bradley parked some way back from the
entrance in case the gate was rushed when it opened.

'LT, you might want to put the magazine in your weapon,' said
Poklewski.

He looked down and saw his M16 was still without a magazine
and quickly rummaged in his pouches to get one and click it into
place. He looked over and saw she had her weapon on her lap. She
had her helmet on and gold Ray-Ban Aviators hid her eyes. A wisp of
blond hair had escaped from under her helmet and hung down by
the gold stud in her ear.

The radio crackled into life and Yip's voice came into the cab
saying that when he was ready, Cunningham should lead the convoy
up to the gate. There was also an ominous message that all routes
around BIAP were now designated "amber" – meaning there was
now a persistent threat of ambush. Furthermore, the roads north of
BIAP up in the Abu Graib slum area were now either "red" or the
highest category "black". Black meant there was either an ambush
actually occurring or that IEDs had been found and were being
cleared. His mind flicked back to the wrecked vehicles in the scrap
heap of the previous evening.

Cunningham looked over his shoulder and saw SGT Andersson's
Humvee behind. He stuck his arm out of his window and gave a
thumbs up and Poklewski drove forward towards the gate. She
stopped just short and waited as the rest of the convoy slowly moved
into position. To exit the camp, she would have to wind around the
concrete blocks of the chicane that were there to stop suicide bomber
ramraids on the gates.

He made one last check on the comms and then the convoy was
moving. There was some whooping and banter on the radio and he

heard Yip's voice coming over, reminding everybody to be on their toes and to keep the airwaves clear of chatter.

As Poklewski pulled out of BIAP, Cunningham was thinking to himself, *OK, this is it.* The moment of truth, perhaps, of whether he really was up for this. Outside the base, it was busy with the early morning rush and that was a good sign. Yip's armored Humvee overtook and blocked the traffic circle, and the convoy trundled through at 25mph. Someone had hung a white sign on the rear of the vehicle:

Stay Back 100m. Danger. Deadly Force Will Be Used.

It was written in red in both English and Arabic. Underneath, in indelible black marker pen, someone had written:

If you can read this, you are closer to Paradise than you think.

Cunningham's eyes were darting from side to side, trying to locate enemy activity or latent threats. He felt sweat running down his back and in his groin and his heart was pounding.

Up ahead he saw two M1 Abrams parked on the side of the road, turrets turned facing the housing. A hundred metres further on were three Bradleys but none of the armor was closed down and so he thought that was a good sign, too. They turned onto Vernon. The convoy had picked up speed now and Cunningham kept a good look out over his shoulder to ensure the vehicles didn't spread out too much. He was relying on Yip's Humvee to block traffic at junctions and traffic circles and occasionally he noticed Andersson's vehicle racing up the outside of the convoy to ensure that gap discipline was kept. Right behind him, the M915 tractor, driven by Chen, kept a steady twenty-metre gap. Luckenbach, the shooter, had the barrel of his rifle poking out of the wound-down window. He pointed it aggressively at any cars that looked like they might encroach out of junctions, thus getting between him and the Humvee in front.

Suddenly, over the radio, came a KBR driver's voice:

<*'Hooollly Crap. Just had a rock damn near come through the windshield.'*>

Cunningham dipped the pressel and said, 'Unknown call sign, please identify yourself.'

<*'Sorry, LT, it's Roadrunner. Some kid just threw a rock that hit the*

windshield. Fucking asshole.'>

<'*Anybody hurt?'*> replied Cunningham.

<'*Negative, LT. Just made a big noise and has split the glass.'*>

<'*Roger that...out.'*>

The road was straight with four lanes and a metal barrier down the median. The vehicles kept to the left to stay away from the more likely areas where IEDs might be hidden. There were wrecked cars every so often, gutted by fire and now red with rust. The road was strewn with rubbish which whirled into the air as the vehicles thundered past and stuck to the radiator grills of the vehicles behind.

Yip's voice came over the air:

<'*All stations, Grandslam Seven Romeo...be advised there is a dead mule carcass on the hardball by the median...move over to the right.'*>

Poklewski changed lanes and hugged the side of the road. She saw the carcass and hoped it wasn't a decoy for an IED in the median or indeed an IED on the other side. There was so much dust and litter, it was impossible to identify for certain that some areas were more dangerous than others. Luck would play a big part in who got hit and who didn't. The rest of the convoy followed her lead and the dead animal was just that, a rotting body abandoned in a decaying country.

As the buildings of the urban area thinned out, the soldiers began to relax out of the high state of tension. Occasionally, young lads would throw rocks, darting out of side streets or from behind cover. Mostly they missed entirely but, on occasion, a rock would thud off the cab of a truck or bounce off the windshields or the protective grills.

<'*We are taking fire...repeat small arms.'*> Cunningham recognised the high-pitched voice of Ciccarelli, the driver of the first M915 tanker. Behind him he heard the crackle of small arms fire. He flicked the safety switch to fire and rolled down his window. He was scanning the buildings for any sign of hostile movement.

<'*Grandslam Seven Romeo Actual, keep driving. Repeat keep driving. Keep the air clear. Report in any casualties. Grandslam 5, copy over.'*>

<'*Grandslam 5 nothing seen yet...'*> Over the air came the thud of the

.50 calibre in three- to five-round bursts. *<'Ignore my last, I have PID, am engaging. Small arms to right.'>* SGT Lieber inadvertently kept his radio pressel switch down.

<'Gil...Gil...>

< what?>

<'Gil, d'ya get anyone?'>

<'What?'>

<'Did you hit anybody?'>

<'No, don't think so...hard to tell.'>

The radio went quiet again. Cunningham had heard the faint thumping of the .50 and the less loud SAW of another vehicle, probably SGT Andersson's. The road was now heading out into the desert and the houses were less densely packed. They rumbled past a disused permanent vehicle check point with an abandoned police block house to the side. There was a concrete plinth with a picture of Saddam Hussein. His face had been shot out. The rest of the convoy thundered past and into the desert.

<u>*<'Grandslam Seven Romeo Actual. We are going to proceed another ten clicks and then box up to assess any damage. Checkerboard One Zero, copy, over.'>*</u>

'LT?' said Poklewski.

'Uh?'

'The escort is calling you...'

'Oh...sure...um...*<Checkerboard One Zero roger that.'>*

'And sir?'

'What?' Cunningham was a bit irritated now. Instead of feeling a modicum of gratitude that Poklewski was gently helping him do his job, he felt a resentment, mainly at himself, that he was continually behind the curve. And he definitely wasn't impressing her. Not one bit.

'Sorry to ask you this...' She had detected the irritation. 'Do you mind putting your safety back on...you know...in case...I dunno.'

'Sheesh, Poklewski, we're in a fire fight, for chrissakes.'

'Sure...sorry, sir.'

Nevertheless, he clicked on the safety.

5

Good Friday, 9 April 2004
Somewhere between Convoy Support Centre Scania and Logistics
Support Area Bushmaster South of Baghdad
1000 Local

'Vehicle...'

A quick check of the rims and the Boss scanned the road. There was an oil tanker coming up through the heat haze. It was at least twenty years old and the large fuel container was streaked with rust over the faded brand lettering on the side. He scanned the cab. There were two occupants as well as the driver. Some sort of red pennant dangled from the rear-view mirror and he could see there was a small fan on the dashboard. All very normal, other than all three were dressed in black and two had green head-bands on.

'Ginge, get Barnie for us, will you?'

Campbell slipped below the berm and wriggled back under the rocky over-hang.

Staff Barnes appeared.

'What's up, Boss?'

'John, this might be the mother of all fucking car bombs.'

'Unlikely here, Boss. What are they going to blow up? It's not used as an MSR by anybody, well, other than themselves, obviously. Which is why we've been fucking sat here for a week.'

'Maybe they're in the oil business and have just been issued the black combats and they thought they might cabby around impressing the birds in their new Gucci kit.'

'Alright, you may have a point. Nothing in this fucked-up place would surprise me, Boss.'

The tanker stopped at the house and the three men got out. All had AK47s. They shouted in and the owner came out. He, too, had donned a green armband. There was some hugging and general loud shouty banter and then the group became a lot quieter. They conversed for about ten minutes.

One of them looked out roughly in the direction of the OP and then started walking towards them. The Boss heard the soft click of the GPMG safety being set to fire. The man stopped, undid his fly, and urinated in their direction.

'I could give him a round right through the bell-end if you want Barnie...' Ginge Campbell had his large frame hunched over the machine gun, his head resting on his left hand, one eye shut, the other peering through the rear site. The index finger of his right hand was caressing the trigger.

'Plenty of time for that later, Ginge.'

The Iraqi zipped himself up, turned on his heel and joined the others. The Boss felt a release of tension and his pulse rate, which had risen dramatically, began to subside. He found his hands shaking.

Two of the Iraqis climbed back into the cab and the tanker drove off towards the raised section. Halfway to the summit, the tanker skewed across the road and stopped. The two men dismounted and walked back down the road. He noted that the driver had unplugged the fan and was carrying it back. He also had the red pennant which the Boss saw was a Manchester United Football Club souvenir.

'Obstacle. They're planning something big here. But I've got to say, it's not obvious what, is it?'

'Maybe they've all converted to Christianity and are going to celebrate Easter with a big fucking firework display.'

'Boss...'

'Yes, Cookie.' The Boss ducked his head below the lip and looked at the patrol signaller.

'Sig in from Zero.'

The Boss shimmied down the incline into the rocky outcrop where the troop had made their home. The radio operator handed him a piece of paper torn from an army notebook. In pencil he'd written a brief message that had just been received in morse code. Cookie had been with the attached SAS Signals Squadron before volunteering for and passing selection. Although badged SAS, he was still, at heart, an old school signaller famous for the speed of his morse.

Cooke sat with his back to a rock in the shade with one ear covered by a headphone. At his feet, on his poncho, lay his rifle in bits. He, too, was cleaning it for perhaps the fourth time that day.

The Boss read the signal. It basically said that someone, probably a US Rivet Joint AWACs, had intercepted mobile phone messages or radio chatter that indicated something going on in their area. They were to remain in position for another two days or until new instructions.

'Cookie, tell Zero we think there's an obstacle on the overpass and remind him there's definitely an IED on the road.'

'Wilco, Boss.'

'And you'd better add that this stretch of tarmac is not conducive to the finer elements of health and safety.'

'Do you mean nobody should fucking drive down this way?'

'That's exactly right,' said the Boss, with a hint of sarcasm.

'Just checking...obviously, I knew that already.'

He wriggled back up to just below the lip of the berm and lay on his back. He took a swig from his water and stared into the cloudless blue sky.

'Another vehicle has arrived. Five more have joined the party. They've also now got three RPGs and two RPKs as well as the dushka.'

'Boss?'

'What is it, Stan?'

'Did you ever bone that bird in the Grapes just before we deployed to Brize? Elaine, small dumpy blonde.'

'No, Stan, I did not "bone that bird" in the Grapes.'

'Oh, just as well. Half the squadron have and I was going to tell you but it sort of slipped my mind at the time. If you did, you might want to have a check-up with the MO. Just saying.'

'Thoughtful of you, Stan.'

'The medic is always here to help, you know that, Boss.'

'Indeed.'

6

Good Friday, 9 April 2004
Route Tampa South of Baghdad
1030 Local

Yip's Humvee drove past Cunningham's vehicle and put itself at the head of the column. After about ten minutes, it pulled over to the side of the road and Poklewski parked close behind it. She sat back, reached for some water and took a long draft. Cunningham sat in silence, looking through the windshield at the distant horizon. He felt a bit guilty for having chewed out Poklewski.

'What the fuck are you doing, sir?' It was Yip, yelling in through his window. 'LT, dismount and get your people in a defensive box. All drivers dismount and face out. Just because you can't see danger doesn't mean it's not there, sir.'

Cunningham jolted out of his daydream, cursed himself for the nth time that morning and got out of the vehicle. His legs were a bit stiff and he limped over to the side of the road and watched the convoy come to a halt and park up. The troops got out and had a stretch and started talking animatedly, hands in pockets, lighting cigarettes and photographing themselves. Some were relieving themselves on the tyres of their vehicles and the women went under one of the trucks to do likewise.

He yelled at his troops, organising all-round defence. Some looked at him, a bit amazed at this new aggression. The M915 gun truck came in last with Zeller pointing his .50 rearwards. SGT Lieber dismounted but the driver, de Rogatis, remained in the vehicle with the engine on.

Yip and Lieber were joined by SGT Andersson and they inspected the vehicles. Some of the Conex containers had small-arms impact marks and one round had narrowly missed a tire having gone through the rear of the front mudguard and exited between the headlights.

'Opportunity sniping,' said Lieber. 'Nothing too organised, they just let rip as we trundle past.'

'See the kids throwing rocks?' asked Andersson. 'I mean, do their fucking moms know what they get up to? Was sorely tempted to give them a squirt from the SAW.'

As if on cue, out of nowhere, some scruffy children appeared holding out their hands. The troops gave them some sweets or some local currency coins. Walking along the road were groups of black clad women with full face veils. A goatherd had his flock of animals off to one side and stood looking sullenly at the parked-up convoy.

Cunningham was crouched by his Humvee, looking out across the sand. In the middle distance was a string of electricity pylons. He was amazed that so many people were busy in this part of the desert some ten kilometres from the nearest house, or so he assumed. There was sporadic traffic on the road going in both directions. Old trucks, many Soviet built, and cars, mostly Japanese or German. For the most part, other than the children, people tended to ignore the Americans' presence. The flies, however, didn't and soon he was swatting away at the irritating small black critters attracted to the sweat under his helmet. He looked over to Poklewski, who was in a fire position facing out into the desert. He dug into his breast pocket.

'Hey, Poklewski, you want a mint?' He proffered the tube.

'I'm good, thanks, LT.' He was disappointed.

He wanted to talk, maybe make amends for the earlier Charlie Alpha. Instead, he rummaged about in a pouch and took out some insect repellent and dabbed it on his face. He looked back down the convoy. All the uniformed personnel were lying facing outwards. The American civilian drivers were standing around in the shade of their white trucks smoking, chatting, and taking pictures with small digital cameras. The TCNs were squatting in the shade, also smoking, but altogether more calmly and quietly. The three senior NCOs were in a group, talking. LT wondered if he should be there, shooting the breeze. He felt it would be too awkward to join the group now, but nevertheless felt excluded.

He got up, ostensibly to check the all-round defence of his men, but really, to stretch his legs, look busy and useful and maybe get invited to join with the NCOs. The sun was up and it was getting uncomfortably hot. And he was getting a headache. He wandered back to the Humvee.

'We have any paracetamol?'

'The CLS will have some.'

'Remind me again...'

'Chen, she's in the truck behind.'

He wandered over and asked for some headache pills. Chen gave him some Naproxen, which he swigged down with some bottled water. He sat down beside her as she lay with her rifle pointing out into the desert, and he let out a soft groan.

'You feeling ok, sir?'

'Yeah, fine. Just a bit of a headache. I think it's the heat and the tension. Sitting in the wagons doesn't help. What's in your trailer, Chen?'

'Dunno, sir. They just loaded a pallet of stuff in there. Probably toilet paper or something important like that.'

'Yeah...probably. Wouldn't surprise me. Did you get rocks thrown at you?'

'Yeah...just kids. Some couldn't even get their rocks onto the road.'

'Not exactly the welcome I was expecting from people who have just been liberated from a brutal dictator, if I'm honest.'

At that point, Yip and Andersson came up.

'Sir, we think we have a slow flat tire on one of the Whites. We're going to be here for at least another hour whilst we change it. SGT Andersson has already detailed a couple of your guys but you may wish to get some sort of rota going. Half in all-round defence whilst the other half can get into the shade and get some fluids down them. Fifteen on, fifteen off. We've still got a long way to go and we don't want anyone flaking out with heat exhaustion.'

'OK, Sergeant Major, I'll see to it.'

'Those not in defence still need to keep their weapons close by and be alert.'

'Yeah, our country needs more lerts,' said Chen quietly to Cunningham with a smile.

'Another thing, sir,' Yip added as an afterthought, 'I'm getting traffic on the other net and on the BFT that we may be diverted off Tampa and on to Jackson.'

'Why's that?' asked Cunningham.

'I'm told the Hajis have blown some bridges around Scania and that Tampa is now Black,' said Yip.

'Eight, to be precise,' said SGT Andersson.

'Eight what?' asked Cunningham.

'Eight fucking bridges. Sir.'

'Where's the junction onto Jackson? And how will we know when we're there?' Cunningham was beginning to feel nervous again about his competency. The trucking battalions were abuzz with stories about how a wrong turn had led to multiple deaths in ambushes. They were only this morning discussing the 507th Maintenance Company convoy which had been decimated in An Nasiriyah a year ago, as Yip had so kindly reminded him when they first met. It had taken a wrong turn and then turned around and gone through the kill zone again. Eleven soldiers had been killed, and almost worse in many people's minds, seven had been captured. And the Blackwater guys in Fallujah didn't bear thinking about.

'There's a Marine base at FOB Kalsu near Al Iskandariyah thirty or forty clicks south of here. They are manning a TCP on the junction of Tampa and Jackson and they'll direct us onto the right route,' said Yip. 'Don't worry, LT, I'll make sure we go down the right one. Just keep listening in on the air.'

Sergeant Major Romaro's confidence made Cunningham feel a little better. So long as they stuck together, he would shepherd them the right way.

Once the tire had been changed, all the crews remounted the vehicles and gunned their engines. Yip's Humvee went to the front of the column and then, after a brief pause, pulled back onto the road.

'Change of plan,' said Cunningham to Poklewski. 'Going a different way.'

'Oh yeah...where?'

'Straight through the triangle of death.' He had meant it to be funny and ironic but he regretted it instantly. It sounded more like misplaced bravado.

'That sounds nice. What's it say it's like in the brochure?'

Cunningham smiled, relieved that she hadn't taken the comment seriously. He changed the subject, for coming the other way, he could see what looked like another military convoy. As the other column approached, he saw that it was British.

'Hey, toot the horn and flash the lights at the Limeys.'

Poklewski did just that when the convoy was about 70 metres away. As they were passing, she waved out of the open window. The British top gunner in the first Land Rover looked at her and then stuck up two fingers, keeping eye contact as they passed and turning in his position to keep the gesture going.

'That's the Brits' sign for victory. They do it the other way round to our "peace sign". Prime Minister Churchill started it in World War Two I believe,' said Cunningham.

'And what's that, then?' asked Poklewski as another Rover in the column opened up a rear door. They were presented with a bare backside.

Cunningham smiled. He had heard the Brits were a bit off the wall.

'That, Private, is literally an asshole.' They both laughed and Cunningham felt some of the tension lift in the cab. He could hear the convoy tooting as the two columns passed each other.

'*<Everyone, this is Magicman. You see them Brits? I mean, what the actual fuck?*' came over the radio with a distant sound of country and western in the background. *<I should have got my shooter to drill his goddam fat white ass.'>*

'KBR,' said Poklewski. 'Kill 'em, bag 'em and replace 'em. What would we do without them, eh, Lieutenant?'

'Damn right, Poklewski. Somebody has got to do the job.'

'Ninety-k a year. I'll do it. Shucks, LT, I'm already doing it.'

After fifty minutes of steady progress south through the feature-less desert, Cunningham saw a vehicle checkpoint up ahead with an M1 Abrams Tank blocking one of the lanes and behind it two Bradleys. An MP to the side gestured to Yip's leading Humvee to pull up.

Cunningham jumped out of his side and marched down the stop-ping convoy, shouting at everybody to get out and go into all-round defence. He looked back and saw Yip talking to the MP. He heard a faint *sir* and saw Yip was gesturing for him to come over. He jogged back down the line, feeling he'd impressed the sergeant major with quick organisation of the men.

'Sir, this is our junction I told you back at the stop. We turn right at the clover leaf up there...' he pointed to an overhead gantry with a blue sign showing the road split in two, 'and we will proceed down Jackson, through some small one-horse towns until we get to Ad Diwaniyah. There the route goes either east to Scania, or west to Bushmaster. The Marines think it may be possible to get to Scania as the engineers are busy putting up Bailey bridges. But if we can't, we RON at Bushmaster or, failing that, Echo just south-west of the town.'

'Copy that, Sergeant Major.' The heat and the jog over to Romaro had made Cunningham start sweating and the toxic mix of sweat and mosquito repellent was now getting into his eyes. He rubbed them with his sleeve but they were itching and watering.

Romaro looked at him, curiously. 'You OK, sir?'

'Yes, fine. Just got something in my eyes. You know, sweat and insect repellent.'

'Oh, OK,' said Romaro. 'And LT? When you have two platoons of US Marines, two Abrams and three Bradleys, you don't have to be so ultra on the all-round defence... Just saying.' He winked at Cunningham. 'Right, let's get down to Bushmaster.'

'Or Scania,' said Cunningham.

'I'm hoping Bushmaster. It's smaller and nicer.'

The convoy mounted up again, and once formed was led by Yip's Humvee right and then down what was ASR Jackson, which, to Cunningham, looked very, very similar to MSR Tampa. They went through a small town at speed, which the MTS identified as Al Hillah. Once again, rocks were thrown by an assortment of teenagers but there was no gunfire. The Humvees blocked off traffic circles so that the convoy could proceed unhindered by cars, donkeys, vans and pedestrians, and before long they were out in the desert again. The next town, Al Qasim, was smaller, but there was still some rock throwing and the possibility of gunfire. Nobody was sure if it had occurred and none of the gunners had managed to engage any hostile targets. Soon, they were out again in the desert and moving towards Ad Diwaniyah.

YIP NOTICED that Hillah had been very quiet compared to the dozen or so times he had been through it before. Sure, there had been rock throwing, but he'd noticed that the kids were older. Mid-teens rather than the eight- to twelve-year-olds. There were almost no women on the streets and the traffic had been lighter than normal. It wasn't a religious day and it made him feel uneasy. On the MTS, he had been getting text updates about a large ambush outside BIAP, and the general word was that things had changed and the clerics were now actively and publicly stirring up violence against the coalition forces.

By the time they were driving through Al Qasim, the town was almost deserted. Only old men could be seen and they stopped and stared surlily at the convoy. He was not getting a warm welcoming feeling at all. Next was Diwaniyah, and he knew that to be a centre of Shi'ite fundamentalism. The cleric, Muqtada Al Sadr, ever since the Blackwater ambush and the big fire fight in Fallujah, had been preaching hatred and resistance to his followers. Coalition Provisional Authority Head Paul Bremer had closed down the Cleric's newspaper and it was now rumoured that the Mosques were telling everybody at prayers that armed resistance to the infidels was God's will. Al Sadr had gone into hiding in order to direct the resistance.

'Where the hell is everybody?' said Gubby, who was still ruminating on how, much against his will, he had been pulled out of his comfort zone of eating pizza and assigned to driving the sergeant major. Not that he minded. Being a "Fobbit" was all very well, but the confines of BIAP and Victory did start getting stultifying and claustrophobic. A couple of days on the road with SM Romaro was a nice break. Providing, of course, nothing bad happened.

'That is the question going through my mind, Gubby. I'm hoping and praying they're not all down in Diwaniyah preparing us a shock and awe shit show.'

'The worrying thing is that the smaller kids have all gone and so have the women. There's no teenagers older than about 15 to be seen. It's all the wannabes...' Gubby had the barrel of his rifle leant against the closed window as he drove.

'Hey, Cale?' shouted Yip to the M60 gunner.

'Wassup?' came the reply.

"You awake up there?'

'Damn right I am, Yip. There's a built-up area up ahead, I can see some taller buildings coming up'

They passed a power station and then they were driving next to a river, which at least gave them some protection from the left. Insurgents would probably not like to occupy the strip of land with no escape.

Yip called on the radio <*'All stations, Grandslam Seven Romeo Actual...be alert for snipers in the tall buildings a click ahead. If we have contact, keep driving through to the junction and we will bear west on Orlando towards Bushmaster.'>* And then, as an afterthought, he added <*'For all you KBRers, west is a right turn.'>*

They went past a petrol station on the right-hand side, its red and yellow cladding covered in dust and blanched by the sun. There were no cars filling up. A dog sat in the shade, chained to a ring in the wall and watched them go past.

<*'Yo everybody, this is Magicman. I can see like a funfair up ahead. Say we stop and have a ride on the ferris wheel?'*

<*'Hi, Magicman, this is Roadrunner, I think that's a mighty fine idea – probably the best you've had since you came to this god forsaken country.'>*

<*'Dude, I'm full of...'>*

<*'Grandslam Seven Romeo Actual, let's cut the chatter. Plenty of time for Disneyland when we get you all safely into Bushmaster. Until then, keep your eyes open and your mouths closed.'>*

<*'Somebody got out of bed the wrong side.'>*

<*'Checkerboard Two Zero. Magicman, I know that's you...just shut it. Out,'>* Andersson barked.

A mile or so beyond the petrol station, a large, gray, imposing three-story government building marked the bend in the road where the dual carriageway of Jackson bent to the right, and south and straight ahead was the town centre with the Ferris wheel now visible to those who were not as high up in a cab as the KBR drivers. The building was made of concrete with large windows on each floor looking out over the road.

Yip, with Cunningham in the Humvee behind, drove past the building. Its gates were closed and there were no flags on the masts. As Chen was driving her M915 past, automatic fire opened from the top story. Almost immediately, Yip's top gunner swivelled round and fired off a burst from his M60. The rounds peppered the upper stories, chipping out the concrete in a cloud of dust and shattering the windows. The empty cases and the black metal links scattered on the floor at his feet.

<'Ambush left...ambush left...'>

Gubby pulled into the side to give the gunner a steadier platform and he was now delivering measured three- to five-round bursts raking the top of the building. Yip was out of the vehicle and, crouching behind the armored hood, scanned the windows for movement or muzzle flashes. Cunningham's Humvee pulled in behind and Cunningham dismounted, running at a crouch towards Yip.

'What the fuck are you doing?' screamed Yip at the startled officer. 'Keep fucking driving, you have got to keep fucking driving...'

Chastened, Cunningham got back in his Humvee and moved off just as Chen's vehicle was coming up behind, and a full-on collision was avoided by Poklewski swerving as Chen sounded the horn. Magicman's KBR vehicle sped past, the driver crouched down whilst his shooter was spraying his M16 out of the window. Ciccarelli's tanker followed and Yip saw it was spilling gas from a hit near the rear of the tank, leaving a dark trail in the dust on the road. The next tractor was an all-female team and Yip saw that the shooter was not engaging. Both soldiers were crouched low in the cab and concentrating on staying as close to Ciccarelli's tanker as they possibly could without being sprayed with gas.

Andersson's Humvee sped past, overtaking the slower trucks, Wavebourne firing his SAW in entirely the wrong direction, spraying a long line of rounds at a warehouse complex on the right. Yip shouted and pointed at the government building, but Wavebourne didn't see him and kept up his assault on the right. Roadrunner's KBR truck followed close behind.

Cunningham looked back and saw Lieber's M915 Skunkwerks gun truck pulling in beside Yip's Humvee. The .50 calibre's deep and slower booming contrasting with the quicker rate of fire and higher pitched sound of the 5.56mm SAW. Zeller was at a higher elevation and had the best field of fire but Yip's gunner, Bastion, was still raking the building, which now had most of its windows shot out. Every five rounds a tracer flashed towards its target and in one of the rooms, a curtain had caught fire.

'Yip...Yip...fucking Yip...I'll see them through, you go ahead because that fucking dumbass officer will miss the turning.'

Yip climbed back in his vehicle and Gubby drove off.

<*'We're taking fire, repeat taking fire from all sides...where the fuck is the support? We need fucking Apaches here now, goddamit'*> Magicman's panic was raising the pitch of his voice and drowning out all other radio traffic.

<*'Checkerboard One Zero, keep driving...'*> came Cunningham's voice.

<*'What the fuck do you think I'm doing you fucking moron?'*>

Yip felt he had to intervene to protect the young officer. <*'Grandslam Seven Romeo, cut all unnecessary traffic. Repeat... all unnecessary traffic...'*>

Gubby was racing past on the outside of the convoy and Yip could tell that this had been planned and may be deep and long. As they were passing Magicman, an insurgent stepped into an open piece of ground with an RPG7 on his shoulder. He methodically knelt down and Yip thought he could see him briefly struggling with the safety catch or trigger before a loud detonation, muzzle flash, and a bigger back blast sent the rocket towards its target. It flew high over the KBR truck just as Bastion trained his M60 onto him. The insurgent rose, dropped the launcher, but was hit in the ankle. Hopping desperately back to cover behind a building, the next burst caught him full in the back and he dropped to the ground. As the Humvee went past the twitching body, Bastion put another burst of five rounds into the corpse, the body shuddering with the impact and loose rounds kicking up the dirt all around.

CUNNINGHAM WAS YELLING at Poklewski to drive faster. Up ahead, he could see an overpass, and he remembered that at some stage they had to turn right and that this was as good a place as any to do it. He saw a muzzle flash to his front right and heard a metallic plink as a round hit the Humvee somewhere. He pointed his M16 at the building and squeezed the trigger. Nothing happened.

'Fuck...fuck!' He slipped off the safety and squeezed again. And again, nothing happened. 'Oh Jesus, please, oh Jesus...' They sped past the building as some of his basic training began to filter into his fogging brain. He cocked the weapon. Jesus and Mary, why had he not cocked the weapon? He pointed the weapon at another building, squeezed the trigger and the rifle fired.

He looked over at Poklewski to see if she'd clocked what had just happened but she was concentrating on the road with her rifle out of the window. Occasionally, almost at random, she fired off a couple of rounds without looking where she was firing. He again heard the plink of rounds hitting the vehicle. He saw a muzzle flash from the flat roof of a house and he raised his rifle and fired a burst. By the third round, his rifle jammed. He felt like weeping. Why was this happening? He pulled the cocking lever and saw a round was jammed in the breach. His action of cocking was now feeding a second round. Desperately, he clawed at it to remove the obstruction. At that point, a round came through the windshield, ripping the sun visor away, and buried itself somewhere in the back of the vehicle.

'Sir, return fire, we got to keep their heads down...please, sir, just fire.' Poklewski was screaming with panic as he tried to get the round out. Suddenly, it flipped out into the footwell and he then let go of the cocking handle and slid another round into the breech. He pointed the barrel out of the window and let off a full magazine into a house in front of them. The M16 stopped with a click and he pushed the magazine release catch, letting it drop to the floor to join the live round rolling around with a bottle of water. He reached into his pouch and tried to retrieve another magazine. It wouldn't come, and he kept tugging at the obstinate yet inanimate object. Finally, he looked down and saw that it was just catching on the lip of the pouch. He eased it out, slammed it into his rifle, cocked the weapon, and fired another burst, this time at a man who was crouching behind a car. He saw the rounds impact the dirt high and to the left, and the man darted out of sight. He didn't appear to be armed.

At this point, they were going under the overpass at the junction of what he previously hoped was Jackson and Orlando. The east-west carriageway was on stilts above them and the right turn he should have made had been and gone without him realising. Cunningham spotted another figure and, taking aim, fired again. The figure dropped and Cunningham felt both elation and horror.

'Alice, I freakin got him. I shot a Haji,' he yelled. The success had a calming effect on him and he searched through the sites for more targets. The shooting seemed to have stopped and Cunningham felt that maybe they had run the killing zone. The houses were thinning out and he now felt a slight sense of disappointment. He continued to scan through his sights, eager to engage another target, and wondered if he should have called Poklewski by her first name.

Yip's Humvee stopped a hundred metres short of the clover leaf to direct the rest of the convoy onto the right turn ramp and up onto the east-west road. The town of Ad Diwaniyah sprawled out to the east and he was relieved the convoy had opted to go west out of the built-up area. He saw that they'd pulled up about a quarter of a mile ahead and the next vehicle, Chen's tractor, was still not yet out of the kill zone. As the vehicle approached the cloverleaf, he saw there were three bullet holes in her windscreen. He couldn't see her shooter...what was he called...Luckenbach, that's right, Luckenbach.

At that moment, a kilometre due south of Yip's position by the right turn, Poklewski said, 'Luckenbach has been hit pretty bad by the sound of it.'

'How do you know?'

Poklewski looked at him in alarm. 'Excuse me?'

'How do you know he's been hit?'

'Chen has just said it over the radio...didn't you hear it?'

'Huh... no, no...I...the gunfire was blocking out my hearing.'

'Sheesh, please let him be OK,' she added to herself as she drove due south as fast as the Humvee would go. Cunningham thought back to this morning, when she and Luckenbach had walked together to the vehicles.

YIP DECIDED he should move forward to beyond the feeder ramp onto the raised east-west carriageway so that he could ensure no vehicles missed the right turn. Bastion was now firing controlled bursts of machine gun fire down the highway east into the main part of the town. The tracer rounds seemed to arc lazily towards their target and then ping up high into the air before burning out. Beyond the junction, the raised eastbound carriageway headed into the city centre, dropping down from the raised bridge section. On the skyline, to the north, was the Ferris wheel, bizarrely still turning. In the foreground, to the east, was waste ground beside the road, littered with rubbish and a few broken down cars, and then, as the raised section levelled down, houses lined the carriageway both north and south of the road. From the end of these houses, automatic gunfire began. The insurgents had chosen their ambush site well as they could fire into the back of any vehicle as it made the slow ascent up the ramp.

Black figures began to emerge from the houses and run toward them across the open space, taking cover in the uneven ground. A flash indicated that an RPG had been fired and it approached more slowly than seemed realistic. It fizzed overhead and detonated some way to the rear of the Humvee. Gubby dismounted and took cover behind the hood of the vehicle, scanning for targets over the iron sights of his M16. This was extreme range for an assault rifle, but just keeping their heads down was useful and the recoil in his shoulder comforting. Bastion was spraying the area with fire and they were darting from cover to cover, trying to get closer to the junction to engage the convoy.

Yip opened the door and leant in for the radio handset.

<'*Thunderclap this is Grandslam Seven Romeo. We are in contact on junction of Jackson and Orlando. Request air support over.*'>

<'*Grandslam Seven Romeo, roger that, wait out...*'>

'Gubby, I need you to monitor the incoming comms. Let them know we have casualties and will require dustoff, and, if they can spare it, CAS. A couple of A10s or Apaches. You got the grid?'

Gubby looked at his map. 'Junction of Orlando and Jackson, west of Diwaniyah.' He studied the map carefully and read out the eight-figure grid reference.

'Good. Make sure they know to approach from the west.'

Yip ran to the side of the southbound carriageway so he could be seen by the on-coming convoy vehicles. Chen's tractor was coming down the road at speed, the windshield's three prominent bullet strikes clearly visible. Other rounds had hit the container on the back and one had shattered the outside mirror. One tire was shredded and the vehicle was sparking on the rim. As it passed, Yip saw a stream of blood had seeped under the passenger door and was streaking the cab horizontally backwards. He briefly toyed with the idea of pulling Chen over and getting Luckenbach out but dismissed it. He couldn't risk stopping in the kill zone and it would be chaos if the others pulled in behind, leaving the ambushers with a static line of vehicles to shoot at.

Close behind Chen was Magicman's KBR truck. It appeared unscathed and was following the military vehicle rather too closely. Yip stood up and indicated for the driver to take the next ramp right on to the flyover and head west. Next was the tanker, which had now been hit several more times, and gas was pouring from the holes. The shooter was leaning out of the window, firing his rifle to the left at the open ground. As the tanker passed Yip and was about to take the right turn, a thunderous whump followed by a blast of heat knocked the air out of Yip's lungs whilst bowling him over on to his back. He knew instantly that an RPG had hit and detonated the lethal mix of gas and air.

The vehicle kept driving but its trailer was now ablaze, sheets of orange flame and oily black smoke streaking back. Yip, still lying on the road, flailed hopelessly, trying to indicate that Ciccarelli should pass the right turn then stop and abandon the vehicle, but she didn't see him and turned onto the ramp. The back tires had caught fire and the truck was now travelling on the rims, sliding over the road, its wheels spinning without grip. It ground to a halt, just as the oily black smoke smothered Yip. Both doors opened and Ciccarelli and her shooter, Keszbom, jumped down. Keszbom still held his rifle but fell awkwardly. He got up limping and staggered towards Yip. Behind him, Ciccarelli, who'd left her weapon behind, was also running in a crouch. Yip staggered back to his feet.

'Get to the Humvee!' he shouted. 'Gubby, Gubby, tell all stations they have to drive through the smoke of the tanker. They mustn't stop or not make the turn.'

'Copy that, Yip. You ok?'

Yip gave him the thumbs up and turned to face up the road.

Through the smoke that was now drifting back over to where Yip's Humvee was parked, the next tractor appeared. The driver, Gamble, appeared, disconcerted by the vision of hell that confronted her. The black smoke was accumulating in the underpass and the trailer was burning furiously in front of her. She would have to drive right by the burning tanker which, in her mind, could explode at any moment.

'Drive through it...don't stop...drive through it!' yelled Yip, even though he knew the drivers wouldn't hear. He was gesticulating frantically for the vehicles not to stop but to turn right and head through the smoke. He was vaguely aware that incoming rounds were hitting the ground nearby, some thumping into the concrete of the overpass and emitting a high-pitched whine as they ricocheted away. The smoke in his lungs made him splutter and cough as he shouted.

The next vehicle was a tractor, too. Yip's heart sank, as that meant a KBR truck was missing. He was hoping the driver had got into one of the passing vehicles as instructed in the briefing. The tractor started slowing and once again Yip began shouting and gesticulating.

'Keep moving, go through the smoke to the right, keep going...don't stop...don't fucking stop...' The driver looked at Yip and gave a thumbs up and pulled onto the ramp up to the overpass.

Screaming down the outside of the southbound carriageway was Andersson's Humvee, with Wavebourne firing the SAW almost continually. They saw Yip too late and over-shot the turning before braking hard and reversing up alongside the other Humvee. With two automatic weapons firing on the waste ground, there were fewer incoming rounds. Andersson got out and Yip saw he'd picked up the KBR driver who called himself *Roadrunner*. He appeared unhurt. Andersson ran in a crouch towards Yip, his M16 in his shoulder.

'Kyle, we need to get the rest of the convoy up the ramp. They mustn't over-shoot. I think we've missed the main part of the ambush over there.'

'That's because they're dumb fucks. You ok, Yip?' asked Andersson.

'Yeah, just a bit of smoke. They were banking on us turning east to Scania. Get to the front of the convoy and find a box lager site where we can land the medivac. Try to catch up with Cunningham. He's gotta be a click or more west of us now.'

Andersson ran across the carriageway, remounted his vehicle and drove off to catch up the lead vehicles.

Yip saw another black oily column of smoke and guessed they had hit the second tanker. He hoped against hope that it wasn't blocking the way and that Lieber in the M915 Skunkwerks would manage to shepherd the rest of the column past it and up to him to get out of the kill zone driving west. Above the din of the SAW and the M60 he could hear the thud, thud, thud of the .50 calibre, so at least Lieber was still operational. More KBRs and M915s came out of the smoke, most having to break hard to make the turn. All had been hit with small arms and one of the Conex containers had an RPG strike. Smoke drifted out of the hole as whatever was in the container was smouldering gently. As it came towards him, Yip saw there was someone on the running plate holding desperately onto the wing mirrors. He hoped it was a pick-up from the tanker but was concerned about where the other crewman was. As the truck braked hard for the turn, the soldier let go of the wing mirror and half fell, half jumped, rolling on the ground as the vehicle slewed right and up the ramp. Impressively, he still had his M16 and, although shaken by the fall and covered in dust, seemed to be unhurt.

'Get over by the Humvee!' yelled Yip over the relentless noise, whilst still guiding the on-coming vehicles. The man ran at a crouch towards Gubby and Keszbom who were in a kneeling position firing over the bonnet. Bastion was still behind the M60 raking the houses and waste ground. Ciccarelli was beside Keszbom but had no weapon. Gubby gestured for him to sprint over to the cover, but the man pulled up from his crouch and stood upright. He staggered for two or three steps and then seemed to collapse down as if he'd been deflated. He lay motionless, face down in the dust beside the carriageway. His rifle discarded a few metres behind.

Gubby immediately raced out from behind the Humvee, kicked the prostrate body over onto its back, and grabbed the webbing behind the man's head. With a concerted effort, he dragged the body backwards. He fell onto his butt but got up and started dragging again.

Yip sprinted the seventy-five metres over to help and between them they got the man over to the lee of the vehicle.

'Gubby, get me the med pack and then make sure the convoy goes up the ramp and heads west.'

Gubby looked up to see Ciccarelli had already got the pack, and she threw it over to Yip. Yip checked the man's pulse, which was faint but discernible. He stuck his fingers in his mouth to check his tongue wasn't obstructing the airways and put his ear down to check the faint rasping breaths. The man let out a whimper, which was a good sign of sorts. Yip tore open the body armour on one side and saw a spreading red stain in the lower abdomen. He ripped open the shirt and then cut away the t-shirt with the scissors from the med pack. The entry wound was just above the pelvic bone and it had exited somewhere further up his back. The immediate danger was bleeding and shock but if the round had missed any of the internal organs, especially the liver, and had not gone through his spine, he may very well completely recover. He ripped open a field dressing and taped it to the exit wound and then another onto the entry wound.

He sat the man up against the rear wheel of the Humvee and was preparing to administer morphine and a saline drip to counteract the shock of trauma when he noticed blood seeping through the t-shirt and down the man's side under the body armor. He lifted the arm and saw a second entry hole in the armpit. The round must have missed the body armor and entered into the chest cavity at an almost impossible angle. This was an altogether worse prognosis. He listened for the man's breathing, but it was impossible with the din of the firefight going on.

'Cale, stop firing. Cale...CALE!'

'Huh?'

'Stop firing for a minute, I need to check this guy's respiration.'

Cale slipped down the ring and out of the rear door and crouched beside Yip.

'He's got two gunshot wounds. Here and in his armpit. I want to see if he's got lung penetration.'

Yip could hear no sucking from a punctured lung and although faint, the wounded man's breathing was regular.

'Fuck...Yip...what about the internal bleeding?' Cale's face was white and he was sweating profusely.

'Get on the air and get the chopper airborne now. Tell it to land on our smoke five clicks west of here on Orlando. We can't risk bringing it in here. Tell em we've got an expectant. Get Lieutenant Cunningham to acknowledge and find a suitable stop for a box up.'

The M60 started firing again and they both looked up to see Keszbom had climbed behind the gun and was now firing at the waste ground.

The chest wound meant Yip couldn't risk morphine that might affect his breathing, but, at least for now, the man seemed unconscious. He reached into the med pack and pulled out a drip and canula. He then searched for a vein in his arm, but the shock had flattened his blood pressure.

'Come on, come on...' Yip smacked the inside elbow to raise a vein. He squeezed just below the bicep with all his strength, willing the increased pressure to present him with an opportunity of sliding in the needle.

Bastion returned and took over. Yip took the needle out and slid it into the flesh.

'Fuck...come on...' A racking coughing fit made him miss the vein. He extracted and tried again while Bastion maintained his vice like grip. He slid in again and this time was rewarded with a rush of blood into the tubing. He connected up the bag and looped it onto the open door. He checked the dog tags: Sneddon. He sat the man up and left him with Ciccarelli to go back to the ramp and get the convoy all going the right way. Bastion climbed back up to his M60, cocked the weapon and started spraying the houses with a renewed aggression, his bursts longer, his eyes misted by tears.

CUNNINGHAM WAS HEADING SOUTH on the dual carriageway, the noise and confusion of the ambush receding behind him. Poklewski was silent and pale but clearly still in control of all her faculties.

<'*All stations, this is Grandslam Seven...proceed five, repeat five clicks west of obvious and go firm...Checkboard one Zero copy, over*'>. Cunningham didn't recognise the voice and hoped that Yip hadn't been hurt.

<'*Roger Grandslam, will go firm in four and a half clicks. All other stations copy.*'>

'Sir, sir,' shouted Poklewski. 'He said west. We've not made the turn yet....'

<'*Grandslam Seven, Checkerboard, we need to bring in a helo for cas dust off, copy.*'>

<'*Roger Grandslam. Out.*'>

The other call signs began to acknowledge, some with the din of the ambush masking most of what was said. But Cunningham was not hearing anything. He jammed on the pressel and shouted into the mic.

<'*Hello all stations, this is Checkerboard One Zero. We've overshot the turning. Am turning round now.*'> He let the pressel go and yelled at Poklewski. 'Stop the goddamn vehicle...'

There were few houses around as the road receded into the

desert. Poklewski jammed on the brakes and all the equipment in the back slid into the rear footwells. There was silence.

'Turn round...we've missed the turn. I told you to turn right...'

'No, you didn't, LT...'

'I darn well did, Private.'

Poklewski stared at him with hatred in her eyes before she shifted it into reverse to turn the vehicle. 'It would be better to drive straight on. We can figure a way to get west further down the highway.'

'Just do as I darn well tell you, Poklewski. We need to get with the convoy. I ain't driving down here on my own!' yelled Cunningham. He then raised the mic again and shouted into it.

<'Hello all stations, this is Checkerboard One. Copy over...'>

There was silence and then the other call signs began chattering.

'Hello all stations...'>

'Sir, they can't hear you...the radio must be damaged. Try the Sincgars...' yelled Poklewski.

As his Humvee overtook, Andersson looked behind at Chen in her M915 and the ominous bullet holes in the windshield where Luckenbach should have been sitting. She was staring impassively back, keeping twenty metres away from the back of his Humvee. As they drove on, Andersson noticed the road rising to another overpass in the distance. There appeared to be a broken-down civilian tanker partially blocking the carriageway.

'Slow down, will you, Kurt? I don't like the look of that tanker.'

The driver slowed right down. He noticed in the rear-view mirror that the twenty-metre gap was maintained by Chen.

'Actually, pull over...'

'We're not five clicks out, Sarge.'

'I know. I just want to get everybody into line before we find somewhere to box up and sort ourselves out. Seems kind of quiet here.'

He jumped out of the Humvee and jogged over to Chen, climbed up to talk to her through the window. He stared at the body of Luckenbach slumped in the passenger footwell. Half his face was missing and he was clearly dead. Chen looked straight ahead, silent. Tear tracks stained her face and she was shaking as she gripped the wheel. There was a lot of blood in the cab and Luckenbach's window was smeared where he'd slumped against it before sliding down his seat.

He shouted back to his driver to organise the convoy as it rolled in and then turned back to Chen.

'Ok, Anne-Lise, we are going to take Luckenbach out of the cab and we'll put him in the Humvee.'

She continued to stare straight ahead, saying nothing.

'Wavebourne, get over here...we need to get Luckenbach into the back of the Humvee.'

Wavebourne stared at the body and then turned away and retched. He reached for his water bottle and took a draft before spitting it out onto the desert floor.

'Oh, sweet lord,' he muttered before reaching past Chen and grabbing Luckenbach's webbing. He rummaged in the pack and pulled out his poncho which he lay on the ground by the passenger's door, and he and the sergeant pulled the body out of the cab and onto the ground. They rolled the poncho over the body and tried to lift the dead weight. By this time, Magicman had pulled up in his KBR truck and jumped out to help. The three of them hoisted the body into the back of the Humvee. Magicman's shooter was Chipunza. He was reduced to a whispered, 'Holy mother fuckers.'

Other trucks were pulling up and people were milling about, swapping their stories of the ambush.

Andersson returned to his vehicle and asked Yip to let him know when he was leaving the junction. He could still hear the firefight in the distance and was pleased that the 50 calibre was still firing. There were other bigger detonations, which he assumed were RPGs. He hoped and prayed that they were missing their targets. Some of the trucks rolled in on flat tires, whilst one KBR vehicle, call sign *Slam-dunk*, was dragging its trailer on rims. It would be impossible for it to continue much further and Andersson thought that when Yip arrived, they would transfer the crew and destroy the vehicle. He set the KBR drivers to change the blown tires and where possible to salvage the vehicles and their cargoes.

'Where the fuck is that bozo, LT?' Andersson said, mainly to himself.

Wavebourne looked down from his gun. 'I've not seen him, Kyle. Must be with Romaro.'

Andersson picked up the radio.

<*'Hello Checkerboard One Zero, this is Two Zero. Send Lockstat, over.'*>

YIP COULD SEE two more KBR vehicles and two more M915 tractors approaching, followed finally by Lieber's gun truck. Zeller was still manning the .50 calibre and, as Yip watched, an RPG rocket fizzed past, exploding several hundred metres beyond its target.

If we can just get these five vehicles onto the ramp and heading out west, we'll have escaped pretty lightly, Yip thought. He was looking at the activity on the waste ground over by the houses when he heard the ominous sound of two very large wine bottles having their corks extracted.

'Mortars...incoming!' he screamed, more out of training than anything else as probably nobody could hear, and if they could, there probably wasn't much to be done other than keep driving. Both rounds landed a hundred metres plus of their targets. Immediately, he heard another two rounds being fired. There was a delayed hang time in the air and then he could hear the downward trajectory rising in tempo. They exploded thirty metres in front of his vehicle. They were ranging in on him and the Humvee. Another two rounds were fired. Yip was flat on the ground and looked over to see that Gubby had also thrown himself down and in the lee of the vehicle. Bastion was maintaining a fire pattern on the waste ground and the houses. Ciccarelli was tending the wounded man. The double thump of the impacts were behind the vehicle and Yip now knew it was time to move. He heard but didn't listen to the radio chatter. SGT Andersson was trying to get through to Lieutenant Cunningham.

'Gubby, we need to get the fuck outta here.'

Gubby flung himself in the driver's seat and Yip, with Ciccarelli's help, loaded Sneddon into the back. He was unconscious now, and deathly pale. There was no time to monitor him, so with Ciccarelli making sure the drip stayed upright, Yip used his hand to sweep the empty cases and links onto the floor of the Humvee. They then loaded him into the back just beside Bastion's feet. Gubby reversed the vehicle into a tight curve and then drove towards the ramp road as two more impacts came in.

As Lieber's gun truck approached the overpass turning, Gubby drove out in front of him and led the way up the ramp, Zeller swivelling round in his seat to keep the fire on the waste ground and the houses. The other four trucks were heading west at a steady 45 mph and soon they would be out of effective range of the insurgents. The tanker was still burning and the column of oily black smoke laid down a partial screen for the vehicles. It was also a good marker for the two A-10 Warthogs that had been deployed following the contact report at the start of the ambush. They announced their presence with their Gatling guns, delivering 60 rounds of 30mm shells per second, each sounding like a fast revving, unsilenced motorcycle. Flying deceptively slow, they turned away over the target as the rounds hit home, spraying decoy flares like fireworks. The detonations could be felt in the vehicle.

'Love that sound,' shouted Gubby. 'Them muthafuckers are going to get themselves ripped new assholes. Here they come again...' Once again, the Gatling guns ripped the air and again the ground shook under the target.

Yip looked up to the sky to see if his casualty helicopter was also airborne, but he couldn't see anything yet. The A-10s were heading for home. He decided he would catch up with the leading elements of the convoy and then stop far enough away so that the insurgents couldn't loop around and have another go.

After a few minutes, he found the convoy's forward elements under SGT Andersson in a box laager. He got on the radio and told Cunningham to get everybody mounted up and then follow him to a suitable place to land the chopper and get the wounded evacuated. There was no answer.

<'Hello Checkerboard One Zero, we are going to go over the raised section across the canal and then we'll stop in a box. Put Two Zero on the summit to ensure nobody tries to follow up the ambush and I'll get Lieber out forward. You need to find a good LZ for the dust off. Hello, Checkboard One Zero? Checkerboard One Zero? Nothing heard; Out.'>

7

'Somebody's getting a right fucking kicking.'

The sound of the ambush was drifting over the OP position. It was difficult to make out who was getting the best of it but the deeper booming of a Five-O Browning suggested it was probably the Americans on the receiving end. Whether they were winning the fire fight, however, was hard to tell.

The troop were stood-to, observing the houses to their front. Further insurgents had arrived, half a dozen or so on motorbikes and the rest in an assortment of vehicles and taxis. As the gunfire rumbled on in the distance, two men mounted a motorbike. The pillion had an RPG launcher on his shoulder. They drove up to the brow of the overpass and stopped about 100 metres from the abandoned oil tanker.

Barnes followed them up with the Aimpoint sight on his weapon. They were crouching down, the RPG horizontal and the motorbike on its side stand. The blue exhaust smoke indicated that it was still running. The driver was standing behind the RPG launcher.

'You don't want to stand there, mate,' muttered Barnes, 'unless you want a face full of back blast.'

The Boss was observing to the front and an assortment of insurgents emerged from the house and began taking up fire positions in the ditch in front and to the right of them. He was beginning to experience the adrenaline rush and felt his hands start to shake and his mouth go dry.

'If they open up, we are right in the line of fire.'

Barnes swivelled his gaze to the ambush, seemingly unmoved by the imminent threat they were facing. The Hilux with the odd door started up and an insurgent leapt on to the back behind the heavy machine gun, his brown shemagh over his face. It drove round to the back of the house and out of sight of the patrol. Lots of confusion and shouting began, as the individuals sought out places to crouch low and wait for whatever convoy came down the road.

The door of the occupied house opened and a procession of black clad women emerged and moved down the road away from the men. A couple of children gripped the hands of their mothers tightly whilst looking over their shoulders at the commotion they were leaving behind.

The troop were mainly in the lee of the roadside out of sight with a couple of sets of eyes on the target. They were, however, coiled, waiting for the counter ambush to go noisy. There were three GPMGs and two Minimis as well as an assortment of grenade launchers on the Armalites. The firepower at their disposal was immense. The backstop was with the vehicles, which would either be used in a fighting withdrawal, or more likely in truth, be moved round to the kill zone in order to exfiltrate following a reorganisation on the objective. War is a brutal business and the advantage was always with those that had the experience and the training. Speed; surprise; momentum; total violence was the mantra.

There was a detonation on the overpass. The Boss looked up and saw the RPG had fired and hit the tanker. An orange fireball rose into the air and black smoke billowed around the impact. The tanker began to burn furiously, orange flames engulfing the cab and the tyres. A few seconds later, a Humvee swerved around the burning tanker and through the smoke. The top gunner was facing forward and fired a short burst at the motorcycle, which was now speeding back down the road. The first burst missed, and the gunner read-justed and gave a longer burst. Around the motorcycle the ground erupted, as the rounds kicked up dust before whining off into the distance. Astonishingly, the motorcycle rode on unscathed, weaving down the road and putting distance between itself and the slower moving American vehicle.

'How the fuck did he not hit that bike?' said Barnes.

'Firing on the move is harder than it looks,' replied the Boss. 'Of course, you wouldn't know that, being all airborne and grunty.'

'He missed it because he's a fackin' crap hat.'

There was now a second Humvee followed by an American lorry pulling a trailer with a container. That, in turn, was followed by a white Volvo articulated lorry. By now, the motorcycle had passed the white stone and the rider hit the brakes, the back wheel locking. Both riders got off and ran to cover. The motorbike toppled over on its side and stalled.

'Bollocks...hold on a sec,' said the Boss and fumbled in his top pocket. He extracted a pair of yellow ear plugs, and with shaking hands, swiftly rolled them and stuffed them in his ears. The effort had also popped out his Silva compass tied through the button hole with a red cord. 'That's better...' he said, rather too loudly, fumbling to put the compass back and flicking the safety off with his thumb.

'Fuck me, Boss,' laughed Barnes. 'You work in from the left, I'll take the right side...watch and shoot...watch and shoot...'

With that, Barnes and then the Boss opened up on the insurgents with their rifles and immediately the belt-fed machine guns started firing. The link was 5:1 ball and trace, so every fifth round a tracer round showed the fall of shot. The effect was not dissimilar to a firework display ignited by a rogue spark and everything going off at once. Red tracer would hit into the impact zone and then lazily ricochet into the sky.

The Boss and Barnes were picking off the targets. Home in on the individual, zero onto the centre of the observed mass, steady the breathing, squeeze off one and then another round. It was a mechanical process honed by hundreds of hours and thousands of training rounds on ranges all over the world. Once it had started, a calm descended on the Boss as he concentrated on the mechanics of the ambush. The rest of the troop were doing the same. The belt-fed automatic weapons were causing havoc with their superior hitting power.

The insurgent ambushers were failing to realise that the direction of incoming fire was not the Humvees. Some were standing to fire their AK47s at the on-coming vehicles. The life expectancy of anybody who opted to do that was a matter of seconds, as the rate of incoming enfilade fire was now overwhelming. Some turned and fled the scene but were cut down before they got more than five metres.

There was a loud detonation as the IED was triggered. The vehicle that took the brunt of the blast was the first American lorry. It continued through the billowing black smoke but half the cab was missing. The tractor slewed sideways and in very slow time, the trailer came round and tipped on to its side and slid, in an agonising display of sound and sparks, down the road before coming to a stop. The shattered windscreen popped out and lay on the road still intact, despite the multitude of cracks.

As soon as the IED exploded, the Hilux appeared from behind the house. The man behind the DShk fired three to four rounds before having to re-cock the weapon, probably the result of dirty rounds. He was firing at a GI who'd jumped out from the front Humvee that had now stopped. The American ran back up to the lorry on its side. The rounds hit around his feet, kicking up dust and debris. He went down behind the cover of the overturned cab. The Humvee gunner was laying down a sustained fire onto the ambush, hitting the house and the road opposite the British ambush position.

All three of the troop's heavy machine guns ranged in on the Hilux. It was being hit by twenty bullets a second and very soon was riddled with holes. Both occupants in the front seats were slumped forward and the rear gunner had disappeared from view at the foot of the pintle mount. The rounds continued to slam into the vehicle, all four tyres bursting, all windows being shot out with large fragments of bodywork and bumper flying into the air.

The second vehicle then appeared and all weapons immediately hosed it with fire. It ground to a halt and the door away from the ambush opened and a figure ran out and into the fields. The tracer rounds followed him mercilessly and he, too, dropped into the grass. The grass began to burn around the body.

'STOP!'

The troop machine gunners all stopped firing on a command from the Boss. There was an eerie silence as the blue cordite smoke, with its pungent odour, drifted away. This was the time when everybody in the ambush was poised, waiting for a movement. This duly happened when a burst of AK fire came from the flat roof. There was a pop as a 40mm high explosive grenade was fired by one of the troop over the parapet. The subsequent detonation on the flat roof was marked by a small cloud of black smoke. Three more grenades were fired in quick succession, one overshooting and landing on the open ground behind the house. Again, there was silence. The Boss began shaking again and felt the nausea of the adrenaline rush. He knew the feeling would stay with him as he came down from the stress. He took a swig of water and tried to steady his hands by gripping his weapon and taking long slow breaths. He knew that his next emotion would be euphoria.

The leading Humvee was still driving down the road towards the position. The Boss stood up and unfurled a Stars and Stripes and motioned for the vehicle to slow and stop. This was always a risky manoeuvre, as a nervous gunner in the Humvee could engage. However, it became clear they'd seen the total annihilation of the insurgent ambush and knew whoever it was, was on their side.

The troop remained on alert for any further insurgents who

might accelerate meeting their maker by taking one last shot at the infidel. Several of the enemy were clearly badly wounded but not dead, though all the fight had now left them. There were also half a dozen bodies in various awkward postures that can only be achieved in death.

'Ginge, take Stan and Cookie and clear the house. Watch out for booby traps. Wolf, bring in the Claymores. Wayne and Ron, check their casualties. Remove the weapons first then arbitrage the wounded'

'You mean "triage", John.'

'That's the trouble with born leader Ruperts. Always right,' he shouted half-heartedly after the troops. 'I mean triage their wounded - obviously.'

The men ran from their fire positions and across the three hundred metres to the house. With well-rehearsed expertise, they began clearing the compound and then the house. The discarded weapons were kicked out of reach by one man, whilst two others kept their rifles in the shoulder looking for sudden movement.

A second Humvee approached cautiously until one of the soldiers signalled for it to stop. The area had not been cleared and for all anybody knew, there may be a second IED.

A young-looking American sergeant stepped out of his vehicle. He appeared somewhat bewildered at the events he had just seen unfold before him.

The Boss ran up to him and, as the American was about to put out his hand to shake it, ran past saying, 'Follow me... get me your medic and keep your gunner pointing east.'

They went up to the overturned vehicle and found Yip, who had now crawled behind the wing of the Humvee and had his M4 in his shoulder. He lowered the weapon on seeing SGT Andersson running towards him with what appeared to be a couple of burly tramps in army surplus clothing.

The Boss ran on to the lorry on its side and stopped. A bit breathless, he composed himself to try to stop the tremors and looked in through the side window of the cab. There was a single driver inside.

He got on his hands and knees and crawled in through the debris, somewhat surprised to find an oriental female. She was missing an arm, which appeared to have been severed at the elbow. He unbuckled her seat belt, grabbed her by her combat jacket, and pulled her out and lay her on her back. She was clearly in shock and made no sound.

'Get the med pack!' he shouted. He then shouted again, louder, 'Someone get me a fucking first aid kit. Oi, numbnuts, double back to your jeep and get on the radio. We need to get the casualty out of here, pronto.'

A second Humvee with a top gunner, had now appeared, and another American had dismounted. He began corralling the incoming vehicles whilst the vehicle with the top gunner drove forward.

'Don't shoot at any of my fucking men,' the Boss shouted as it drove past him.

The troop had secured the ambush site and the Desert Patrol Vehicles had been sent round to cut off any counterattack from the west. One of the Rovers drove up the raised section and the Boss was glad to see it was Stan at the wheel.

'There's a couple still alive down in the kill zone, but the rest are dead. The command wire operator on the roof was also slotted.'

'Stan, we have a casualty with a severed right arm trauma here.'

Stan dismounted and rummaged for the med kit.

'All right, love?' he asked. 'What's your name?'

She stared at him, deathly pale. He read her name off the name tag on her body armour.

'OK, Miss Chen, I'm just going to stem the blood from your arm with a tourniquet and then do a quick check to see if there's anything else.'

'Anne-Lise,' she whispered.

'That's better, Anne-Lise. You're going to be fine. We've got you a chopper that'll take you to a hospital and then before you know it, you will be out of here and back home with your family.'

He produced an elastic tourniquet and positioned it around the arm above the wound to stem the blood. Both he and the Boss did a surface check for further wounds but aside from what looked like an ugly wound in her thigh and another in her calf, as well as glass fragments and possible blast fragments on the face and upper arms, she looked as if she might have had a lucky escape. Some of the blast fragments had been stopped by her body armour.

'Anne-Lise, stay awake for me now. Come on, keep concentrating for me. You are going to feel a small jab in your elbow.'

Stan administered the drip into the other arm at the elbow and then took a syrette of morphine and jabbed her in a vein. He took out an indelible marker and wrote the dose and the date time group in large black letters on her forehead. He then cut away her combat trousers and put a field dressing on her thigh wound and another on the calf. The fragment appeared to have gone in and then out of her calf but the other fragment was probably still embedded in the thigh. It was dangerously close to the femoral artery for him to want to dig around to get it out. He reached for her neck and looked at the dog tag. *A-L Chen. O positive.*

Stan looked up and saw a circle of people watching him.

'She gonna make it?' said one, who seemed to be an older civilian in army uniform.

'Yes, mate, she'll make it, but I need you to make sure this drip remains upright and above her and you need to monitor her. If you think she's having a reaction, you scream for me, Ok?'

'Sure, buddy.'

'Keep reassuring her, the chopper will be here very shortly and we'll get her back to a field hospital in Baghdad quicker than greased weasel shit. They need O positive plasma.'

'We should be getting a bird in here real soon,' shouted one of the Americans.

8

Good Friday, 9 April 2004
Somewhere South of Ad Diwaniyah towards Al Hamzah
Route Jackson
1610 Local

Cunningham felt rising nausea at the realisation that he'd done the one thing that everybody dreaded. He had become detached from his unit. He noticed an acidic coppery taste in his mouth. Poklewski slewed the Humvee around and drove the wrong way down the carriageway back north towards the ambush site.

<'Hello Grandslam Seven Romeo, over.'> There was no answer and more worryingly, there was now no chatter in the headphones. Not even static. He looked behind him and saw the radio had been severely damaged by one of the bullets that had come through the vehicle. Poklewski was right. He should try to text on the SINCGARS.

'LT, there's vehicles coming towards us...'

Cunningham looked up and saw three double cab SUVs driving at speed towards them. As he watched, one of the SUVs drove across the median onto the other carriageway to block him. The flatbed cargo areas contained three or four heavily armed men each. He felt the nausea rising in his throat and picked up his rifle but didn't put it into his shoulder.

Poklewski began to slow the Humvee to avoid an inevitable head-on collision. One of the vehicles turned sharply to block them from behind. As the Humvee came to a halt, it was surrounded by Iraqi fighters. They were pointing their weapons at the windshield and all were shouting and gesticulating with their barrels. Both the doors were wrenched open and numerous hands reached in and pulled the two Americans out and onto the road.

Cunningham felt the first of the blows and tried to curl into a protective ball with his arms over his head. His helmet and body armor took some of the brunt, but soon he felt both his arms pinned down and grasping fingers undoing his equipment. His helmet and sunglasses were ripped from his head and he felt the body armor go next. Denuded of protection, he was once again subjected to a battering of fists and boots. Blood entered his mouth and through the pain of the blows, he vaguely heard a woman's screams coming through the ringing in his ears.

It seemed an eternity before the blows stopped. The cacophony of shouting continued as he felt himself being hauled upright. At first, his legs seemed unable to carry his weight but hands under his arms held him aloft and he was dragged toward one of the vehicles. He opened his eyes and looked through the swollen slits as he was shoved up against the back and then hoisted onto the floor of the cargo area. He felt a rifle butt smack into his back just above his kidneys and the overwhelming pain made him black out for a moment.

He awoke to the realisation that the vehicle was driving down a road at some speed. Next to him was Poklewski, stripped down to her t-shirt. Her once pretty face was a morass of bruises and welts. Her nose was bleeding and one eye had already closed.

'Alice?' He reached out a hand but was rewarded by another kick in the back and someone attempting to stamp on his fingers. A black hessian hood was put over his head as someone removed his watch.

9

Good Friday, 9 April 2004
Somewhere between Convoy Support Centre Scania and Logistics
Support Area Bushmaster South of Baghdad
1615 Local

'Yip? Yip Romaro? You've got to be fucking shitting me.'
'Is that Scouse Barnes I see before me?' said the American sergeant major looking up at his British counterpart. 'Well, I'll be damned.'

'How many times do I have to tell you I'm not a Scouser, I'm not black, and I don't play football for Liverpool? Fucking hell, I would have thought you'd have learned that by now.'

'Or Leicester...' said the Boss.

'You mean Watford,' said Stan. 'Barnes never played for Leicester.'

'You sure, Stan?'

'Course I'm bloody sure,' said Stan. 'I used to be a season ticket holder at Filbert Street.'

'You mean the Walkers Stadium.'

'OK, Boss, you are right, the Walkers Stadium. But it was fucking Filbert Street when I had me season. What's it about Ruperts that they always have to be right?'

'Because we *are* always right.'

'You're thinking of Emile Heskey,' added Cookie.

'OK...he did play for the Foxes and then Liverpool. And was also black.'

'Only I'm not called Heskey. Or Emile,' said Barnes.

Yip gave a small cough to let everybody know he was still there.

'It's got to be ten years, no? When did we do that jungle trip then? '93? '94?'

'Anyway, back to the present, how the fuck are you, you stupid Yank crap hat?'

'I'm good, thanks for asking so politely. How about yourself, you Limey dipshit? I've got to say, you freakin' stink like a bobcat.'

'Well, I'm not so shabby either, health wise. Still getting older. And the smell...we've been in that OP for a week now. You know how it is.'

The Boss looked at the two of them. Words failed him.

'You couldn't make this up...' he mumbled.

'Hey, Scouse,' said Yip.

'Yeah, what?'

'Come over here where I can talk to you... See that truck on its side? Look in the back...there's a present for you. A pallet load of hundred-dollar bills. They know it's coming down so you can forget about stealing it. Well, not all of it. Just remember me in your will.'

Barnes stood up and looked at the crashed tractor and the little group tending Chen.

'Go on, it's in the back. It's for you Limeys, present from Uncle Sam, delivered with my compliments.' Yip gave a theatrical wink. 'And buy some soap and take a shower, maybe clean your teeth. Swear to God, you really do stink like a hobo.'

Barnes' faced cracked into a smile.

'What the fuck are you talking about, Yip?'

'I'm talking about there being a large amount of US dollars in the back of the trailer. Sixty-four million dollars to be precise and it's meant for you Brits in Basra. My convoy is shot to fuck so I'm considering that it's now delivered. All I need is for you to sign my manifest and you can take it away.'

'Great...where do I sign?'

'Actually, fuck the paper work. We would have had to burn it anyway along with most of these vehicles and their contents.'

'Seriously, I can't carry a large amount of money and I'm not going to Basra.'

'Well, take what you can and hand it over to whoever.'

At that moment, the young American sergeant ran up. 'Yip, we are missing the LT...'

'What? Oh fuck. You sure, Kyle?'

'Can't find him anywhere, nobody has seen him since the ambush and there's no response from the radio.'

'Has anybody seen his Humvee? Or his driver?'

'He was at the front of the convoy. He must have driven straight on rather than west on the overpass.'

'Excuse me one moment would you, sir,' Romaro said to the Boss.

'Boss,' Barnes shouted, 'come with me...'

'There's never a moment's peace.'

The two of them walked over to the trailer on its side, went around the back and tried to lever open the door. With much pushing, they eventually managed it and the heavy door fell open with a clang. They looked inside to find a pallet which had been partially hit by what looked like an RPG strike to the container. There appeared to be several thousand US dollars scattered about.

'What the fuck...?' The Boss climbed in. There were bundles scattered loosely around but the majority were still on the pallet sealed in by plastic. He picked up a bundle and opened it. It was a wedge of hundred-dollar bills.

'Fucking Nora, there's got to be millions of dollars in here.'

The Boss shouted over to Stan.

'Oi, Stan, cordon off the road, the Yanks need to get a chopper in. Get Ginge and Cookie up here pronto with their pinkies.'

The British soldiers closed the container doors. The Americans were milling about chatting, presuming the British were ensuring their safety.

An American sergeant approached the Boss and introduced himself, passing on the information that there was a chopper now coming in to evacuate the wounded and that an armoured platoon had been dispatched from some base called *Echo* and would be with them in ten or fifteen minutes. However, there was a missing American vehicle with an officer and his driver that may have been diverted during the first ambush and was now lost. Sergeant Major Romaro was asking for instructions.

The Boss came up to Barnes and murmured, 'John, lets load this dosh into the back of the pinkies. We've got ten minutes max. We might as well take it. I'm fucked if I'm leaving it here for the locals to help themselves. And the Yanks have got a problem. They're missing a wagon and two personnel. We can decide what to do with the cash later. I'm sure Hereford could find a use for it if we can't get it to Basra.'

Barnes summoned up two of the DPVs. He got the troop into a circle and explained the plan briefly.

'There's millions of dollars in the back of the container. The Yanks are going to fuck off shortly and probably burn the vehicles that are BLRd. I'm told this money is assigned to UK forces but they are now not going to deliver it and they want us to do it for them. Apparently, it was originally going to a US base, probably Scania, and then sent on to Basra Palace. The Yank sergeant major told me that as far as he was concerned it was now our responsibility. He's got enough on his plate as he's missing two of his men. What is certain is that I'm not leaving it here. We'll think about what to do with it once we get back to SHQ.'

'Ok,' said Cooke, 'let's get it into the kit containers. Split into three we should be able to hide it from view until we get out of here.'

'Yeah, we can reorg tonight in the Ulu.'

The troop began carrying the bundles to the vehicles and stowing it away from view. They were astonished at the amount of money each contained. The US chopper and a QRF from the Americans would be arriving in a very short time and it was essential that the remains of the convoy moved off before last light.

'Barnie...those are tracks.'

'Say again, Boss?'

'I can hear tracks...Ginge, Stan, get in the Rover and go up to the summit of the overpass. Be careful as you crest – I don't know who that is. If it's Americans, let them know we are down here. But it could be Iraqi T55s or BMPs. Make sure you take the Javelins. If it's enemy armour, get out of there pronto.'

'Roger, Boss... Right, Ginge, mount up.'

Ginge slung the dismounted GPMG in the footwell so it wouldn't be pointing forwards if they encountered the Americans, but made sure the shoulder-launched anti-tank weapon was within reach as well. The Rover sped off with the two troopers in the front out past the final US Humvee and up the raised section. Just before the crest they stopped. Ginge unfurled a Stars and Stripes flag, normally used as an air maker to prevent blue-on-blue attacks and threaded it through the whip antenna on the front wing. He stood in the passenger seat and held it so that it was visible as they drove slowly over the crest. Anyone observing would see the flag before the vehicle.

'Steady, Stan...easy mate...ok, stop. I don't want to die today, it's me wee bairn's birthday.'

'Really? How old?'

'She'll be six. It's important I don't actually kark it today.'

Ginge could see the top of the turret of an armoured vehicle and was relieved to see it was an American Bradley. There was another behind. They were closed down and the nearest turret moved slightly to make him the centre of observation.

'OK, Stan, slowly does it...let's show these muppets that we're nice and friendly.'

Ginge held the flag open and the Rover moved slowly into sight. Just before Stan could see the top of the turrets it stopped again. Ginge got out and slowly walked towards the American vehicles. He had his Colt Canada but held it one handed by the pistol grip, pointing at the ground to his side. He was staring down the barrel of the Bradley's main armament. On the glacis plate of the Browning 50 was drawn a big black arrow pointing to the gun and written were the words: *Iraqi Photos. Look Here. Smile. Wait for Flash.*

Had it been a British vehicle, he would have felt perfectly safe but the Americans didn't have the best reputation when it came to target recognition and positive identification. He stood still, his weapon still pointing down and to the side, hoping his stance was so alien to their idea of a threat that they wouldn't open fire. He gave a small wave with his other hand.

The right-hand hatch opened and a helmeted head popped into view. He walked slowly forward.

As he approached the front of the AFV, he noticed, disconcertingly, that the co-axially mounted machine gun was minutely adjusting to keep him in its sights.

'All right there, gentlemen? I've been sent up here just to warn you that, right now, further down, it's not that safe as there have been some IEDs. We've secured the area but there are some US casualties and we've radioed in for a helicopter to extract them.'

What the American commander heard was:

'Areet da genmn, eeee jush tae warn youse, reet noo, is nae see briwant safe wi the eedees an the like. Webin gon an secured ti an we got ae chooper en fur di cashties.'

The American looked at him, baffled.

'What the actual fuck are you saying? Are you Polacks from Echo?'

By now, Stan had appeared and was walking towards Ginge.

The American shouted at Stan, 'Fuck over here...you, get the fuck over here...you, Terps, get over here.'

Stan jogged over to Ginge.

'Yo, dude, you the interpreter? Where you from? You Polacks or Ukrainian or something?'

'Me?' said Stan, prodding himself in the chest.

'Yeah, fucking you, Einstein. Who the fuck you think I mean?'

'I'm from Melton Mowbray,' said Stan.

'Excuse me?'

'Melton. It's near Leicester.'

'You some fucking sort of comedian?'

The other hatch of the Bradley opened and a very large black head appeared. The owner grinned. 'They are fucking with you, Sarge. They're English'

'Excuse me, ya fookin yanki coonts, eem fro'Dundee in Scootland,' added Ginge, helpfully.

The commander ignored him and asked Stan, 'You fucking with me, muthafucker?'

'Not really...but, in case it helps, we are both serving with UK SF.' He pointed to the Union Flag on his shoulder. 'My ginger colleague here...'

Ginge raised a hand as if in a game show and said, 'Atsh me pawl, an ahm sorry aboot the swearin.'

'... and I have come to warn you that there are some IEDs and RPGs in the area just down in the low ground,' continued Stan.

'You seen an American convoy? There's a convoy been hit bad and we are tasked with securing the area for extraction,' said the commander.

'Yes, it's down in the low ground to the west...we've secured the area and the chopper's coming in for the casualties...apparently already airborne. We'll take you down there, if you'd like to follow us.'

The two turned and walked back, chatting. 'Fuck's sake, Ginge... no need to call him a cunt straight off.' Behind them, the Bradley revved, shooting out a jet of exhaust and adjusting on its tracks to follow in their footsteps. The other vehicles also set off in a slow-moving clanking column which Stan hoped would alert the lads down in the low ground that the armour was friendly. As they walked, they became aware of the recognisably low thud of a UH-60.

'That'll be the casevac. The boys will have heard it.'

The two soldiers started up their vehicle and executed a swift about turn on the road and headed down the gradient to where the convoy was boxed up. The American armoured vehicles followed in their tracks, dodging the detritus left by the insurgents as obstacles for the convoy. There was a small pile of medical litter and discarded water bottles by the cab of the over-turned lorry where Chen had been treated. The tarmac was stained by the lost blood and was already attracting a swarm of flies. The Americans were in all-round defence, with Andersson's vehicle blocking the road. Wavebourne was still behind his SAW and traversed the gun so that they were not in the line of fire. The British vehicles had moved away towards the west and the doors to the upturned trailer were closed.

The casualties were laid out by one of the American Humvees and fifty metres to the side of the road, somebody popped a smoke grenade and orange smoke fizzed out marking the LZ. The whack of the rotors whipped up a swirling dust storm as the large helo came in, the front side doors open. Above it circled an Apache gunship to ensure that any attack on the medevac would have an instant response.

The Blackhawk touched down and the rear-side doors slid open. A flight surgeon emerged in combats wearing blue latex gloves. Behind came the medics carrying rolled up stretchers, crouching down instinctively. There were three casualties and one dead body to pick up. Sneddon was the worst and was unconscious, Ciccarelli still stoically holding up his drip.

The flight surgeon knelt beside him and put a pulse monitor on the casualty's finger. One of the medics took over from Ciccarelli on the drip and two others opened a stretcher. Very carefully, they hoisted the wounded man onto the stretcher and then, with one at the front, two at the back, and one holding the drip, carried him back to the helicopter. Next, they came back for Chen. As they lifted Chen onto the stretcher, Wolf came up to her and put something in her top pocket.

In the noise of the rotors, the flight surgeon shouted into the ear of Sgt Major Romaro: 'On the flight in over the town, we saw an abandoned Humvee a couple of clicks south of the intersection with the burning tanker. That one of yours?'

Romaro had a sinking realisation that his day was very far from over.

'Did you see any of our guys in it or near it?'

'No; it was on the wrong carriageway, or, at least, pointing the wrong way on the right carriageway. I didn't have the time to take a proper look as we were coming in on your smoke.'

'Which way was it heading, do you suppose?'

'I think north, but it was on the southbound. The doors were left opened. Looked like it had been abandoned.'

'Fuck! Fuck! Fuck!' shouted Romaro.

The M915 Skunkwerks gun truck drove up.

'What the fuck is that?' asked Stan.

'Looks like it belongs in Mad Max,' agreed Cookie.

'Fucking state of that.'

'Hey, fellers...' shouted Zeller from his dog house, 'I've got three Hajis you Limeys whacked. Barely alive, like I give a fuck. Apparently, we need to load them onto the medevac.'

Stan shouted to the medics and they came with the stretchers. The flight surgeon re-emerged from the helicopter.

'This one is deceased,' he pronounced. 'You searched the other two for grenades and the like?'

'Yeah,' said Zeller. 'They're clean.'

The other two were loaded onto the stretchers. Stan looked at them. They were barely out of their teens. They wore simple baggy clothing with dirty, white, western trainers of an unrecognisable brand on their feet. Both had been hit at least three times and were losing blood quickly. They stared at their captors with wild eyes, expecting to be executed on the spot. One had been hit in the hand and was missing all but one finger. They had armbands to denote they were mujahedeen, which not five hours before had been the proudest moments of their young lives. There was a pool of urine swilling about with the blood in the back of the truck.

The medics were gentle with the boys. They wrapped them in gold foil blankets to offset the cold of the helicopter and then loaded them into the back, stacking them next to the soldiers they had been trying to kill half an hour before. They would get the same treatment as the Americans.

The dead body was unceremoniously dumped beside the road and would be picked up by the Iraqi police. Once identified, he would be returned to a grieving mother as soon as the foreigners had disappeared. A grenade was used to destroy the heavy machine gun in the back of the Hilux. The AK47s used in the ambush were collected and put in the back of the gun truck, where the blood and urine had begun to attract a swarm of the ubiquitous flies. In the house, a cache of detonators, det cord and Semtex was found and destroyed. The interior had been badly damaged by the machine gun bullets and what small amount of possessions the owner had were also mainly destroyed. The command wire on the roof was removed but the body remained there, missing two limbs from grenades, the tiles black with blood and yet more flies.

Back at the convoy, the Boss and Barnes approached a huddle of Americans, including SM Romaro, Sgt Andersson, and the platoon commander from the Bradley detachment.

'We're just going to have a quick headcount, get the rest of the guys in and then we will be out of your hair,' said the Boss to Romaro.

'Scouse... Sir... We have a situation developing here,' Romaro said.

'Go on...' said the Boss.

'We think one of our men, Lieutenant Cunningham, and his driver, overshot the turn during the ambush and may have been captured.'

'Fackin Ruperts...' said Barnes.

"Scuse me?' said the Bradley LT.

'Nothing...in-joke,' replied Barnes.

'The helo reported seeing an abandoned Humvee just south of the crossroads and there's nothing on the radio. It's got to be his. Scouse... John... We may need your help. With the Bradleys and your vehicles, we might have a chance of finding them if we leave now.'

'No chance, Yip.' replied Barnes. 'They'll be chained to a radiator in some basement by now.'

'We have to try, though...we have to try. I can't not give it my best shot. I'm calling command to inform them of the situation and then we should leave asap.' The American was visibly shaken.

Barnes let out an audible sigh. 'Fackin Ada,' he murmured under his breath. 'Boss, I'll take two pinkies to back up our American cousins. You take the rest of the troop back to basha up at Echo.'

'Fuck that...I'm coming with you.'

'No, you are not.'

'I'm wearing the pips, last time I looked, it was me that was in charge.'

'You're nominally in charge. I'm actually in charge, that's the way it's always been...'

'I'm not going to carry the can for all the shit that happens and then not get to go on the good bits. Fuck that, I'm coming with you and that's an order!'

'I can't believe you've just said "that's an order" like we're in a John Wayne film. OK, ok, fucking born leaders. Jeez, what happened to the officers doing as they were told.'

'It's the new model army, don't you know.'

'There's two hopes of finding them anyway, and Bob Hope is playing golf, which leaves them with fuck all hope. Ginge, get the lads in for a briefing.'

'Boss... Boss... We've got company,' Cookie was shouting from one of the Rovers blocking the approach from the west. There was a general rushed preparation for a hostile encounter. Barnes and the Boss went to the side of the road and adopted fire positions, and Andersson got in his Humvee.

'Poles,' said the Boss to Barnes.

'How on earth can you tell that? Or you just bluffing as per?'

'It's a Dzik.'

'A what?'

'Dzik. And a ZWD. With a big Polish flag on the side. And the last vehicle is an Iraqi police Toyota Landcruiser. You can tell by the big blue stripe and the flashing lights on the roof.'

'That "Zit" looks like the Pigs we used in the Province.'

'You should recognise them from all the AFV Recognition lectures you obviously so assiduously attended. They'll be from Echo. I'm pretty sure the Poles are at Echo, which is a few clicks from here, actually.'

A Polish officer dismounted from the ZWD and came up to the Land Rovers. He was followed by two Iraqi police, who had dismounted from the Toyota. Cookie pointed up to the convoy and the officer gave a sharp salute, got back in, and drove on up to the vehicles. He dismounted from the front vehicle which had a Polish red and white recognition decal.

'Good afternoon, gentlemen,' he announced in a slight accent. 'We have been tasked to escort you back to Forward Operating Base Echo. The IP will deal with the indigenous casualties. Who, might I ask, is the officer commanding here?'

The Boss stepped forward and proffered his hand. The Polish officer tried valiantly to hide his distaste and reached forward and shook it.

'Poruchik Stanislav Dabrowski of the Polski Kontyngent Wojskowy based at Echo.'

'Nice to meet you, Mr Poruchik. I'm Captain Tom Smith serving with the British.'

The Pole smiled. 'Poruchik is my rank, Captain. It means Lieutenant in English. Please call me Stanislav, or Stan, if you prefer.'

The Boss grimaced slightly, acutely aware of the smirking troop sergeant beside him. 'Stanislav it is then...we already have a Stan and one's about as much as we can handle at the moment.'

SM Romaro jumped in.

'Good afternoon, LT, I'm currently commanding this US convoy detachment. We have a number of civilian contractors driving the trucks and some inexperienced Transportation personnel that I would love you to escort back to either Echo or Bushmaster.'

'Bushmaster is not problem but Echo is better. We have also the Bradleys? I think it will be quiet trip.'

'Stanislav,' said Romaro, 'we are missing two Americans back in the town and I'm going to take the British, our Bradleys and gun trucks and try to locate them. We've probably got a couple of hours before they disappear for ever.'

'May I suggest, in that case, Mr Romaro and Mr Smith, that I join you with my Iraqi police colleagues? They are local to Ad Diwaniyah and will be very useful. Kassim,' he raised his hand and summoned over one of the Iraqi policemen, 'the British and Americans need to go into Ad Diwaniyah to find two men they appear to have lost.'

The Iraqi officer spoke to his subordinate who returned to one of the vehicles. 'We are calling in the police to remove the bodies to the police station. I would be honoured to help you find your missing men. My sergeant will organise a recovery operation from our maintenance troop at Echo for your convoy.'

'In which case,' said the Boss, 'there is a dead insurgent on the roof of the house over there.'

'Come in my Humvee, Stanislav, and we can put Kassim in with the British.'

'I think it better that Kassim stays with us, Mr Romaro. He is of high birth and I feel that he may neither appreciate nor enjoy the trip with the British. I feel that their attention to personal hygiene is not up to his standards.'

'Ha...he's certainly right there. There should be room in with us if you don't mind my top gunner standing in between you both. He has, however, taken a shower this morning.'

'I think we take our car,' said Kassim. 'It is better for the peoples to know that the police are here. Safer for you, too.'

'OK, we will follow you,' said Yip.

The British loaded their equipment into the Land Rovers. The automatic weapons were remounted on the pintles and the bergens were stowed. The Boss got in the front passenger side with Cookie driving and Wolfie in the back. Barnie had Ginge driving and ManBat on the gun. The others similarly mounted in the vehicles and they headed due east, up the raised section, past the burning tanker.

'Fackin Tom Smith?' said Cookie.

'It's my "nom de guerre".'

'Your what?'

'It's what I use in civvy street when I'm, you know, giving it large.'

'Giving it large? Are you for real, Boss? Nobody's going to be impressed by some Rupert called Smith. You should think up something better than that. "Hoo doo yoo doo. My name is Captain the Lord Fotherington-Cholmondley-Twitbasher. Yoo must be Cordelia and yoo must be Araminta. Might we engage in some shaggage after a small aperitif of sherry?"'

'Very good, Cookie, but slightly let yourself down at the end there. Actually, the general commanding British Forces in the first Gulf War was called Rupert Smith. Just pull over here, will you? Let the Yanks past with the IP'

'Oi, Wolfie?' said Cookie.

'Yes, mate?'

'What did you put in that casualty's pocket? You know, when she was being loaded onto the chopper.'

'Her wedding ring off her severed hand. Thought she might want to keep it,' said Wolf, matter-of-factly.

'Fackin' hell,' murmured Cookie.

The two Humvees and the Skunkwerks gun truck went past in a cloud of dust, covering everything in the open vehicle with the fine grit of the Iraqi desert.

'SLOW DOWN, GUBBY...' They were approaching the intersection where the ambush had taken place. The tanker was still burning and acrid black smoke had filled the void in the underpass. There was no sign of any insurgents and the only sound was of the convoy's engines and the thud of the rotors of an Apache that had joined them to give top cover.

<'Hello, *Firefly Seven Zero*, this is *Grandslam Seven Romeo*.'>

<'Go ahead, *Grandslam*.'>

<'We are at the junction with Jackson and will turn south. Can you place your assets on this location whilst we try to identify the location of Checkerboard...over.'>

<'Copy that. We can you give you two hours, Grandslam, and then we have to RTB'>

<'Roger Firefly, just need some top cover to make a statement of intent and watch our asses.'>

Gubby steered the lead Humvee down the ramp of the cloverleaf and south down the carriageway heading out of the conurbation. After a few minutes, they could see the abandoned vehicle about a kilometre in front. Both the doors were open. There was a crowd of young Iraqis surrounding it, no doubt trying to pillage anything that was movable. Two were on the roof and a few others were climbing onto the bonnet and chanting. The youths watched the approach of the vehicles, slowly backing off from the abandoned Humvee as they neared, but continuing their shouting and chanting and throwing stones.

Yip signalled for the Skunkwerks to overtake and go static beyond the abandoned vehicle. Zeller on the .50 was scanning to the front and sides and the driver, de Rogatis, had his rifle sticking out the window also scanning east. The crowd backed off leaving the abandoned Humvee.

'Stop here, Gubby... <All stations, this is Grandslam, I'm going to dismount and check the vehicle. Be aware of snipers and booby traps...Out.'>

Gubby pulled up a few metres in front of the abandoned Humvee and kept the engine running as Yip dismounted. The two Brit vehicles pulled in behind him. The open topped Land Rovers appeared very exposed with the machine gunners standing without any protection at all. Yet the Brit soldiers gave off an air of insouciance that the two Americans could only admire. The Boss and Barnes got out and joined him.

A few stones landed close by, but the crowd was keeping its distance. An ignited bottle of petrol was thrown but landed well short. The black oily smoke drifted back into the crowd. Lieber reversed the gun truck back towards the abandoned Humvee and the crowd slowly encroached forward, all the while shouting and chanting.

'What do you reckon?' asked Barnes.

'No major battle damage,' said the Boss. 'There's some 556 brass in the footwell...oh, and a live round and an empty mag. Looks like the radio's knackered. They've been taken, if you want my opinion.'

'Agree, Boss. No blood in the vehicle, either. Give us the mag then. Always good to have spares.'

'In which case,' said Yip, 'we have a hostage situation.'

'They don't normally end well,' said the Boss.

'Stanislav, Kassim?' said Yip. 'What do you suggest?'

Kassim pondered for a short while and then spat onto the tarmac. 'They will be now in the hands of the Jayesh al-Mahdi. It is likely two outcomes. Execution or traded to the Iranians.' He spat again. 'Give me an hour to ask in the town. I can make no promises.'

'Tell them there's a reward for any information that leads to the release of my men. You good with that, John?'

'Sure...though I thought we didn't pay ransoms,' said Barnes, and gave Yip a wink.

'How many dollars?' asked Kassim.

'Dunno,' Yip answered. 'What do you reckon?'

'Offer a hundred fifty thousand.'

'Ok,' said Yip. 'One hundred and fifty grand it is. Got it right here. Tell us where they are and it's theirs. Swear to God, it's as simple as that.'

'Tell you what,' interrupted the Boss, 'if they release them and tell us where to find them, nobody needs to get busy trying to identify who took them. We can all go about our business as normal. No harm done.'

Kassim looked at the Europeans as if they were simpletons and said, 'I will ask the Khams' elders if they know of the whereabouts of your men. I will meet you back at Echo this evening.'

'I'm not leaving without my guys,' announced Yip.

'My American friend, nothing will be accomplished with your troops in the town. You must think of this now as a commercial transaction. There are almost half a million people in this city. You have no chance of finding them. If whoever has taken them think you are close to finding them, they will slit their throats and dump the bodies.'

'There's a certain logic to that,' said the Boss.

'As I say, the situation in Diwaniyah is complicated. Us police still have our friends both among the Mahdi and the Badr.'

Another petrol bomb landed but closer this time. There was a big cheer from the crowd who were edging forward again.

'Reminds me of the good old days,' said Barnes. 'Just need a couple of baton guns to get the show started.'

'Come on then,' said the Boss, 'let's split. Yip...we'll meet you up at the junction.'

'Copy that, sir,' said Yip. 'Let's get this vehicle rigged up to the gun truck and tow it out. Ain't no way I'm leaving this here.'

The teams returned to their various vehicles. The Skunkwerks bobtail reversed up and came under a renewed hail of stones. Zeller cocked his .50 and fired a short burst into the air, dispersing the crowd. They ran for the cover of the nearest houses and looked nervously around walls to see if anybody had been shot by the Americans. Lieber and de Rogatis reversed the truck and the Humvee was hitched to the towing bar. The truck and the other vehicles drove back up the carriageway north, under the bridge passed the still burning tanker, and up onto the flyover where the Bradleys were static, their main armaments surveying the scene to the south, their generators still on to power the turrets.

The two British vehicles stopped and Barnes got out.

'I think we should stay overnight at Echo,' shouted Yip above the din of the armoured vehicles. 'You guys can get a much-needed shower and some decent chow. Guess you've been on MREs for a while now.'

'It's that or another night in the Ulu. What do you reckon, Boss?'

'I don't know. Or should we just leave it to the Americans and head for home? I mean, we're not going to be much help, are we? Not really, if you think about it.'

'We can't just leave them. Think of the international ramifications of that.'

'True. I suppose we could go to Echo for the night and see what the IP turn up. I have a feeling that we've long since missed the boat. If they are still in the town, they'll probably be moved out tonight.'

'Depends who's got them. If it's just a bunch of local heroes, they may try and sit it out for a ransom.'

'The local militia will take a very dim view of that, I think. Live US prisoners are not a commodity that can just be traded with anybody. Far too valuable for that. No, they'll be handed over. It just depends to whom.'

'Right,' said the Boss. 'Executive decision. We go back to Echo with Yip, get some scoff, replen the ammo and POL, and look at the problem in the morning. I'm fairly sure the Yanks will be getting their arse in gear for a hostage release situation starting with the SigInt, but probably the most relevant gen will be found at Echo.'

'Sounds like a plan,' agreed Barnes. 'Everybody mount up.'

Yip came over to the Land Rovers. 'The Bradleys will escort us to Echo and then go on their way to Bushmaster. Echo is a multinational camp under command of the Poles but it does have a Stryker company located there as well as the Polish armour, so we can use those assets if required. And, I'm told, it has a reputation for one of the best MWRs in Iraq.'

'OK, sounds good,' said the Boss. 'We'll follow you.'

10

Good Friday, 9 April 2004
Battlefield Interrogation Facility
Baghdad International Airport
1720 Local

Barbara's pager had sounded just as she was finishing her weekly update report. She looked at the four numbers, indicating she was required immediately in the signals room. When she got there, she was informed, as she had suspected, that the Clocktower number had rung four times before hanging up. This was the signal that he would call again in thirty minutes exactly. She hadn't heard from him for a while.

It had given her just enough time to get some dinner from the cookhouse before taking the call at five-thirty. She now sat in the signals room with a cup of tea waiting for the call.

He rang thirty seconds early.

'Hello, this is me.' She recognised his accent and knew it was him. 'I am just calling to let you know about my day.'

The first sentence indicated that he was not under duress and was able to speak without being overheard. He was probably in his house having swapped his usual sim for the one she had given him.

'Have you had a busy day?' she enquired.

'Yes, yes. Very busy.'

'Were you at the party in the middle of town today?'

'No. No. I was not invited. They are not my friends.'

The guarded talk, she knew, would fool almost nobody, especially not the Americans who were definitely listening, but it was a habit with Clocktower and she played along. She instinctively knew he had something important to tell her.

'So, anyway,' she continued, 'what's new with you?'

Clocktower paused on the other end. 'We have a new visitor. A tourist.'

'OK, that's interesting. Anything else you can tell me?'

'I think it better if you meet me at the place. Very soon. Very, very soon.'

'It's going to take me a bit of time to get to you.' She had already started doing the mental arithmetic. She could probably get down to Camp Edson, North of ad Diwaniyah tonight. Edson was the main postal outpost for the area and handled dozens of container loads of mail for the US Marines. There was probably a chopper going down tonight or early tomorrow to pick up or deliver mail, and if not, she could quickly get clearance to organise a flight. Everybody knew that the Americans had two soldiers missing in the area and, although they were playing their cards close to their chests, she knew Vauxhall would let their Allies know they had some HumInt that might prove invaluable. Co-located with Edson was camp Hope, which catered for the Iraqi police working with the US forces. It would be perfectly normal for US and Iraqis to mix at Hope without causing suspicion.

'I might be able to meet you at the post office tomorrow morning. Can you get there?'

'Yes. Yes. No problem. Bring dollars.'

'Call again in two hours,' she said, then hung up.

11

Good Friday, 9 April 2004
Forward Operating Base Echo
Head Quarters Multi-National Division Central South
1730 Local

The column of Rovers, Humvees, the gun truck and the Polish vehicles drove through the main entrance of Echo, past the concrete plinth with its palm tree logo announcing Camp Echo was headquarters of The Multi-National Division Central South. The camp security was manned by troops of unrecognisable origin.

'Where they from then?' asked Rocket, as they were directed towards the vehicle park.

'Fuck knows,' replied the Boss. 'Look like they may be Asian perhaps. Sri Lankan? Oi, Stanislav, where are the gate guards from?'

The Polish officer smiled. 'They are the Mongolian detachment. There are many nationalities in this camp. We Poles are the biggest but we have also Americans, of course, and also Norwegians, El

Salvadorians, Spanish, Ukrainians, Danes, Lithuanians, Estonians, and many, many others.'

'You don't really hear about all those other nationalities, do you?'

'Many countries have been persuaded by the Americans to send small contingents to make it look like a global effort run by the United Nations, but, in reality, they do not achieve much. Even us Poles are only here for diplomatic reasons and because your Uncle Sam is paying.'

'Let's make one thing crystal clear, Stanislav, old mucker, so we don't get off on the wrong foot. It's not our Uncle Sam. If truth be known, we are probably in a similar situation to you. We may have a bigger contribution to offer but we're all doing it for the Americans,' said the Boss.

'Understood, my English friend. We only follow the orders of our stupid politicians.'

'Amen to that.'

'Mr Smith, I suggest you put your vehicles here. We have no over-head cover but there has been little in the way of mortar or incoming rockets so far. Then I can take you over to our mess hall and you should also meet our intelligence officer. Nobody knows more than her about the current state of politics in Diwaniyah.'

'Her?' said the Boss.

'Yes. She is a formidable lady but you will get on well with her. I sense you share the same world outlook.'

'Can't wait...take me to your leader.'

Sgt Barnes came over to the two officers. 'I've told Cookie to set up the 319 and clock in with the squadron, let them know where we are. The others are going to do last parade on the vehicles, clean up a bit. Stanislav, mate, would really appreciate some fuel for me jerrycans, water and ammo replen. I take it those fackin' AKs of yours take 5.56 and you've got 7.62 link?'

As soon as they heard their sergeant, the other requests came in thick and fast. 'John,' shouted Stan, 'can you ask him for a medical replen, too? Running low on gauze, and some morphine wouldn't go amiss, neither. ManBat, can you get all the gash bags sorted in the dump? Stanislav, where are your burn pits?'

'Leave the rubbish here, I will make sure someone comes to collect it. I will try to get you everything you require that we can offer, John, if I may call you John. Our quartermaster sergeant will be requested to make all supplies available to you.'

Stanislav spoke in rapid Polish to his driver, who ran off towards the main camp.

'John, I think we should go and check in with their int officer and get the ball rolling. Apparently, she's a bird, so try to keep your effing and blinding down to an acceptable level for civilised society.'

'You can fucking talk, Boss. Your language is some of the worst! Ginge? Me and the Boss are going up to HQ block. Get the vehicles and the replen sorted. We'll probably be about half an hour. Yip, you coming along as well? Where the fuck is Yip?'

'He's with the Yank convoy protection just over there,' said the Boss. Barnes wandered over to round him up for the briefing.

'Boss?'

'Yes, Stan?'

'Can you ask if the Norwegian Army Women's Beach Volleyball team are stationed here? I think I heard they were?'

'I've been reliably informed that they're playing Sweden away, this weekend.'

The Boss stowed his rifle in his vehicle, put his pistol in his chest pocket just in case and then, with Barnes and Romaro, followed the Polish officer over to a cluster of single-storey buildings where they were shown into the office of the intelligence officer. The Boss saw that one entire wall was dominated by a large map of the town of Ad Diwaniyah and a slightly smaller map of Iraq. There were two desks and behind one sat a woman, whom, he assumed, was the intelligence officer.

She stood as they knocked and ushered them in with a wave of her hand. She spoke in Polish to Stanislav, who saluted, and said, 'Gentlemen, I will leave you in the capable hands of Major Duda.'

The Boss put out his hand. 'Captain Tom Smith, from the British contingent in Basra. This is my troop sergeant, Staff Sergeant Barnes.'

'And I'm Sergeant Major Javier Romaro from Camp Victory Baghdad, up at BIAP.'

'Welcome to Camp Echo, gentlemen. Magdalena Duda. I'm the current intelligence officer for Echo.' She shook his hand and similarly shook Barnes' and Yip's, too. 'Please be seated. Can I get you some refreshment? Tea, perhaps?'

'Bottle of water would be grand,' said Barnes.

'Same for me, but could I also have some tea?' asked the Boss.

'I would love a Coke, if you have one,' said Yip.

'Of course.' The occupant of the other desk was dispatched off to find the refreshments. 'Tell me, what brings you to Echo? Were you caught out by the bridges being blown?'

'Er...no. To be honest, I didn't know any bridges had been blown, although we sort of guessed something had happened when we heard the detonations. We got caught up in an ambush on the Americans and met up with Mr Romaro.'

'Much has happened in the last twenty-four hours,' the major pointed out. 'As you may know, there has been a Shi'ite call to arms earlier in the week and the country is in upheaval. Most Allied forces are in lockdown as there has been a spate of ambushes. An American convoy was destroyed in Baghdad this morning with many dead and some missing. Another American convoy was hit here in Diwaniyah this afternoon. Also, some dead – three I think. The camp is now on lockdown too, but I think we will raise it tomorrow to continue patrols.'

'Yes, we came across the American convoy ambush just west of the town, that was the ambush I was talking about,' said the Boss. 'We've been operating an OP on the Diwaniyah-Najaf road for the last week, so we've missed much of the recent intelligence updates.'

'That was my convoy,' Yip interjected.

'They are now here, or what is left of them,' said Magdalena. 'They were brought in by our recovery section after we were alerted by a Bradley platoon from Bushmaster. They are mainly civilian drivers and even the troops seem very inexperienced. It sounds as if they were lucky to get away at all.'

'They've only been in country a few weeks and are mainly from a National Guard transportation battalion and KBR. Not even regulars. But thank you for taking them in. Appreciate it. I thought they had gone to Bushmaster.'

'No, they are here. We will do our best to get them back south. I think we have a liaison team up in Baghdad who will co-ordinate their return to their units.'

'Magdalena, we have a problem. We have two missing personnel who were taken after a wrong turn in the town. We found their vehicle but not them.'

'Yes, I have seen initial reports for missing US personnel from this area. I'm sorry they are your men, Sergeant Major.'

'One is female,' answered Yip, hoping this might, in some way, influence things.

'This is not so good.'

'Do you have an inkling who might have taken them?' asked the Boss.

'There are a number of possibilities,' replied Magdalena. 'How much do you know about the local situation here?'

'The square root of nought-point-jack-shit,' replied Barnes.

'Excuse me?' said Magdalena.

'He means, not very much, which is not quite the case, is it, John?' the Boss answered on Barnes' behalf.

'It is really, Boss. We don't know about the local politics, really. Do we? If we are honest.'

'My team is already liaising with the Americans in Central Command. This means that the ears of the US military will be tuned into Diwaniyah. Mobile phone and internet traffic, where possible, will be intercepted. FOB Loyalty in Baghdad is liaising back to Fort Meade in the States and I'm reliably informed that General Quirke himself is taking a strong interest in this. He's reporting straight into Rumsfeld and Wolfowitz at the White House and bypassing the NSA.

But the situation remains complicated, volatile and fluid,' Magdalena explained.

The refreshments came in and were laid on a small table. The Boss took a sip of his tea.

'Mmm...not a bad brew. Barnie, you should have had one.'

'Compliments indeed from an Englishman.'

Magdalena got up again from her desk and walked over towards the map. The Boss did a quick survey and saw that she was medium height – five-seven, maybe eight. Probably late thirties, early forties with a bit of timber on her, but several months into an operational tour he was not going to quibble. Also a wedding ring...but you never know.

'The situation is the following...' The Boss snapped out of his daydream to see Barnes glaring at him. Yip had a face of puzzled amusement. 'Diwaniyah is a mainly Shi'ite town that was never very fond of Saddam Hussein,' she started. 'The local politics and indeed, the commerce, is dominated by the Hakim family, which is headed by Abdul al Hakim. They are a proud and independent people but today they are heavily influenced by Iran. Next to us here at Echo is stationed the 8th Division of the Iraqi Army. They are also supposedly our friends but sometimes we wonder. They are commanded by my friend General Oothman Ali Farhoud. He is not to be trusted but I can tell you he is very fond of American dollars. For the moment, it seems he is co-operating with us.'

'OK,' said the Boss. 'So, who would be interested in taking US military personnel and should we just offer a ransom.'

'It is more complicated than that, although a ransom would get at least half the town excited.'

'US Government never pays ransoms officially, but unofficially, we've already let the IP know we would pay for a quick solution,' said Yip.

'Also in the town,' continued Magdalena, 'we have the Jaysh al Mahdi.'

'Moqtada al Sadr's lot...' said the Boss.

'Yes, indeed. Universally known as JAM. Here in Diwaniyah we think they are led by someone called Qais Khazali, but we can't be sure. We think he's been funded and possibly trained by the Iranian Revolutionary Guards Quds brigade. We know that they are looking at attacking coalition forces, and intelligence from Central Command tells us that they are developing a VBIED threat. Furthermore, we are getting intelligence that the Iranians are supplying a new type of anti-armour road-side bomb called *Explosively Formed Penetrators*, or EFPs. On top of that, we think the JAM are recruiting Special Groups that are better trained and equipped than the average JAM militia. It is almost certain that it was a JAM Special Group that blew the bridges.'

The Boss found his mind wandering back to the major's tight camouflage trousers. He was startled out of his reverie by Barnes surreptitiously kicking his foot.

'It's a right old shit show,' he murmured.

'Which bridges were blown?' asked Barnes.

Magdalena pointed to the map. 'Eight major bridges over the Euphrates and its tributaries. Here...' she said, indicating with a pointer, 'here and here. They seem to be trying to stop the flow of supplies from Scania, here. If you look at the town,' she pointed at the other map 'this is the Al Jaza'ir district. The prisoners, if they have been taken by JAM, will probably be being held in this district, here.'

'You say "if they have been taken by JAM". Who else would have taken them? Local opportunists?' asked Yip.

'It gets more complicated, I'm afraid, Sergeant Major.'

'Fucking great,' whispered Barnes.

'We are in the Iraqi province of Qadsiyah. As I explained earlier, this area has always been Shi'ite and against the Ba'athist party of Saddam Hussein, looking to Iran for support. The Shi'ites have always been a majority in Iraq but have always been dominated by the Ba'athists. Now they see their chance but they are acutely aware that the Sunni, though a minority, form a majority in the new Iraqi Parliament. The Americans have announced elections to a new Parliament next year and so we are finding that the Sunnis, represented by Al Qaeda, and the Shi'ites, will engage in a power struggle. This is why al Sadr formed JAM.'

'Have you seen Al Qaeda activity down here, Major?' asked Yip.

'Not yet. There is another dimension. As part of the Shi'ite struggle against Saddam Hussein that was nurtured in Iran but now moved back here, the *Islamic Supreme Council of Iraq*, or ISCI was founded. The Governor of the Province is definitely a member of ISCI and ISCI is headed by our old friend Abdul al Hakim. ISCI are running death squads called Badr Brigades. The Badr brigades are quasi-official. We know they exist and we know that they answer to the 8th Division next door. There's a group called *Wolf Brigade* who seem to be doing a large number of summary executions in Diwaniyah. A week ago, they organised the total destruction of a village called Kawali. Totally razed it to the ground and anyone that was not quick enough to flee was murdered.'

'So, let me see if I've got this right, Magdalena,' said the Boss. 'You are saying that either JAM or Wolf Brigade might have taken the hostages. They don't talk to each other but of the two, Wolf Brigade is more inclined to us?'

'Mainly right, Tom. If the Wolf Brigade have them, they may well take them over the border to Iran to be used as human capital by the Revolutionary Guard. However, they may, may, I stress, be prepared to hand them over to the Iraqi Division and we can get them back. Possibly with a "consultancy fee" for General Oothman.'

'And if JAM have them?' asked Yip.

'We have a much bigger problem. Al Sadr is behind the current attacks on the Americans today. He has no interest in payment. He will probably execute them although not immediately. I'm afraid they will go into a JAM safehouse where they will be kept until al Sadr is ready to film and upload their execution to the internet.

'So they're fucked, then?' asked the Boss.

'Sorry?' asked Magdalena, a puzzled expression clouding her features.

'Excuse my language but it sounds like we've lost them?'

'It's not that simple, I'm afraid. The local people, here in Diwaniyah, the Jabouri tribe, are no friends of al Sadr or JAM. It might well be that we can find the safe house with their help. It is difficult to keep secret having two American prisoners.'

'And if the Wolf Brigade have them, we might also have a chance of getting them back too, Boss,' added Yip.

'Right now, the Americans will be monitoring the mobile phones and internet cafés for an increase in chatter. This may well be the best clue to their whereabouts. Our own int platoon at Echo is very adept at listening in to their comms.'

'Let's hope it's the Badass brigade then,' said Barnes.

'It's the lesser of two evils, really. If they have them, they may well end up in Iran.'

'Could Al Qaeda have them?' asked the Boss.

'Unlikely, but not impossible,' Magdalena answered. 'Al Qaeda and JAM and Badr tend to shoot each other on sight.'

'Best guess then, Major Duda?' asked Yip.

'We are fairly certain JAM organised the Ambush on your convoy. The insurgents would have seen the vehicle make the wrong turn and would have sent people after it. Therefore, I would say, they are being held in a house somewhere in Jamhouri Street district by JAM. That would be in my best guess.' She pointed to the map. 'Here. But it is only a guess.'

'But impossible to go door to door?' asked Yip.

'Yes, I'm afraid so, Sergeant Major. We don't have the men to lock down such a large area and it is almost certain that even the Americans would not risk inflaming what could turn into a very volatile situation. Diwaniyah is considered pro-coalition at the moment. Smashing down doors would change that instantly. We've had quite an increase in violence lately, not directed at coalition forces, yet, but the town is seething. I've already mentioned the massacre at Kawali. That was only ten or so kilometres from here.' She pointed at the map to a village south of the camp. Nobody knows how many civilians the JAM killed.'

There was a heavy silence.

'I think the best we can do now, gentlemen, is to wait for further intelligence coming from the SigInt from Ballad and Loyalty. There is someone I want you to meet. LT Brian Mendoza is the platoon leader of the SigInt platoon here at Echo. He is what you would call a very smart cookie.'

'He'll be smarter than our Cookie, that's for sure,' said Barnes, with a grin.

'He's smarter than most cookies,' continued Magdalena, not quite getting the joke. He has a master's in math from Stanford and a PHD in cryptology from MIT. The Americans are not generally good at intelligence gathering and we find it hard to get anything much out of their chain of command, but Brian is a genius. He will explain tomorrow at the BUB.

'For now, we can get your men settled for the night. The camp is run by KBR and we will get CHUs for your men. We have the second best DFAC in Iraq I'm told, and it being Friday, I think they have a bit of a party in there. The SPO will get your men settled and fed. We have a very good ice cream bar, too.'

Magdalena issued some orders in Polish to her second and he left the office and returned shortly after with a portly middle-aged man in civilian clothes.

'Hi, I'm Frank. I'm the KBR representative on the base here. Nice to meet you guys. Brits, right?'

The Boss did the introductions.

'Great,' said Frank. 'Welcome to Echo. I very much hope we can make you welcome and comfortable. We have choos for the officers and NCOs but the other ranks have to make do with the tented accommodation. We have been promised more choos but they've not yet come up. The DFAC operates 24/7 and gets a bit crowded...' he looked at his watch...'just about around now. But it clears quickly and we don't lack food. The base has a bit of a party in the evening, it being Friday. Alcohol served until ten local. Should be steaks tonight but other stuff is available, including vegetarian and a full menu Pizza Hut.'

'An advantage of being run by us,' said Magdalena, 'is that we have a perhaps more relaxed attitude to alcohol than the Americans.'

'That certainly is an advantage,' said Yip, who had been sitting quietly on Magdalena's desk.

'Everything else, Mr Romaro, is courtesy of the US of A. And don't get me wrong, we are all very grateful. The Polish Army would supply none of this luxury.'

'Excellent,' said Barnes. 'Haven't had a beer for months now.'

'But I would remind you that this is a multi-national base, gentlemen. There are over a dozen countries represented here from Mongolia to Latvia. Please ensure your men behave appropriately.'

'Of course, Magdalena. We are very civilised, despite how we look.' The Boss gave her a wide smile.

'We had a company of a Scottish Regiment here, the Black Watch. Everybody was very glad when they left. Much less drunken fighting.'

'Oh, yes. The Black Death, as we call them. I'm afraid they are renowned for that sort of behaviour and they are feared equally in the British Army as they are by the enemy. You don't get a finer fighting man but it's not always certain they don't kick off spontaneously. Especially if you add drink.' The Boss made a mental note to keep Ginge off the whisky that evening.

The Boss noticed an enlarged photocopy of a newspaper article in German pinned to the wall.

'Do you mind, Magdalena, if I asked you what this is?'

'That is an article written in the German newspaper, *Tagesspiegel*. I have it up as an inspiration.'

'Oh, what does it say?' asked the Boss.

'It's about the Polish presence in Iraq, especially as we are in command of the Central area. The Germans don't like it at all.'

'The Germans declined to help in this particular theatre, didn't they?' said the Boss.

'Indeed. It's titled *The Trojan Ass*. The Germans think we are a Trojan Horse for the Americans to split the EU. It starts "A Nation of illegal workers and thieves are set to rebuild Iraq".'

'Blimey, that is a bit strong.'

'Old enmities die hard, Tom.'

'No love for the Germans then, Magdalena?'

'I am afraid there is little from me. Tom, let me take you to the officers' accommodation block.'

'I'm fine thanks, Magdalena. I'll stick with my men.'

The Boss felt a small nudge from Barnes. 'I think, Boss, you should have a night in the mess. I think the boys deserve a night away from you. Ma'am, the Boss would be delighted if you could show him the Ruperts' Mess.'

'Ruperts?' asked Magdalena.

'Officers,' said Barnes.

'Like the bear?' said Magdalena.

'Yup...same trousers but not quite so good at soldiering.'

'Ignore him, Magdalena,' said the Boss. 'I would be delighted for you to show me to the mess.'

'It might not be quite what you are thinking but we have our own rooms with good air conditioning.'

'Barnie, what are you going to do?'

'Those bashas sound very inviting. All the lads are NCOs in their parent units so if we can get into the sergeants' mess or whatever it's called around here, that would be grand. But I'll detail a couple of volunteers to sleep with the vehicles.'

'You detail volunteers?' asked Magdalena.

'Old Brit Army tradition; they get voluntold,' replied Barnes.

'We've got two-man CHUs for the NCOs, but they still have working aircon and the shower block is pretty decent. So if you would like to follow me,' Frank added.

Frank led them both out of the office and over towards a group of single-storey blocks. 'Frank, I think we can put them in here. Tom, follow me, officers are just around the corner,' she said.

Inside the container, the Boss was surprised to see a large made bed, a wardrobe, small desk and chair, and a full height fridge. The room was almost too cold from the air conditioning.

'I'm opposite. Let me know if you need anything, like the laundry facilities. The women's accommodation is not that crowded as the rest of the world doesn't have the same view of women in the military as the Americans.'

'Or the Poles,' said the Boss.

'There are very few of us in the Polish military and not many units we can join.'

'I'm going to get my stuff and then get cleaned up. Hopefully see you soon.' And he added, as a parting shot, 'At least let me buy you a drink in the bar.'

'I have asked for Fatima to come over for the laundry. She can do a quick turnaround for a few dollars and can have your men's uniforms washed and pressed by six o'clock tomorrow morning.'

'I'll get the lads' stuff over here pronto. It might be quite a challenge. I hope she's used to smelly kit.'

'Don't worry, Fatima has seen it all before...'

The Boss went out and found the others by the NCO block.

'Barnie, get the lads to put any dhobi they want done in a pile. Make sure it's all name marked with indelible ink.'

'Wilco, Boss. Gotta say, the bashas are right Gucci.'

'Not bad, eh?' agreed the Boss.

'Not quite as nice as BIAP but hey ho, nobody's complaining,' said Yip.

'Meet in the scoff house in half an hour? First round on me?' asked the Boss.

'Wilco, Boss. You can get a round in and I'll call the Guinness Book of Records.'

'Oh, how we laughed...' retorted the Boss.

12

Good Friday, 9 April 2004
Jaysh al Mahdi Safe House
Somewhere in Central Ad Diwaniyah
1730 Local

C unningham lay on the steel flatbed floor of the Hilux, which was still warm from the sun and covered in a fine grit, trying to remember the briefing he had been given "in the event of capture": *Name, rank, date of birth. Nothing more. The first twenty-four hours is the best opportunity to escape. Don't antagonise your guards. Try to figure out which guard is the nicest and work on him. If things get really bad, then slow release of information sown heavily with disinformation.* The trouble was, he felt as if he'd been beaten half to death and as well as a migraine and severe abdominal pain, he thought he may have dislocated or even broken his left shoulder. He tried to keep track of time and the turns of the vehicle, but the incessant chatter and the occasional blow made it hard to concentrate and he now had no idea how far they'd come or how long he had been in the vehicle. His hands were tightly bound behind his back, probably with cable ties, and along with his shoulder, his wrists felt as if they would be severed by the restraints. He could see very little out of the hood, which was stifling hot. One eye had closed and out of the other all he could see was his legs and boots. He tried to shift position to see if he could see where Poklewski was. He wriggled a bit, trying to make it appear that the vehicle was bumping him around. But all he could see were the flip flops and trainers of his captors and occasionally their rifle butts.

After a short time, ten minutes perhaps, but who knew, the vehicle stopped and he heard the rear trunk latch open. He was hoisted to his knees by the cable ties and nearly fainted from the pain both in his wrists and his shoulder. He cried out, only to receive a boot in the small of his back propelling him forward and out of the Hilux, onto the dust of the roadside. He lay still in agony, not knowing what to do. There was more shouting close to his head and again the hoisting to his feet by the cable ties. Once more, he felt he may faint but he was held up by what seemed to be two people. He looked down and could only see his boots. They had specks of blood on them. The absurd and random notion went through his head that at least his boots looked like they belonged to a veteran rather than the FNG.

He heard Poklewski being hauled out of the vehicle. She began to cry and said, 'I'm a US citizen and part of the Multi-National Force in Iraq authorised by the UN Security council. I request that you take me to the nearest American military installation.'

Cunningham heard a slap and a cry of pain and fear.

Then she said, 'The US military will compensate you with US dollars if you return us to the Americans.'

There was the sound of masking tape being ripped off a roll and then he felt Poklewski trying to struggle as her hood was lifted and the tape placed over her mouth. His own hood was then also lifted, allowing him a glimpse of his surroundings, and his mouthed taped. There were no readily identifiable landmarks. He could be in any town he had driven through in the last week. Low level brown buildings of two stories, a dusty and empty road strewn with litter and a stream of sewage. He could see no people other than those close to him. There must have been six or eight of them, all young men of about twenty to twenty-five years old. Most seemed to be wearing predominantly black. All were armed with AK47s except one, who had an RPG7 on his shoulder.

The hood was pulled back down. He had to struggle to pull air in through his nose, as the dried blood crusting it made getting enough oxygen in difficult. He was turned roughly round and pushed forward. He looked down under his hood at his feet to try to keep his balance and realised he was being led off the road and into a building. He was gripped by a terrifying fear of what awaited him once inside and started to shake and struggle. He felt a rifle butt smash into his back but he nevertheless shouted, 'I am a US citizen that is being kidnapped. Help!'

The masking-tape gag prevented anything intelligible escaping but he already knew he could shout as loudly as he wanted and nobody would come to his aid. His guards didn't even bother to hit him.

Poklewski was still sobbing behind him as he felt the coolness of what he assumed was a courtyard. He was pushed through a door into a building, which, judging from the floor tiles, was an occupied house. He was stopped and then he heard a door being unlocked and a light switched on and then he was walking down some stairs into a basement. He realised with dread that he could no longer hear Poklewski. Another door was unlocked and he was shoved into a room. Then he heard the door lock and the light faded. He stood in the dark for a few minutes, listening. He attempted to call Poklewski but there was just an overwhelming silence. He shuffled forward until he felt a brick wall, turned around and slid to the floor. Then he began to cry.

13

Good Friday, 9 April 2004
Forward Operating Base Echo
Head Quarters Multi-National Division Central South
1800 Local UK

The Boss put his bergen on his bed and unpacked a green, canvas, Claymore mine bag in which he kept his washing kit. It was sparse. Disposable Bic razor, toothbrush and toothpaste, and a stub of soap. He took off his shirt and admired his squaddie suntan. Brown face and arms, ghostly white torso. His exposed skin was still striped from the camouflage cream he had applied in the OP two days ago. His dog tags and an opium syrette, on green para cord, dangled around his neck. He went to the shower cubicle and began running the water. *I'll borrow some shampoo off the major*, he thought, and still shirtless, left his room and went across to the major's and knocked tentatively on the door.

'Who is it?'

'Hi, Magdalena, just me. I was wondering if I could borrow some shampoo?'

The door was opened by the major, dressed in a white dressing gown with a towel turban wrapped around her hair. Clearly, she'd just come out of the shower.

'Oh, I'm sorry, excuse me, I didn't mean to...'

'Relax, Tom. Let me get you some shampoo.' She left the door open and turned back into the room and towards her shower cubicle.

The Boss popped his head into the room and noticed it was sparsely furnished with two photographs of young children, a boy and a girl. There didn't seem to be a photograph of a husband, however.

She returned with a bottle labelled, *Szampon Joanna*. The Boss flipped the lid and sniffed.

'I'm going to get a right load of stick smelling of this.'

Magdalena laughed. 'I promise you,' she said, 'that it will be an improvement on the way you now smell. Now, off you go, or tongues will wriggle.'

'Er, I think you mean "wag".'

'I look forward to my drink with you shortly.' She smiled then removed the towel, revealing a cascade of damp, brown hair as she closed the door, leaving him standing on his own.

The Boss turned on his heel and sauntered back to his CHU with a spring in his step.

BARNES WAS OVER-SEEING the vehicle park. The Rovers had been checked for fluids and pressures, the gash disposed of, the ammunition replenished, and the weapons were dismantled and cleaned. The boys had declined the offer of both the tented accommodation and the CHUs. Fatima had collected their combats and they were in an odd assortment of civilian shorts and t-shirts. Most wore flip flops but some had kept their combat boots on.

'Prefer to basha up here, to be frank,' said Ginge, who was wearing an orange Dundee United football shirt. 'I'm going to sling my hammock between the wagons and get my head down. But not before I've eaten my body weight in steak. Will see if I can call the bairn, too.'

The rest of the troop agreed. The fuss and bother of decamping to the accommodation, rotating through stags throughout the night, and, crucially, getting out of the habit of life in the field, made it easier, in their minds, to stay put.

Barnes detailed the stag roster for the night to keep an eye on the wagons and the weapons. Stan and Ginge were doing the first stag, and consequently the most uninterrupted sleep, as they were the two most senior after the troop sergeant. ManBat and Ron, the two newest arrivals and the youngest in the troop, had been allocated the "drag stag" between 0100 and 0300. Barnes would take the final one and made a note to remind the Boss to join the troop at about 0500. Reveille was set at first light, which would be around 0445, but the troop would be up before then.

'Right,' he announced, 'get the weapons stowed and let's go to the cook house for some scoff.' They wandered over to the restaurant building and found it less than half full. The queue for food was non-existent but the amount and variety on offer was surprising.

'Fackin' 'ell, this makes the cook house in Shaibah look a bit measly,' announced Ron, piling his plate high with food.

'Certainly makes a welcome change from compo,' agreed Cookie, with an equally large plate. 'But no tea. Fucking philistines.'

Yip spotted them and walked over. 'The guys from the convoy and my rat patrol would love to buy you a drink for saving their asses.'

'Rude not to,' said Barnes.

'See you in the MWR in ten minutes?'

14

Good Friday, 9 April 2004
Jaysh al Mahdi Safe House
Somewhere in Central Ad Diwaniyah
2030 Local

The single overhead bulb flickered into life and slowly penetrated through the fog of Cunningham's mind. He didn't know how long he'd been sitting, semi-conscious, with his back to the wall in the dark. His head still throbbed, his mouth was sandpaper dry and ironically, he was bursting to urinate. He heard activity the other side of the metal door and the key scrape in the lock. The door was violently kicked open, presumably in case he was waiting the other side to surprise and overcome his captors, a possibility so remote it had not even occurred to him. He pushed his head back so that he could see under the hood and watched as two men entered. Both were armed and both had black head scarves covering everything but their eyes. An empty plastic bucket was thrown in his direction and then the two men approached. Both were armed but the second man had his weapon slung over his shoulder and carried a bottle of water and a bowl. He wore scruffy blue Nike trainers.

Cunningham stayed seated so he could observe his visitors. One gripped him by the arm to make him get up and then took the hood off his head. His eyes were not yet ready for the light, dim though it was, and he screwed his lids shut. More shouting made him force them open. They turned him round and cut the cable ties on his wrists with a pair of pliers. The instant relief was immense but as he moved his arms from behind his back, the pain in his shoulder was unbearable. He stood before them blinking and panting and then was given the bottle of water, which he accepted.

As he twisted the plastic lid, he noticed the seal had already been broken. He sniffed cautiously at the liquid but his thirst was such that he readily gulped down the first mouthful. It was lukewarm and a bit brackish but didn't seem obviously drugged or poisoned. He reasoned that they could just shoot him anyway, so wouldn't go to the bother of anything more sophisticated. His second thought was that if the water was contaminated, he could get a stomach upset and that could get really messy.

The bowl was placed at his feet and he saw it contained a brown stew-like substance. A slice of flatbread was laid beside it on the bare concrete floor. The second man said, 'Eat,' pointing to the food, and made a motion with his fingers. Then he pointed to the plastic bucket. 'Toilet,' he added.

They turned to leave the room and Cunningham blurted out, 'Thank you,' which prompted them to look at him, and then they turned again and left. The door was locked but the light remained on. Cunningham used the bucket to relieve his bladder and then picked up the bowl. It appeared to be a goat stew and despite the bones and lumps of fat, he wolfed it down. He used the bread to scoop it into his mouth and then his fingers to get everything left behind. Finally, he licked the bowl and took another swig of water. He judged the time to be evening and realised that he hadn't eaten properly since leaving BIAP that morning. It seemed an age ago.

He sat back down with his back to the wall, wondering what had happened to Poklewski and whether the army knew they had been kidnapped. They must know, he reasoned. Right now, there would be a US Special Forces team honing in on this house and the next person to come through his cell door would be dressed in black with a flashlight on his weapon. He wondered if his parents had been informed that he had disappeared, presumed captured. Or perhaps they had been told "missing in action, presumed dead". He thought about his mother, who had begged him not to join up and go to Iraq. His father who had been proud of him doing just that and the tension between the two that it had caused before he left. His mind turned to his sister, who was at school at the University of Madison, in South Dakota. He hoped she wouldn't get told. She'd let him know that her friends, like most of the students, were very anti-war and that she felt she couldn't tell them he was in Iraq. Why hadn't Poklewski turned right? She had been briefed, same as him. He was in the middle of a firefight. It was her fault they were in this mess. He couldn't be expected to navigate and be in a firefight. He wondered if his captors were the same people he had been firing at. Whether they realised he had killed one of their number and whether there would be retribution. Maybe a show trial followed by execution. Surely there was honor amongst soldiers, they would realise that. And they wouldn't want that US Special Forces troop finding them if they'd just executed two American prisoners. Definitely not. Maybe he and Poklewski were the lucky ones. Maybe the convoy had been shot to pieces and everybody killed. It certainly sounded as if it was taking numerous casualties before the goddamn radio got shot out. If they were all dead, maybe nobody knew he was here. But they would do a body count, right? Yet it took the army four days to get those bodies back out of Fallujah. They were left hanging from that bridge. Maybe they would hang him from a bridge for all the world to see. Maybe they just wanted a ransom. The army would pay up rather than have him executed. Where were they holding Poklewski? Maybe she was in the next room.

He got up and went over to the door. He listened and then gently tried the handle. It didn't budge. He gently called her name and then listened again. He heard nothing. He became aware in the distance of the sound of traffic and could hear the faint sound of car horns. He'd noticed that Iraqis used their horns as much as the emergency services used a siren, to let everybody know where they were and to make sure they got out of the way. He called Poklewski's name a bit louder and then listened again. Still nothing. He knelt down and peered through the keyhole. He could see nothing. Presumably the key was left in the lock the other side. He didn't dare risk anything else. If she was nearby, she may well be asleep or unconscious. He didn't want to attract attention to himself. He had to be a gray man, not rile his captors; to win them over, maybe bond with them. He went back to where he had sat before and slumped down again, resisting the temptation to drink more water as he didn't know when he would get another bottle. The cable ties were still on the floor, and he picked them up, wondering if they might be useful. He put one in the side map pocket of his combat trousers just in case. His shoulder still ached and his head still throbbed. He got up again, trying to take his mind off the pain, deciding to check the walls of his prison. He walked around the small room hitting the wall periodically with the side of his fist. It all sounded solid to him. He paced the room to measure it out and decided it was about ten by twelve feet. He went to look at his watch and then remembered it had been stolen. He went through all his pockets. Nothing. His wallet, notebook and pens were gone, his map, even his dog tags had been taken. All he had were two cut cable ties, a bucket half-full of piss, a bottle half-full of water, and an empty bowl. He wondered what the procedure was for defecating. The time would come shortly and there was no toilet paper. He sat down again and looked at his wrist to see the suntan marks where his watch used to be then closed his eyes and tried to sleep, but his headache was all he could concentrate on.

He got up again and decided to see if he could summon the guards, a decision that had him walking up to the metal door and banging on it loudly.

'Hey, hey, guards. I need to talk to you. Hey, hey, can you hear me?'

He stopped to listen but only heard the distant roar of the traffic. He banged again, louder this time, but the pain resonated through his shoulder, even though he was using his good arm. He listened again. In the distance he could hear the call to prayers. That should indicate to him it was before midnight. Unless it was the next morning. He didn't really know what time the Muezzin made their calls. Was it five times a day? He couldn't remember. That lecture in Camp Virginia seemed another lifetime ago and to be honest, he hadn't really paid much attention to the in-country cultural briefings. Two types of Haji out here, he remembered. Sunni and Shi'ite. Sonny and Cher, they had joked. He had no idea which were holding him, though he had a vague idea they might have been in the Sunni triangle when they were ambushed. He remembered the Sunni were the bad guys. OBL's lot. But thinking about it again he remembered that the Shi'ite were down in the South because he remembered on the way up they went through that area first. The Shi'ite were more disposed toward the Americans. Or were they? He remembered they were pro-Iran and Iran absolutely hated Americans. But America had been well disposed towards the Marsh Arabs in the South and part of the "no-fly zone" before the invasion was to protect them. In which case, why had they ambushed the convoy? There was nothing remotely friendly about that ambush. Or maybe he had been rescued by pro-American Iraqis who were grateful for being liberated and they were keeping him safe until they could hand him over to a patrol. Or, maybe they were going to execute him and send video footage to the world's press.

He sat back down and wished he had Poklewski with him for company. The solitude was just beginning to wear him down and he felt himself slipping into despair as he leant against the wall and closed his eyes again.

15

Good Friday, 9 April 2004
Forward Operating Base Echo
Head Quarters Multi-National Division Central South
1835 Local

The Boss felt considerably better after a hot shower. He hadn't bothered with the razor so still sported a scruffy and patchy beard, and as he had no hair brush, he looked like the bastard child of Jimi Hendrix and David Bellamy. But the shower had worked wonders and he ambled over to the main part of the camp.

A sweat shirt bearing the slogan *HellCats*, which seemed to be the nickname of the current US cavalry unit, caught his eye in the small shop at the entrance, so he bought it with one of the several ten-dollar bills he always had whilst on operations and put it over his t-shirt. He contemplated a coffee from the Green Bean Café but decided against. He walked past a number of booths, which appeared to be some sort of internet café where soldiers were chatting with home. Times had changed so quickly in the decade he had been in the army. Back then, communication home had been mainly via "blueys" if you were a pad, and not at all if you were single. Now, soldiers were using the internet to talk to loved ones, both email and the more immediate and generally more favoured, instant messaging. He used ICQ instant messenger but you could also now use the internet to make free phone calls. One of the Scaleybacks had been telling him about a programme called Skype that had been developed by some Scandis with which you could talk and video at the same time and all for free. Barnes, the philistine, thought it was all black magic and, being very old school indeed, preferred to keep communication with his wife for when he got back off operations.

'What's the second thing you do when you get back off ops? Put your bags down.'

He wandered into the bar area and saw the boys sitting around a couple of low tables pushed together. They were with some Americans, some of whom must have been part of the ambushed convoy judging by their age and dress. There were also, inevitably, some females in the group too, and he could tell there was some serious chatting up about to commence.

'Nice sweatshirt, Boss.'

'Thank you, Ron. Just bought it in the PX Naafi shop thingy.'

'HellCats is a bit better than *Cherrypickers* don't you think, Boss?'

'Cherrypickers?' said one of the American girls. 'That sounds kinda, like, pervy.'

'It's a two-hundred-year-old regimental nickname when pervy wasn't really a thing,' said the Boss. 'A reconnaissance squadron caught eating cherries by the French in the Peninsular War.'

'Oh, right...' said the girl with a vacant expression, clearly having never heard of the Peninsular War.

'The Boss is right posh,' explained Ron. 'Hangs about with all the duchesses and princesses back in Blighty. It was him that they got to murder Lady Di...'

'Oh. My. God,' said the girl. 'So all that shit about her being murdered was true?'

'Look, man...' interjected ManBat, picking up the theme, 'we shouldn't be speaking about secrets in front of uncleared civvies.'

'How did you get the car to crash?' continued the girl.

'Um...cut the brake cables...not sure we've been introduced.'

'This is the Boss,' said Ron. 'Boss, this is Shannon, Sharelle, and, er...um...'

'Mindy...' said the third of the trio.

'Yeah, Mindy...mind went blank there for a moment, Mindy, don't know why.'

'Probably because you are a thick Welsh twat,' said ManBat.

'Are you "the Boss" as in some kind of mafia way, or because you don't look like Bruce Springsteen? I've noticed you Brits always say the opposite of what you mean.'

'Look, it's because he's a gay Nazi clothes designer, isn't it, Hugo?' said ManBat.

'Oh my god, does your dad own the clothes company? I love their clothes,' said the gullible one he now knew was called Shannon.

'Um...no, it's because...'

'So, you're not really a Nazi?' continued Shannon. 'I mean, I'm all for freedom of speech but a Nazi might be a bit of, like, a problem. I think my cousin is a white supremacist.'

'Just so we don't get off on the wrong foot,' began the Boss, 'I'm not Bruce Springsteen, gay, a Nazi, a royal murderer, or in the mafia.'

'I love your names, though. Why do they call you Bat?'

'His full name is ManBat,' said Ron.

'Not Bat Man?' asked Sharelle.

'Definitely not Bat Man!' said Ron

'Look,' said ManBat, 'my adoring but, shall we say, sheltered parents, Sandy and Eileen Bruce named me Wayne...Wayne Bruce. Living on a tobacco farm in what was then Rhodesia, they didn't even have a TV so hadn't even heard of Bat Man.'

'Oh, I get it. I see what you're doing there, like it's Bat Man backwards.'

'And what are you called?' Mindy asked Ron.

'He's called Rocket Ron,' answered Cookie. 'Rocket Ron Stevenson.'

'Okaaay' said Mindy, not quite getting it.

'You know, Stevenson's Rocket? The first train?'

'Whatever...' said Mindy, none the wiser.

'Ask him why he's called Pocket Rocket,' carried on Cookie.

'Why's that, then?' said Shannon.

'Um...who would like a beer?' interrupted the Boss, quickly. 'Do they do beer here?'

'You can get Bud and Coors but they only sell to non-American personnel,' Shannon replied. 'But it's ok for you to get them and just put 'em on the table. We just, you know, like maybe try them out once you've got them. So long as it's not in your face obvious, nobody minds.'

'OK,' said the Boss. He looked around and saw Yip talking to some Americans that he assumed were the protection from the convoy. He remembered Lieber and recognised the top gunner on the gun truck, and wandered over.

'Evening, Yip. Evening, gentlemen. Can I get you lads a beer?'

'We should be buying you a beer for saving our asses,' said Yip. 'However, US military personnel are not permitted to purchase alcoholic beverages on this site. Unless you want a Coke?'

'No thanks, Yip. I'm just getting a round in for the lads and getting extras in for the ladies. If you want to join us, be my guest.'

'We may come over in a minute,' said Yip. 'We're just going over the events of the day. Word on the street is that there's a TF Green hostage release team being assembled at Edson, the Marine camp north of the town. We'll learn more at the BUB tomorrow A.M.

'TF Green?' asked the Boss.

'1st Special Forces Operational Detachment. Also known as Delta Force. Is John joining you at all?'

'He said he'd wander over but he's just sorting out the wagons at the moment.'

The Boss went to the bar and ordered a dozen Buds and looked at the array of TVs on the wall, all of which seemed to be tuned into either an ESPN sports channel or an MTV music channel. There was a country and western song playing over the speakers.

By the time he got back, Cookie, Bat and Rocket had cleverly sliced and diced the three girls and were each concentrating on one girl each. He marvelled at the continuous stream of banter and how they bounced off each other.

'You smell nice,' said Cookie, getting into the no-fly zone around Mindy.

'Aww...thank you. It's Calvin Klein. My boyfriend back home sent it to me.'

Cookie brushed the set-back aside. 'It really suits you.'

'You smell nice too,' said Mindy. 'What have you got on?'

'He's got a hard-on!' said Ron.

'But I didn't know you could smell it...' added ManBat.

'Eww...that's gross...' said Mindy, clearly not minding at all, her far-away boyfriend forgotten for the moment.

The Boss put the tray on the table and handed round the beers. 'So, how long have you all been out here?' he asked, immediately regretting such a lame question.

'You know the difference between an officer and a senior NCO?' asked Cookie.

'Go on then...' said Ron.

'The NCO knows everything about fuck all and the officer knows fuck all about everything.'

'Very good, Cookie. Shouldn't you be twiddling your knobs?'

Just then he noticed Magdalena Duda coming into the hall. She looked around, spotted the group, and began to walk over. She'd scrubbed up well and with her hair down and a bit of eye makeup, she looked fabulous to someone who had been in the desert for as long as he had. He clocked again her generous curves.

He thankfully left the group to intercept her and asked her if she wanted a beer, offering a Budweiser.

'I think, perhaps, I would prefer a glass of white wine,' she said.

'I'm impressed they sell that here. One glass of chilled white wine coming up. Is there a choice? Do you have a preference?'

'There's not much of a choice but a glass of Chardonnay would be perfect. Thank you, Tom.'

'My pleasure. I was sitting over there with the lads but we can sit elsewhere if you prefer.' He paid the bartender with another of his ten-dollar bills and they both turned to survey the room.

'Your men are quick movers, it would seem, Tom.'

'Er...yes, I suppose so. You know, the common soldiery is the same the world over, I suspect.'

'I would hate to take you away from the party.'

'Oh...don't worry about that. I'm almost certainly cramping their style and I'm sure they would prefer me to piss off.'

'Let us sit here. I've worked out that this table is where the music is the least loud,' Magdalena suggested, and they both sat down. 'I'm hearing the Americans are assembling a Delta Force team at Edson, which is based at the University of Diwaniyah.'

'Yes, Yip Romaro, the American sergeant major, told me as much.'

'The Americans really do not want more captured soldiers. Have you heard about the battle in Baghdad today?' she asked.

'No. Nothing.'

'An American fuel convoy was ambushed just outside BIAP. There were numerous casualties, almost all the vehicles were hit, most destroyed, I'm told. I think some of the drivers are missing. There were tankers ablaze on the flyover around Abu Graib district.'

'Do they know who organised it?'

'Initial int reports suggest al-Sadr. Tom, this marks a big escalation in the insurgency. The ambush down here and up there on the same day indicates an organisational ability that we had no idea about.'

'How come you speak such good English, Magdalena?' the Boss asked, to change the subject. The current spate of ambushes was rather depressing and it could wait until the briefing tomorrow. He was still trying to come down from the intensity of the fire fight and didn't want to talk shop right then.

'I did my master's degree at King's College, London.'

'That would explain it. What in?'

'Defence Studies, of course.'

'Of course. Did you enjoy London?'

'I loved it. It is a great city, especially for a quiet girl from Wroclaw.'

'The British and the Poles have always got on well. As you say, a shared mistrust of the obvious lot in the middle of us...'

'The Germans?'

'I wasn't going to say so, but now you mention it.'

'The Poles fought alongside the British in the war. We flew your Spitfires and we invaded with you in Normandy.'

'Indeed. And always gave a good account of yourselves.'

'We were the troops that took Monte Cassino, after the New Zealanders, British and Indians had failed.'

'Also true.'

'And then you sent us back to the Russians after the war.'

'I wasn't alive then, Magdalena.'

'The Russians murdered five thousand Polish officers in the woods at Katyn. They killed a further ten thousand prisoners in their concentration camps. Nobody remembers this holocaust.'

'There's a Polish War Memorial in West London. It's a famous landmark and it gets mentioned on the radio every day.'

'I doubt that is true, Tom.'

'It's sort of true. If you listen to Capital Radio breakfast show with Chris Tarrant, well, the traffic bird, who I happen to know is called Kara Noble, mentions it because it's where the traffic comes to a halt on the A40.'

'I don't think a traffic jam is a suitable memorial for the Polish war dead, Tom'

The Boss felt this was not going well. At all well. Time to stop digging or try to dig yourself out, perhaps?

'It's just that if you ask anybody in London where the Polish War Memorial is, they know. That's all. Nobody knows where the French one is. Let me get you another drink.'

'No, Tom. Let me get these. I'm sorry about the little lecture.

Sometimes, I think the crimes against the Polish people by the Russians and Germans are ignored. Now, we have joined the EU.'

'You joined last year, didn't you?'

'Yes, almost exactly a year ago. But we are now going to be the German pets again. They haven't invaded but they might as well have. And they can feel they can write those insulting articles in their press about being Trojan Asses and criminals.'

'Wouldn't worry about that, Magdalena. The press in my country are far worse. It's the nature of the beast. How would you employ all those people who are too lazy to be traffic wardens and too stupid to be tax inspectors?'

She laughed. 'Time for that drink...' and got up to go to the bar.

The Boss sat back, relieved that he might have avoided a catastrophic fail incident. Barnes, Wolfie and Stan came in and walked over to the table.

'Just proffed meself a poncho liner from the stores,' declared Stan.

'Did you get me one?' asked the Boss.

'Did you ask me to get you one?'

'No, obviously, I didn't ask you. I didn't know they were there.'

'In which case, it's lucky I look after you. John and me got the whole troop one each.'

'Well played, Stan. Good drills,' said the Boss.

'Looks like the boys are getting stuck in,' observed Barnes. 'Getting any traction with Acorn?'

'Difficult to tell. Slow progress being made perhaps.'

'Oops, switch to radio silence, approaching enemy forces...' muttered Barnes as Magdalena came back with a glass of wine and a beer.

'My apologies, gentlemen. I did not see you arrive. What can I get you to drink?'

'That's OK, ma'am,' said Barnes. 'Stan and me are just going to go over and see the lads for a minute. We might join you later, if that's ok?'

'Of course.'

Barnes, Wolfie and Stan wandered over to the group.

'Time's up, Cookie-dough,' announced Stan, pointing to his watch. 'Ginge is over by the vehicles.'

Cookie got up, drained his beer in one draught, said his goodbyes to the Americans, and went back to stag-on with Ginge.

Barnes left the group and walked over to Yip. He was introduced to the members of the rat patrol that had accompanied the convoy down from BIAP. They were intending to RON at Echo and head up in the morning after the BUB. However, it seemed the general opinion was that the main routes in the North were no longer safe and that they would probably be stuck at Echo for a few days at least. Whilst they didn't have any extensive kit with them – expecting only to be away 48 hours - the delay was not as bad as it could have been. The FOB would be a cushy and safe place to stay overnight for a few days and anything they needed could be bought in the PX or issued by the stores.

'How are the casualties? Any word on that driver that lost an arm or the GSW?'

'I think they'll be medevacked to Kuwait and then back to Ramstein, Germany,' Yip replied.

'I've heard that the driver, I think he was called Sneddon, didn't make it,' said Gubby. 'Checked out on the dust-off flight.'

'Doesn't surprise me. He was in a bad way. Round went through the armpit of his body armour, missed his sapi and probably blew away most of his lung and severed an artery,' said Yip.

'Sorry to hear that,' Barnes offered. 'You know, in this business, so much depends on luck. You can't calculate the odds of a round going through the one chink in the armour. Doesn't matter who you are, in a fire fight, luck plays a big part.'

'A sucking chest wound sure is an indicator that you've fucked up a fire fight. No shit,' said Gubby, taking a swig. 'Chen, the driver that was hit by the IED, had her driver shot in the cab right at the start of the ambush. Probably those Hajis firing from the top floor of that government building. Could easily have hit her, missed him, missed them both. Just don't know.'

'Think there was another KIA driver. One of the tankers. Don't know his name.'

'KBR?' asked Yip.

'Don't know,' said Gubby. 'Don't think so, though.'

'What do you make of the missing personnel, Yip?' asked Barnes.

'I think they missed the turning in the ambush and were taken where we saw the vehicle. Given it was on the wrong carriageway, I suspect they knew they'd fucked up and were trying to get back. Should've kept driving like they were briefed. The spent shells in the footwells would suggest they put up resistance but probably were out gunned. The only good thing was we found no sign of blood in the Humvee or the surrounding area.'

'I hear there's a Delta Force team just up the road.'

'To be honest, John,' replied Yip, 'I'm no longer in that loop. I imagine they were scrambled as soon as the sitrep went in that we'd lost a vehicle. But yes, I've heard that too.'

'I think we're going to stick around in case we're useful. Major Duda will brief us tomorrow on the latest intel and we'll take a view then. We don't want to be superfluous to requirements but I've got some highly trained men familiar with hostage release drills if it's required.'

'It's a kind offer,' said Yip. 'Your Boss seems to be keen on the int officer,' he continued. 'From where I'm sitting, it looks like he may be on to a good thing.'

'He's normally shite at chatting up birds,' said Barnes, 'but he may be on to a lucky one here. Let's keep to tradition and go and fuck it up for him.'

'That's not very loyal of you, John, but, if you insist and you say it's a British Army tradition, then who am I to disagree?'

The two of them wandered over to the Boss and Magdalena. She stood up as they arrived.

'Don't move, ma'am, I'll draw up a couple of chairs...'

The major looked at Barnes and said, 'I'm calling it a night, Sergeant. I trust I will see you at the briefing tomorrow for an overnight update on the hostage situation?'

'Oh...yeah, ok.'

As Magdalena left, Barnes quietly said, 'Have you fucked that up as well, Boss?'

'I'm not sure it's entirely dead in the water but probably, John. Thank you for your concern.'

'It may be for the best.'

'How do you work that out?' said the Boss. 'Anyway, I'm going to have one more beer with the boys and then also call it a day. I'm utterly cream crackered.'

'We'll see you at the TOC for the BUB then,' said Yip. '0700 local'.

'Right you are,' said the Boss. 'John, get the lads to turn in shortly. I don't want them shitfaced in the Naafi and then giving it the one-yard gormless look rather than the thousand-yard stare tomorrow.'

'If they've not secured a knee trembler or a nosh by 2300, then I'll get them back to the bashas. Bruce and Stevenson are on the drag stag anyway, so they'll be leaving shortly.'

'Night then, all,' said the Boss, and wandered out of the hangar and towards his accommodation in Chuville.

He was in his shorts, just washing his face in the basin using the stub of his soap, when there was a gentle knock at the door.

'Who's that? Come in...'

Magdalena opened the door and entered. She was in the white dressing gown again and the Boss noticed it was not so secured at the top as previously. One might even assume it was slightly open deliberately. Not too much but then again, not tightly secured, either.

'I was hoping to retrieve my shampoo,' she announced. 'And wondered if you would like to share a little night cap of Polish vodka?'

'Well, if you insist, just a small one then... let me just get the shampoo.'

'Forget about the shampoo, Tom.'

'Oh, ok...' The Boss wondered if this was what it looked like it was. She was obviously coming on to him and he couldn't help but notice there was a little white band where her wedding ring had once been worn.

She sat on the bed and his eyes were drawn mesmerically to the large amount of thigh on display. The clincher would be if she had omitted to wear shreddies, he considered.

She waved her hand in front of his face.

'Hello, Tom, over here...' She laughed, offering him a small tumbler of ice-cold vodka.

'Twoje zdrowie,' she said, raising the glass.

He raised his own glass and drank it down in one. The cold, powerful liquid made his eyes water and burned on the way down.

'My God!' he muttered.

Magdalena was leaning forward with the bottle to refill his glass. Nope, definitely not wearing a bra. No bra, no wedding ring. That was amber, flickering green in anybody's book. He felt the rush of excitement and remembered the old classics lesson at school. In Plato's Republic, the great writer had quoted the philosopher Sophocles, who had said, in the loose translation by Kingsley Amis, *Having testicles was like being chained to the village idiot.* This particular village idiot was definitely now making himself known.

'Cheers,' he said, raising the glass. 'To the Polish war dead.'

'And to the Queen of England.'

They both fired down the second shot. That also made his eyes water and he let out a small gasp as the liquid slid down his throat for a second time. The village idiot was now definitely interested because alcohol made Idiot Control lose power.

'Boy, that's quite powerful.'

'This comes from Wroclaw and is the best vodka in the world. Don't be fooled by that Russian shit.'

'I won't be,' he replied, sitting down on the one chair in the small room. The ice-cold alcohol was already beginning to take effect. 'So, tell me, Magdalena,' he said, trying to think of something to say, the village idiot now swiftly taking command of most of his faculties, including that of rational thought. He was never quite sure at what point in these types of proceedings that it was acceptable to let it be known that the idiot had now taken over and was in charge.

'Yes?'

There was suddenly an unmistakeable noise of an incoming

round and a loud detonation, which he judged to be about a hundred metres away. The camp siren started and then a second detonation, this time further, perhaps a hundred and fifty metres. He looked at Magdalena and she was smiling.

'Should we go to the shelter?' he asked.

'Only the US Airforce go to the shelters. It's a tradition that the army don't. The chances of a direct hit are very small and they normally only get to fire three or four bombs before escaping as the QRF get crashed out.'

Magdalena stood up to offer him another shot of vodka, the chilled bottle now frosted with condensation. A third round came in and exploded, nearer this time, the shock rattling the room. Magdalena involuntarily – or was it voluntarily, jumped at the sound, spilling some vodka on the Boss. He caught a full-on glimpse that proved she had come wearing at least some underwear. But it was also now very apparent to him that it was only for a bit of show and was very definitely not Polish Army issue. She hooked up a leg and sat astride him on the chair and whispered into his ear, 'I think we should mop up that spilled vodka... Oh...is that a gun in your...'

'It's actually my Sig Sauer,' said the Boss, fishing the pistol out of the pocket of his combats. He flicked off the magazine, cocked the weapon, caught the unfired round as it was ejected, flipped it back into the magazine, put his finger into the stock, and released the hammer forward before replacing the magazine.

She put her arms around his neck and let the gown fall open. 'You seem to have a second Sig Sauer about your person, Tom...'

It must have also been apparent to her that this manoeuvre was totally acceptable to him/the idiot as well. He stood up, with her clinging on around his neck, her legs hooked around his back, and he carried her the few steps to the bed and laid her down, all without spilling either his or her vodka. It was the cherry on the icing of the satisfaction cake. Idiot Control shut down for the night.

16

Good Friday, 9 April 2004
Jaysh al Mahdi Safe House
Somewhere in Central Ad Diwaniyah
2315 Local

L T Cunningham awoke from a fitful sleep at the sound of the key in the lock. The bare lightbulb was still on, filling the room with its harsh, yellow light. He had no idea what time it was. His shoulder still hurt badly and his headache had not subsided. He looked at the door as the handle turned and it opened to reveal three men, one of whom he recognised from earlier by his blue sneakers.

Two of the men carried Poklewski between them. She was clearly finding it hard to walk and her feet dragged across the concrete floor as they entered the room. She was in her white t-shirt and desert cam combat trousers and boots. Everything else had been removed. Through his puffed-up eyes, he noticed that she was conscious but obviously very much subdued or sedated, making no effort to keep herself upright. There was a little spot of blood on her earlobe where an earring used to be. Her face was badly bruised and her hair had been half released from the bun she had made, when...yesterday? Much earlier today? He had no idea. She looked at him with vacant eyes and he noticed her mascara had smudged down her cheeks.

The two guards laid her down on the ground next to him, her back against the wall. She sat with her arms at her side and stared into space as she let out a quiet sob, much like a child coming to the end of an epic bout of crying.

Cunningham stared at the guards. In his mind he shouted at them, *What have you done to her, you animals*, but nothing escaped his lips. They put another bottle of water down next to his empty bowl, turned around and left without a word.

There was silence. Poklewski let out another sob, still staring straight ahead. He turned to face her, wincing at the pain in his shoulder.

'Hey, Poklewski. They're going to get us out of here.' He didn't sound too convincing but he continued anyway. 'Right now, the whole of the goddamn US Army is looking for us.' He reached forward for the water. 'Here, have a bit of water,' he said, unscrewing the top before offering her the bottle. He looked at her face again and saw tears trickling down her cheeks, little rivulets of smudged mascara through the caked-on dust. She made no attempt to take the water or wipe away the tears. Another racking sob escaped her cracked and blood-stained lips.

'Drink a bit. Hey, Poklewski, look at me. Look at me...' She turned her head and stared vacantly at him. He noticed her nostrils were full of coagulated blood too, and he thought he probably looked equally as bad.

'Have a bit of water. It'll make you feel better. We'll be released in a few hours.'

She mumbled something incoherent at him, which he couldn't hear. Then he leaned forward and over to her to get closer. She mumbled again, scarcely a whisper: 'They... raped... me.'

Cunningham felt a red-hot surge of anger. Impotent anger. He had no words for her. Finally, he spluttered out, 'We'll find those sons of bitches and the US Army will try them and convict them for War Crimes. They won't get away with it, Alice. Not on my watch.' Even as he said it, he felt absurd. With much effort, he got to his feet and hobbled over to the door and banged on it. The noise sounded very loud in that little room. He listened and then banged again: silence.

'Hey, you sons of bitches...' he screamed. 'Hey, you come here right now and open this goddamn door. Do you hear me? Right now!'

Again, he listened, putting his ear to the metal door. There was silence.

'Goddammit, Alice, they're not getting away with this. They'll be tried in a military court. Yeah, they will, and I will testify. Probably an Iraqi court and they'll be sentenced to death. Hell, yeah...these sick wackos have made a really big mistake. Probably the biggest of their miserable little lives.'

Poklewski stared at him, saying nothing. He walked over to the metal bowl and kicked it. It flew across the concrete floor and came to a clattering rest in the far corner. He stood facing the wall, his arms supporting him and his head hanging down, thinking. But his mind was blank. His voice seemed out of place in the silence. His rantings were the lame posturing of a weakling and a victim and he hated himself for it. The black despair came over him again and he turned and slid back down next to Poklewski, his knees up and his back hunched slightly forward.

The silence and heat were palpable in the small space. Having both of them in there somehow made it worse for him. He felt awkward and closed his eyes, wishing for the blessed relief of sleep, but it wouldn't come. He replayed in his mind how they had missed the turning. How he'd hit the Haji. Had he killed him? He didn't care. He felt only bitterness and hatred towards this godforsaken country and its people. He thought of back home. Would they know he was MIA by now? Maybe he had been reported as dead. Yesterday had been Good Friday. His folks would have gone down to the church at eleven and then home for roast lamb lunch. They always did that. His big sis would have been over with her family and his little sis would be on her spring break. The US was behind about eleven hours, so if it was the middle of the night here – maybe four in the morning, that would make it...what? Five in the afternoon. They would be watching TV, probably the news. He knew his mom watched every news bulletin looking out for what was happening in Iraq. If they thought he was dead, he knew that things would be very different from a normal Easter Saturday. His folks would take comfort in the local church. Neighbors would be coming round to console his family. But they would never pronounce him missing presumed killed without some evidence. No, they would be looking for him right now and his folks wouldn't know he was even missing yet.

Poklewski got unsteadily to her feet. He opened his eyes as she got up. She hobbled over to where the bowl had landed and then picked up the water bottle. She then started undoing her combat trousers.

'Hey, Alice, what are you doing?'

She ignored him and turned her back, then dropped her trousers down to her knees and pulled down her underwear. Cunningham looked at her and turned away, ashamed. But his gaze was pulled back to her white butt. There was blood on the inside of her thighs. She picked up the water and poured some into the bowl and then using the palm of her hand, she began to delicately wash away the blood.

'My god, Alice...' was all he could say. She poured more water and washed herself more vigorously, scrubbing viciously as if to try to rid herself of the stain on her soul as well as the mess in her trousers. She pulled them back up and undid her combat boots and then she stood up again and removed her trousers and her underwear, which she threw into the corner. They were soiled with all the sordid by-products of the crime that had been inflicted on her. She poured more water and continued scrubbing with her hand.

'Hey, Alice, easy on the water, that's all we've got...'

She ignored him still. Finally, when all the water was gone, she redid up her combats and then sat back down again, further from

Cunningham than before. She stared ahead. He got up and sat next to her and reached for her hand. She pulled it away, violently. Embarrassed at the rejection, he got up and again went over to the door and started banging.

17

The Boss awoke from a bad dream. He couldn't remember what. Trying to avoid an invisible ill-defined threat. It was still dark outside but the camp was beginning to come to life. Magdalena had left at around midnight, so he'd had a decent four and a half hours' kip. He got dressed in the neatly ironed combats that had been returned and left outside his door, before doing a quick scan of the room and the shower to make sure he'd left nothing behind. Then he slid out into the night towards the vehicle park. As he approached the troop wagons, he heard a murmured 'Is that you, Boss?' from Barnes, who was taking the final stag of the night.

'Yes, it is.'

'What's the password?'

'I don't fucking know...um...Who Dares?'

'Wins. Correct. Advance friend and be recognised...'

'All OK, John?'

'Yeah, quiet enough night. I presume you weren't so otherwise engrossed as to not hear the mortars? Half the troop didn't even wake up.' He handed the Boss his steaming, plastic mug of tea.

'What, even through the siren racket?'

'Did you get lucky then?'

'You know I couldn't possibly comment. Strictly need-to-know basis. If you need to ask, you don't need to know.'

'So that's a yes, then?'

'What time's the briefing?' the Boss said to change the subject.

'0700 in the TOC.'

'I guess we need to get everybody up, send the sitrep and go over to the cookhouse for a bit of brekkie.'

'Reveille set at 0515, so in about five minutes.'

Barnes went around the troop, shaking them awake by the foot. Ginge had indeed slung a hammock between two of the vehicles but the rest were sleeping on the hard, sandy ground. 'Come on, you lazy twats. Hands off cocks and on socks.'

There was a general muttering and some splendid breaking of wind.

'Man, you are a fucking rancid pig, Ron. Jesus, that smells like a rat has crawled up your arse and died.'

'I'm not used to this American scoff, Bat. It's playing havoc with me insides. I think that one might have had a skin on it.'

'Fucking hell, Ron,' added Cookie. 'Mate, honestly, you need to go and see the MO and get a good pulling through with a Christmas tree.'

'Right, get over to the cookhouse and get some breakfast. The Boss and me will stay here. Want you all back for 0645. Ginge, get some scoff for us, will you? And don't forget the crates from the cookhouse.' Barnes handed him a mess tin and the Boss dug out a small frying pan from his kit and his black plastic mug.

'White coffee, no sugar, please, Ginge.'

'You tap off with that Polish bird then, Boss?'

'Which Polish bird, Ginge? Come on, get a gildy on. Haven't got all day.'

'The int officer one.'

'Fucking get going, Ginge. Don't forget the crates.'

'I'll take the wagon,' said Ginge. 'Come on, Ron, let's go.'

'OK, Ginge. Once we've got the crates and some scoff, could you then run me over to the accommodation block?' asked Ron.

'I'll only do one run, Ron, I'll only do one run,' Ginge replied with a broad grin.

Ron broke into a tuneless song: '*I met him on a Monday and my heart stood still. Da do ron-ron-ron, da do ron-ron. Somebody told me that his name was Ginge and he was a twat, da do ron-ron-ron, da do ron-ron.*'

'I'm here all week,' chirped Ginge, still very pleased with his joke.

'Stick with the day job, Ginge.'

Ginge still had a smug grin of satisfaction on his face as he put the Rover into gear.

Once the troop had left, the Boss began stowing his kit on his Rover.

'What are we going to do with the money?' asked Barnes.

'We're going to hand it in to the CO when we get back.'

'What? All of it?'

'Yes. All of it. You got a better idea? Other than stealing sixty-odd million dollars from HMG?'

'Let's say, just for a theoretical discussion on the matter, you know, playing devil's advocate and all that, we keep a couple of mil for ourselves? Not saying we should but nobody knows how much we've got stowed in the wagons. So, we can hand in most of it and keep some back.'

The Boss remained silent for a good minute. His face was inscrutable.

'How would you get it back to Blighty and where would you keep it? You can't have a massive wad of unused US dollars stowed in your garage, John.'

'So you're not horrified by the suggestion?'

'I didn't say that. We are, I think I remember you saying, discussing theoretical options.'

'We are. But I've not much longer in the field before they put me in the stores or behind a desk. And you, Boss, well, your next posting will be some sort of staff job. Probably in some backwater like Aldershot or Wilton.'

'Have you even begun to think this through, John?' asked the Boss. 'If we get caught, it's a minimum of five years in Colchester, dishonourable discharge, no pension, front page of the Daily Mail. Probably find it hard to get a job even as a security guard. Why risk it?'

'Because, Boss, every now and again, life hands you an opportunity. Nobody knows how much money survived the ambush. Fuck's sake, we don't even know how much we've got. It'll just go to some corrupt fucking war lord who's going to spunk it on prozzies and booze.'

'Isn't that what you are going to do with it, as well?' the Boss asked, grinning.

'I wish. No, what about we set up a secret fund? Look after the lads' families if they don't make it back from an op.'

'That's what the Clock Tower Fund is for,' replied the Boss.

'Yeah, I know. But that's often not able to make a difference. We could do things that really makes a difference.'

'OK. Let's say we prof some. How do we get it back? You know that there's random searches of kit after ops.'

'We make it a deniable op. The government are always putting us in situations where if it goes tits up, they're going to deny we're anything to do with official policy. We stow it somewhere, if it gets found, nobody knows who put it there. I dunno, an MFO box of Rover spares.'

'So you've put some thought into this?' asked the Boss. 'So, we get it out of Iraq. Then what?'

'I was hoping you might come up with the answers to that. What about all those yuppies you know in the City? Maybe they could help.'

'Well, you would be asking them to break the law as well and then they'd lose their job, never work in the City again, and probably do a spell in Ford Open Prison with George Best.'

'You know he's had a liver transplant?'

'Really? How to waste a God-given talent.'

'And a fortune. "I spent a lot of money on booze, birds and fast cars. The rest I just squandered".'

'I guess we could ask.'

'Who? George Best?'

'No, you wazzock. I have a mate who works in the City that I can trust. Are we decompressing in Cyprus, do you think?'

'Almost certain to,' said Barnes. 'Probably a week in Akrotiri.'

'Cyprus is renowned for slack financial regulations. There's a lot of stolen Russian money pouring into the banks there, no questions asked.'

'Not Switzerland then?'

'Swiss have tightened right up. They're not going to accept cash from a clear reprobate like you. I mean, just look at the state of you.'

'You can fucking talk, Boss, you are the scruffiest Rupert I've ever met, and actually, I scrub up quite nice. Or so the missus tells me.'

'This will make you a criminal, John. Get caught, and you go to Colchester, lose the pension, get kicked out of the Regiment in disgrace. You really prepared to gamble all that?'

'You've asked me that already,' said Barnes. 'You know...maybe. We could hand most of it over, and just keep a little BFU.'

'BFU?' asked the Boss.

'Bit for us. I looked into one of the bin liners whilst on stag. It's all in hundred-dollar bills and packed into ten-thousand-dollar bundles. One million dollars is nothing, weight and space wise. If you filled the spare bergen we could get five million in there easy.'

'Let's just keep an open mind for the moment. But I think we tell the lads that it's all going to be handed in. Then, if there is a BFU, as you call it, left over, we need to think seriously about how a, we keep it secret and b, how we get it back.'

'That's your job, Boss, above my pay grade.'

'First, John, you need to think if it's all worth it.'

'Boss, I'm coming up for retirement. I'll probably get to be an SQMS at one of the TA regiments, probably 23 then get put out to pasture. I don't even own a house.'

'You are putting dark thoughts into my already addled brain, John. The risks outweigh the rewards, in my opinion.'

'You're probably right, Boss. Forget we ever had this conversation.'

THE TROOP WERE WANDERING BACK to the vehicles as the sun was just beginning to rise. The Boss and Barnes downed a large plate of eggs, bacon and hash browns, with two mugs of coffee in quick time. They washed the containers with water from the jerrycans and then stowed everything on the wagons.

'Bruce, can you stay here and watch the wagons? The rest of you, let's tab over to the TOC for the briefing.'

'Wilco, Boss,' replied ManBat, settling into his rear-facing seat on the wagon.

When they got to the briefing room, it was already filled with close to a hundred people. There were rows of red plastic chairs and the troop found an empty line towards the back. There were a multitude of different types of uniforms and badges on the assembled troops. Nearly all appeared to be officers but nobody seemed to mind that a bunch of insignia-less and rank-less troops had come into the briefing.

The briefing started with the camp commandant, a Polish colonel, giving an update briefing from Central Command in Baghdad. Most were surprised to hear that yesterday had been one of almost country-wide attacks, which was a sudden change from the usual dull routine. An American major gave a briefing on what appeared to be an extremely well-organised ambush of a US military fuel convoy taking supplies up around BIAP. The Mahdi Army had dropped eight bridges around Scania to prevent the US resupply columns getting to the 1st US Cavalry Division in the North. As a result, the 724th Transport Company had been tasked to escort 17 fuel tankers from Anaconda to BIAP. These had been hit in a complex and well-organised ambush in the suburb of Abu Graib just outside BIAP. Five civilians and one US soldier called Goodrich had been killed and twelve soldiers and four KBR drivers had been wounded. It sounded from the initial reports that Goodrich would win a posthumous gallantry award. Furthermore, three civilian contractors and two US soldiers were missing, presumed captured.

'Fucking hell, Boss,' whispered Barnes.

'You were right, John. Those explosions were the bridges,' the Boss replied. 'This changes everything. It's a clear statement of intent and the gloves are now off.'

Next, Magdalena gave a daily update on the occurrences in the TAOR around Diwaniyah. She gave a brief summary of the convoy ambush at the road junction and gave a description of the two missing US personnel, a Lieutenant called Cunningham, who looked from his photograph like your average Midwest preppy American, and a private called Poklewski. Poklewski looked like she might have belonged to the local team's cheerleaders, blonde, tanned and with perfect white teeth.

'She's a good-looking girl,' whispered Ron.

'Marks out of two? I'd give her one,' said Wolfie.

Barnes glared at him to prevent any further indiscretions.

Magdalena went on to describe small incidents of hostility and violence on yesterday's patrols in the area and then gave an account of the mortar attack on the camp the previous night.

'Surprised she noticed,' Ron said, winking at the Boss.

'Ron, can you shut the fuck up, please?' the Boss hissed in response.

The briefing concluded with the OC of the US Stryker company giving the US assessment of events in the area and orders that the camp had notched up its security and all patrols outside the wire were to be especially vigilant for either ambush or IEDs.

There was a general scraping of chairs as everybody got up to leave. The Boss and Barnes noticed Yip had been in the other half of the room listening. He came over to chat and Magdalena also came over with an American officer.

'Guys, I want you to meet Lieutenant Brian Mendoza. He's the US SigInt platoon leader.'

The LT was a short man of about twenty-six years old, with round glasses and closely cropped hair. He shook everybody's hand and said that Magdalena had asked him to give an intelligence briefing on what was happening over the airwaves. He had a slight nervous stammer and, the Boss noted, didn't look you in the eye.

'Gentlemen, if you would like to follow me, I've got a little set up in the smaller briefing room next to my office.'

'Stan, take the lads and meet us back at the wagons. Cookie, can you get in touch with HQ and see if there's an update from our side?'

Once they had all settled down, facing a wall mounted computer screen, LT Mendoza began the SigInt briefing for the last twenty-four hours.

'I gather Magdalena spoke to you yesterday about the general situation in Qadsiyah Province in general and Diwaniyah in particular. We've got a number of players in the area, including JAM "Special Groups", BADR, and possibly rogue elements of the Iraqi Army not affiliated to BADR. Added to that, we can also add in organised crime affiliated to ISCI and the al Hakim family which is generally confined to the local Jabouri tribe.'

He paused and took a swig of water from a bottle. 'Excuse me, are you all good for water? Or can I get you a coffee or something?'

'No, that's very kind of you,' said the Boss. 'We're fine, just had breakfast.' Despite this, LT Mendoza went over to a cabinet fridge and pulled out four bottles of water and put them on the table.

'Help yourself whenever. It seems we have everybody wanting to know what's going on in our little bit of the world,' he continued. 'I have had to brief Baghdad prior to this and I've been told that General Richard J. Quirk III himself has ordered that he is to be kept up to date on any developments. As you know, the US Army lost a number of dead yesterday in various ambushes but much more scary is the fact that there are at least seven Allied personnel missing, presumed captured. POTUS has taken a personal interest in this as well and that means a whole lot of shit flowing downhill towards us via Fort Meade.

'The truth is, I'm afraid to say, we have absolutely no idea what is going on here and the SigInt of the Central Command is one big fuck up. There is currently a meltdown at Balad and it's even worse at Loyalty. I'm hearing that the computers are down at Loyalty and that there are not enough resources, especially cryptologists and inter-preters. Half of them are rotating through on OIF2 right now. You couldn't make it up.'

'Sounds worse than the Green Slime,' Barnes quipped to the Boss.

'So, what have you got up your sleeve then, Brian?' the Boss asked.

'Well, to be truthful, we've been working by ourselves for a while now because of the shit show further up the chain of command. I do have a few contacts in Balad and Loyalty but mainly we listen in down here. Up there, they have a whole base full of useless kit. They shipped over tonnes of scanners to intercept Iraqi Army radio traffic but nobody is using that kit anymore. Our Rivet Joints are in the air but nobody has much to report back. They know we'll listen and so, even if they had the kit, which most of them don't, they wouldn't use it.'

'What about mobile phone intercepts?' asked the Boss.

'Again, we do pick up some cell phone traffic but it's mainly a blank or just useless chatter. The cell network is patchy around here and again they know we are on it.'

'So how do they communicate?' asked the Boss.

'Mainly through either the internet or using walkie talkies. Around here they're using Japanese manufactured ICOM handheld radios. The trouble is, they don't operate on the military bandwidths used by the Iraqi Army, as you would expect, so most of our scanning equipment is useless. I've managed to get a couple of scanners sent over from home that my dad bought for me in RadioShack. It's as basic as that.'

'Fuck me sideways,' said Barnes. 'You're telling us that the greatest military power with the largest budget in the world has to buy scanners from the fucking high street?'

'I'm telling you exactly that, Sergeant. And we sit with the terps translating for us. Even that doesn't get us much. They only use it for urgent command decisions of limited intelligence longevity, "go here" or "do that" or "watch out someone's coming".'

'What about HumInt?' asked the Boss

'We do get a lot of low quality HumInt. US dollars go a long way in this country. However, we think much of it's either fabricated to get the payment, or old and useless, or they're trying to get their neighbour arrested for making them pissed at something. We also get a bit from pocket litter. Our biggest source, though, is the internet cafés. My friend at Balad has worked out that Al Qaeda are operating a crude type of intranet we call *Obelisk*. I must remind you that this is designated "Top Secret". It seems that JAM are using a similar system here via the internet cafés in the towns.'

'How does that work then?' asked the Boss.

'What they have done is set up an online email account that's password protected. But rather than email each other, they compose messages and then save them to drafts, and leave them for the next operator to pick up. In that way, the message doesn't enter in the realm of the world wide web. It's simple and clever. All they need to know is the log on and the password and they can see the message. It's the perfect dead letter drop.'

'I have absolutely no fucking idea what you are talking about,' said Barnes.

'Me neither,' said Yip.

'Do you not have an email account?' asked the Boss.

'Nope,' said Barnes.

'You really are a dinosaur, aren't you?'

'Why do I need an email account? What's wrong with the Mark 1 pencil?'

LT Mendoza let out a little cough. 'The point being is that we can intercept their messages if we can crack the usernames and passwords. It's something I've been working on and generally I can get into some of their accounts and read some of their messages.'

'Anything on the whereabouts of our hostages then, LT?' asked Yip.

'Nothing yet. We picked up some chatter on the ICOM scanners yesterday, which related to the ambush on the highway junction. There was talk of a crusader jeep heading down to Nasiriyah, so I'm assuming that was when they were taken.'

'Yeah, we found the Humvee south of the main junction,' said Yip.

'Brian,' Magdalena asked, 'who do you think is behind the kidnapping?'

'It's definitely JAM. I know this because we were without doubt listening to the JAM ICOMs. We think we're into a JAM email account but there's nothing yet been left.'

'Do you think it's a "Special Group"?' she queried.

'Um...excuse me, just remind me again, who is behind the "Special Groups"?' asked Yip.

'It's a part of the Jaysh al Mahdi set up,' replied Mendoza. 'They've been trained by the Iranian Quds to be a pain in the ass. They're sort of the elite of JAM.'

'I thought Iran was behind the BADR groups?' said the Boss.

'They are as well,' replied Magdalena, 'but they miss no opportunity to make our lives difficult and dangerous. I told you it was complicated, Tom.'

'The "Special Groups" are directed by Qaid Khazali. He was trained in Iran during the nineties. Iran will support any Shi'ite organisation that opposes the Infidel presence in the Middle East.'

'OK, let me see if I've got this,' said the Boss. 'We know they're in the hands of JAM and that they're probably somewhere in Diwaniyah. It's likely that they will be interrogated, filmed and executed, and the footage released onto Al Jazeera.'

'That is the worst-case scenario,' said Mendoza. 'I don't know if you remember that Marine, SGT Fernando Padilla-Ramirez?'

'Can't say I do,' said the Boss.

'He was captured in Nasiriyah this time last year. He was filmed being dragged through the streets and then hanged in the town square at Ash Shatrah. Just here.'

'Oh yeah, I do. From that convoy, right?'

'Yeah,' said Mendoza.

'Don't forget those two 33 RE lads, Allsopp and Cullingworth,' said Barnes.

'The Brit engineers? Yeah, there was quite a lot about them on the official channels. The authorities said they died in a fire-fight but it's well known that they were captured, tortured and executed. The bodies were dumped at Al Zubayr – which is here.' Mendoza pointed to the map.

'That's about halfway between here and Basra,' observed the Boss.

'Cunts,' Barnes said.

'Central Command has offered a reward of one hundred thousand US dollars for information that leads to the release of the prisoners,' Magdalena announced.

'That's less than the hundred and fifty k we told Stanislav's mate, wotsisname, in the Iraqi police,' the Boss pointed out.

'Kassim?'

'Yeah, him. Hundred thou' is still worth having.'

'Has that come from General Sanchez?' asked Magdalena.

'So I'm led to believe,' said Mendoza.

'Will that increase the chances of someone dobbing them in?' Barnes asked.

'It will, but also it will dramatically increase the amount of bullshit reports we get from every Haji trying to fuck over their neighbours or trying to get their hands on the cash. It's really a ransom offer to the hostage takers. We would need a proof-of-life video, though, Mendoza said. 'Do you mind me asking what you were doing in the area to the west of town?'

'Oh, you know, this and that,' replied the Boss.

'Everybody in this room is cleared to the highest levels including with JSOC. If that makes it easier for you.'

'Do you know about Op Crichton and Op Hather?' asked the Boss.

'I know that Crichton is the name for UKSF operations in Iraq and that you all work through JSOC. I've not heard about Hather.'

'Op Hather is a UKSF operation in the South, reporting into Basra,' the Boss stated. 'We are tasked with 3F and helping Box...er, that's our Secret Intelligence Service, similar to your CIA with their int picture. On top of that we're trying to find the WMD. What do you know about Op Ashton?'

'Not heard about that either, I'm afraid,' said Mendoza.

'Ashton was a house assault by some of the lads in B squadron, 22 SAS,' said the Boss. 'We were tasked with breaking an Iranian pipeline that was ferrying foreign fighters into the country. There was a bit of resistance, but we captured two LeTs.'

'LeTs?' asked Magdalena.

'Lashkar-e-Taiba,' said the Boss.

'It's a Pakistani-based jihad group that is beginning to get involved in Iraq,' said Mendoza. 'Funded by Osama bin Laden, it literally translates as "Army of the Righteous". They did that attack on the Indian Parliament in 2001.'

'Right,' said the Boss. 'Do you think foreign elements like that could be involved?'

'We've not had any pick-up on that sort of activity down here,' said Mendoza. 'The Iranians don't really allow any competition on their territory.'

'Our two strategic objectives are to find WMDs and specific senior Ba'athist Party members,' continued the Boss. 'You know, the old pack of cards.'

'What do you know about WMDs?' asked Barnes.

'There are no WMDs in my humble opinion,' replied Mendoza.

'It certainly looks like it,' agreed Magdalena.

'Were you looking for anyone specific?' asked Mendoza. 'We may have picked up something here.'

'We had it on good authority that Sabawi Ibrahim al-Tikriti, the six of diamonds to you, was moving from Nasiriyah to Najaf via the route we were watching.'

'We've not heard anything about him down here. Magdalena, have you heard anything about Sabawi?' asked Mendoza.

'No, Brian. Nothing on the daily int updates that I can recall.'

'Doesn't mean he's not in town, I guess,' said Mendoza. 'Can we mention the US 800th Military Police brigade, do you think, Magdalena?'

'It's going to come out sooner rather than later, so whilst we're all being open and honest with each other, we might as well.'

'The MPs at Abu Graib?' asked Yip.

'Yes,' she replied. 'It is still classified as secret but General Taguba has been commissioned to report on the abuse of detainees at Abu Graib prison. I'm told it makes very grim reading.'

'Who is General Taguba and why does that affect us?' asked the Boss.

'Well, Tom, Taguba is second in command Coalition Land Forces Component Command based in Kuwait. He's been looking into mistreatment of prisoners and his report is a detailed analysis of prisoner abuse including torture, rape, sodomy, humiliation and numerous other human rights abuses. It's going to be a bombshell. Command think that the report has been leaked to the American media. It contains some damning and lurid photographs of US soldiers abusing detainees. Everybody is just waiting for it to appear on primetime TV.'

'Who's got it? Al Jazeera again?' asked Yip.

'No. This time it's CBS News.'

'Will they show it?' asked the Boss.

'Sure, they will show it,' said Magdalena.

'Nobody can really stop them,' added Mendoza.

'So, when that breaks, then the insurgency will double in fury yet again,' said Yip.

'Fucking hell,' said Barnes. 'Just when you thought this cluster fuck of a war couldn't go any worse.'

'We really rather need to find those two quite quickly, then,' added the Boss. 'So, what's the plan?'

'We are the best positioned to locate the prisoners because of Brian's work on building up a detailed picture of active players in Diwaniyah. I'm told there is a Delta Force team either moving to or already in Edson, just north of the town. They will have their own int and typically, they share nothing with us. It is very unlikely they will even let us know they are here. Normally, it's the rumour mill that lets us know they are about,' Magdalena said.

'But you've not been told to stand down by any higher authority?' asked Barnes.

'Not as yet,' replied Mendoza. 'I think we can best help by just going about our usual business. My SigInt platoon will keep listening and the routine patrols have been briefed about reporting unusual activity, though it's unlikely much will be gleaned from the street, you never know. Especially with the reward now out.'

'Any chance some of my guys can go out on a patrol with your troops?' asked the Boss.

'What I was going to propose is that we take the Kiowa and have a fly around to familiarise you with the town,' said Magdalena. 'I have asked for it to be ready at 1000 hrs.'

The Boss looked at his watch and saw it was just gone 0900. 'OK, we'll see you at the LZ at 0955. We'll go back and brief the troop and get them stood-to for possible patrol today with you Poles.'

18

Easter Saturday, 10 April 2004
Jaysh al Mahdi Safe House
Somewhere in Central Ad Diwaniyah
0720 Local

T he key scraping in the lock alerted Cunningham out of his dozing state. He was thirsty and still had the headache. He watched as the door was kicked open, again, he presumed, so there was no surprise waiting the other side for the guards. As if he and Poklewski had the strength and guile to overcome three armed Hajis. Old Blue Sneakers was back with his two sidekicks. There was also a female in a black abaya. She was carrying a basic tin tray on which there were two bowls, two chunks of flat bread, and two more bottles of water. The guards checked that they could see their two prisoners before letting the woman into the room. She placed the tray on the floor between the two Americans. Cunningham looked into her eyes to see if he could detect any sign of empathy but she avoided his gaze.

'We need medical attention. I demand, in the name of the Commander of the United States Army and the President of the United States that we be taken to see a fully qualified medical doctor and we are treated in accordance with the Geneva Convention.'

The woman looked at him and then walked over to the bucket, looked inside, picked it up and backed away. The three soldiers stood still until she had left the room and then, one by one, backed out of the door.

As they were leaving, Cunningham jumped up, ignoring the pain in his shoulder.

'Goddammit, listen to me. I demand we be seen by a doctor.'

His sudden movement caused one of the guards to raise his AK. For an instant he was looking down the barrel and into the wild eyes of his captor. Then they were gone again, the door slamming shut and the key rasping in the lock.

Cunningham sat back down next to Poklewski. He picked up a bottle of water and drank. He then tore off a morsel of bread and put it into his mouth before picking up the bowl and sniffing the contents. It appeared to be some sort of vegetable soup. He dipped the bread into it and ate. It was nicer than it looked and reminded him of his hunger. He tore off more bread and used it as a sop for the soup.

'Hey, Alice, come on. You've got to eat.' He picked up the other bowl and the bread and offered it to her. Neatly folded under the bowl was her underwear, washed and ironed. It must have been brought in by the woman.

'Hey, Alice. They've bought these back for you...' He indicated to the knickers under the bowl, feeling that to pick them up might somehow add to her existing feelings of violation.

She continued to look down at her boots which still had the laces undone. She then reached out and stuffed the underwear into her pocket.

'Here, have some water.' He offered the plastic bottle to her, which she took.

'Atta girl...you told me I need to watch out for dehydration during the trip down south.' He found it hard to believe that was probably only yesterday, or perhaps the day before.. He thought about the stops in the desert, the all-round defence, his anxiety that he wasn't getting things right. It was all meaningless now. He'd made the biggest mess of everything possible and there was nobody to bail him out.

'We need to be ready for when the Seals come through that door. I can promise you, Alice, that is going to happen today. They'll know where we are and they'll kick some butt when they get here.'

She still didn't speak but raised the bottle and sipped a little water.

The key scraped in the lock and Cunningham looked up. Again, the door was kicked open and one of the guards threw in the bucket. It rolled across the floor and came to rest at the wall as the door closed.

'It's not exactly the Holiday Inn, hey, Alice? This room service is total crapola, if you ask me. I'm gonna give it zero stars on TripAdvisor. You seen that site, Trip Advisor? Lists all the hotels and diners and you can leave comments and ratings. This one is sure getting zero from us. Hey? Alice?'

Poklewski kept looking straight ahead, sipping on her water.

'You gotta try to eat something. You're gonna need your strength for when the rescue team turn up.'

'Don't feel hungry,' she replied. Cunningham was relieved that at least she had replied. A fly landed on his bread and he shooed it away with a wave. It must have come in with the food as there had been nothing buzzing throughout the night.

'You might not feel hungry, Alice, but you need it for the strength. We don't know when the next food will be coming.'

She was still fixated on the wall opposite avoiding any eye contact. The fly buzzed around and landed on the bread again. 'Goddamn shit fly!' He made a grab for it but it evaded his grasp with ease and circled again. This time it landed on the soup bowl. Very slowly, he moved towards it, but again, as he swiped, it avoided death and hopped onto the bread.

'This Iraqi shit fly is as good as dead!' He stood up and slowly moved his hands above the fly and then clapped. The fly again evaded his hands and flew off to the bare light bulb.

'You not going to eat your chow?' he asked.

'You have it,' Poklewski replied.

'I feel kinda bad but we can't waste it.' He tore off a bit of her bread. 'This soup ain't so bad with the bread.' He offered her the morsel, but she turned her head away and stared at the other wall. Cunningham ate the bread and the soup.

'Hey, Poklewski, do you mind but I've got to pee.' He got up and wandered over to the bucket, turned his back on her and then looked back over his shoulder to make sure she was looking the other way. His urine was dark brown. His urination made him also feel the urge to defecate but he held it in for the time being. That would be an awkward moment for him. He wasn't sure if he could actually go with someone watching. Whilst he had both hands occupied, the fly returned and landed on his lip. He blew hard and it took off, circled and landed back on his lip. This time, he decided to ignore it. He finished and did up his combats and placed the bucket in the corner of the room.

'You let me know when you need to go…it's all natural and I guess we're gonna have to get used to living like this for a short while.'

He sat back down and remained silent, wondering if he could return to the trance-like semi-sleep he had been in before the food was delivered.

At some point, he heard a helicopter overhead. There was a nearby burst of gun fire and the sound of the rotors changed pitch and faded.

'Hey, Poklewski, hear that? That's the Seals looking for us.' She said nothing but her eyes moved to the ceiling as if trying to see through the concrete. 'They definitely know where we are now because of that gunfire,' he continued. Gradually, the sound of the rotors faded until they could hear them no longer.

The room returned to silence. Just the three of them and a bare electric light bulb. The fly was now happily settled into the remains of the soup and Cunningham had decided to ignore it unless it came to bother him.

The key scraped and the door flew open. The woman in the black abaya came in with two more bottles of water, leaving them on the floor before she collected the trays. As she backed out, one of the guards threw a garment at Cunningham.

'You. Wear.'

The door closed and was locked again. Cunningham picked up the garment to discover it was an orange jump suit. It was roughly his size, possibly a bit too big and looked home-made. He held it up to himself to check it for size and then rolled it into a ball and threw it to one side.

He had just sat back down when the door flew open and the three guards came in with a fourth person they hadn't seen before. He wore the black of the Fedayeen and carried a tripod and video camera.

One of the guards picked up the jump suit and handed it to Cunningham. He refused to take it and received a vicious slap across his face that made his ears ring and his eyes water.

'You. Wear.'

Cunningham took the garment and put it on over his combats. The guards took him by the arm and led him to the far wall and pushed him down on the ground. He sat with his back to the wall looking at them. The coppery taste of fear was back in his mouth. He watched as they set up the tripod and camera. He began to have an overwhelming dread that they were going to film his execution and he started shaking uncontrollably.

One of the guards pulled out a rolled-up newspaper from his back pocket and handed it to Cunningham.

'Hold.'

Cunningham took the paper and stared straight ahead at the camera, the paper shaking in his hands. The little red light flashed for a few seconds and he assumed he was being filmed. The man in black also pulled out a little Canon digital camera and took a few photographs.

'Hold up paper.'

Cunningham decided that obeying orders was the wisest thing to do. He was somewhat relieved they were filming *him* rather than filming his execution. He managed to control his breathing and steady the shaking, although he now felt nauseous.

'You,' the man said to Poklewski.

She looked at him, slowly got up, evidently still in some pain, and hobbled over to where Cunningham sat. She took the paper and sat down.

A guard came over to Cunningham and prodded him with his foot. 'You. Move.'

He shuffled sideways and the man in black moved the tripod slightly. Again, the little red light flashed for a few seconds for the couple of shots with the Canon. Then he folded up the tripod and the group left the room and relocked the door.

Once it was locked, Cunningham got up, walked hurriedly over to the bucket, and vomited into it. His eyes watered and he began to shake violently once more. He took his bottle of water, drank a bit and spat it out into the bucket, then he sat back down to wait.

19

Easter Saturday, 10 April 2004
Forward Operating Base Edson
Ad Diwaniyah University
0745 Local

Clocktower approached the American camp slowly. His clapped-out Toyota Crown, though typical of most of the private cars in Iraq, would be treated by the camp gate guards as a potential vehicle borne IED. He waited in turn and then drove round the concrete blocks of the chicane and came to a stop by the barrier. There was already a long queue of Iraqis on foot waiting patiently to enter the camp. Many had small businesses selling tat and street food to the foreign troops, others worked in administrative jobs such as cleaning or interpreting. Others were there to help with the reconstruction of the damage that the looting had inflicted. The university, one of the best in the land, was stripped of everything movable and all the books and papers burned. It was reported that only one door remained, hanging by a solitary hinge and that a series of heavily-laden donkey carts had taken away the rest. Now they queued up patiently each morning from about five o'clock. Clock-tower showed his ID and told the guard that he was here to meet with the Allied CIMIC office.

He got out of the car whilst the guard used a mirror to check the underside of his vehicle, and then opened the boot for another inspection before lifting the bonnet. Finally, the guard raised the barrier and under the watchful gaze of machine guns in the towers above the entrance, he drove to the building where he had, on previous occasions, met the English lady.

He parked his vehicle on a central parking lot away from any buildings and walked the hundred and fifty metres to the three-storey block. He was hoping the lady had brought some dollars. He was toying with the notion that if she had not, or if the sum was paltry, he would hold out his information. He needed dollars for his escape fund for when he could take his family out of Iraq and over to Europe, or better, the US. There was still a chance of a ransom and he would like to have his share of any large pay-out.

On entering the building, he spotted her waiting for him. First, he had to empty his pockets and then walk through an airport-style security arch. He was patted down and collected his car keys and phone. He knew better than to take the pistol he now carried for protection. Security had been dramatically stepped up in the last few weeks.

'I've booked us an interview room,' she said without preliminaries. He still didn't know her name. He followed her down the corridor and into a spartan room with a table, on which two bottles of water had been placed, and four chairs.

'I've brought you these,' she said, delving into her small rucksack and producing two packets of Marlboro cigarettes. 'And this.' She produced an A4 manilla envelope, folded in two and taped together. 'It is eight hundred dollars.'

'I need more. I risk everything. I risk my family...'

'You know I can't get you more. We've been through this. Little and often is the best way to get money out of my government. If it were up to me, of course, I would, you know, but it's not. It has to be signed off in London.'

He took the envelope and put it inside his jacket without checking the contents. He then unwrapped one of the cigarette packets and lit up.

'So, what have you got for me?' she asked, whilst twisting the top off a bottle of water and pushing it across the table to him.

'The men of Al Sadr have taken two Americans.'

'Yes, so I am aware. Do you know where they are being held?'

'No. But we will find. The Iranians want the Americans. They have sent an important agent. He is here, now, in Ad Diwaniya.'

'Do you know his name? Or where he is staying?'

'No, no. But he is talking with Wolf Brigade. Wolf Brigade will find the Americans and then sell them to Iranian man.'

'Do you know why the Iranians are interested in the Americans?'

'Iranians are always hating the Great Satan. They will take the Americans to Tehran. They will put on TV. Maybe they try them and put in prison or execute.'

'How will the Wolf Brigade find the hostages?' Barbara took a swig of water and tried to stay out of the constant stream of smoke coming from the man opposite her.

'They will find, no problem.'

Barbara knew the Badrs had infiltrated the highest echelons of the local police and military. As the security situation across the region descended into chaos, it was the militias that were stepping into the vacuum. The struggle for power and money meant that instant feuds sprang up between the competing factions. Much as a fragmented industry will eventually coalesce into a few larger players, so the competing factions began to shift allegiances. Not doing so or choosing the wrong side could end in a violent death. The Badr were particularly indiscriminate and violent in settling scores.

Just after taking Clocktower's call last night, she had signalled

DIS in London and asked Eric Scott-Douglas to prepare a briefing paper on the various power factions. His preliminary message laid out the family, tribal and religious factions. She knew the Wolf Brigade's main recruiting push was with the local Iraqi Police. She also knew that the Iranians were financing some of the Badrs, including the Wolf Brigade. Clocktower's snippets of information, especially concerning Iranian activity, had proved to be reliable and accurate. Both Vauxhall and DIS were extremely interested in anything he had to say.

What Barbara didn't know was that Clocktower was a member of Wolf Brigade.

'I will tell you when they find Americans,' he said. 'I need more money. Very dangerous work for me and my family.'

'I will see if I can get another eight hundred dollars. Can we meet again this afternoon?'

'I don't know. Maybe. I bring you good information. The best. You should pay more.'

'You know I can't just do that for you.'

'What if I find where Americans are? You can pay more?'

'Can you do that?'

'Maybe I can. I know people who know but very dangerous. I have family.'

'If you can tell us where the Americans are, we can perhaps get you emergency funding. I might be able to find a way of getting you a reward.'

'They say the Americans will give hundred thousand dollar reward.'

'The Americans never pay rewards and even if they did, you know we are not the Americans. We can't talk to the Americans about you. I've told you that. It is too dangerous. The American intelligence is not secure for you.'

'I find you the Americans, you get me more money. You ask Americans for the reward.'

'Well, let's take this a step at a time. Find me the hostages and we will see about the reward.'

'I must go now.' He stood up, stubbed out his cigarette, and turned to leave.

'I have to see you out. But let's see if we can meet this afternoon. Text me when you can.'

20

Easter Saturday, 10 April 2004
Forward Operating Base Echo
Head Quarters Multi-National Division Central South
1120 Local

The Bell helicopter touched back down at the pad in FOB Echo and Barnes and the Boss thanked the pilot for the trip over the town. An hour earlier, they had boarded the aircraft and had flown over the general area, including both ambush points. From the air, the blackened tanker was clearly visible beside the cloverleaf junction and the burning petroleum had left a large black smear on the tarmac. Also visible were four or five mortar impacts. Over the other ambush site, where they had lain for almost a week, the Iraqi tanker was still there but the KBR trucks had been recovered. They flew over the house and the body on the roof had been removed but the black stain of his blood remained. Below them, the town of Ad Diwaniyah was a bustle of activity and was surprisingly large. They could see the ring road around Echo and caught sight of a Polish patrol making the hourly rounds on its anti-mortar reconnaissance. Next to FOB Echo was the Iraqi Army base where the Iraqi police were co-located, and probably and unofficially a BADR group as well. The pilot flew over the east of the town, across the river where there was a large slum of low, dun-coloured houses. They were close together and the roads and tracks between them were hard to discern. It must have been laundry day as there were clothes hanging on washing lines, drying in the hot breeze. They spotted the Ferris wheel towards the north of the town and the road heading south to Basra.

The helicopter banked hard to the left and rose sharply as a stream of tracer arced to the right of them. It was impossible to see where on the ground the fire had come from.

The pilot informed them over the headphones that the slum they were flying over was the al Jaza'ir district, which was very much Al Sadr territory. He hadn't been engaged from the ground before over the town and that it was an indication of the recent escalation. The rest of the town was less sympathetic to the Cleric and was controlled more by the Al Hakim family, head of the local Jabouri tribe. They continued east until turning over the town of Afak, which the pilot told them was a known JAM stronghold.

'You guys seen enough?' the pilot asked through the helmet intercom.

'Yeah, thanks,' replied the Boss. 'We can't make out much from up here but it's good to get a general feel for the ground. Looks really busy.'

'Half a million Hajis live down there,' the pilot pointed out. 'It's fucking chaos on the ground. Just one big fucking shithole.'

'How defined are the areas between loyalties?' asked Barnes.

'"Scuse me?' replied the pilot. 'Not sure I understand your question.'

'How much mingling between the different areas, you know, how likely is it that an al-Sadr supporter goes to another part of town, say one loyal to the Iraqi Army?'

'I don't think there's much stopping them doing that. There's little

Arab on Arab violence down here. I'm hearing up North there are roving death squads, but we are not seeing that down here apart from that massacre in Kawali a short time back. Apparently, the Iranians control everything. The Hakim family are the head honchos but I don't think they argue with Tehran. Besides, they don't like their businesses fucked with. Providing business is making money, people tend to rub along fine.'

'Much like anywhere,' said Barnes.

'Guess so,' agreed the pilot, as he skilfully landed the helicopter with barely a bump.

'Thanks for the trip,' the Boss said, opening the door and clambering out, quickly followed by Barnes.

The two headed back to the vehicle compound where they found Cookie was waiting for them.

'Where are the lads?' asked Barnes.

'Just me and Stan here. The others have dispersed like a mad woman's shit. I think a couple are tabbing around the perimeter track and some are in the gym. Nice to have a bit of time off.'

'So long as they know to check back in every so often,' Barnes said.

'I've told them to make sure they clock in on the hour,' said Stan. 'Though it's not helped by the fact there are personal trainers in the gym. I think Bat and Ron are having a good sniff around.'

'Didn't they get enough last night?' enquired the Boss.

'You know, another day, another dollar, Boss.'

'I guess you don't get personal trainers in Basra Palace,' the Boss replied.

'Boss,' said Cookie, 'big signal in from Basra for you and John.' He handed over a couple of sheets of paper. The first words were, *For UK Eyes Only*. The Boss took them and signalled to Barnes to join him.

'Get a brew on, Stan, would you,' shouted Barnes.

The signal was a mix of instructions and updates, some routine and some pertinent to the current situation.

'They're telling us that Box have some HumInt on the hostage takers. Confirmed as JAM. There's also a Regiment-wide order that we are to cease handing over prisoners to US Special Forces. You know those two Pakistanis from Aston? The LeTs?'

'Yeah,' said Barnes.

'They've been special renditioned over to Bagram in Afghanistan for interrogation. The UK Government are not pleased about it. "UK forces are to avoid handing detainees over to JSOC", it says here.'

'Bit late now,' Barnes replied. 'They should've thought about that before making their way over here to kill coalition forces. They've probably also caught wind of what your Polish bird, the Intelligence Rupertess, was saying about prisoner abuse. If that gets out it'll be a total cluster fuck.'

'It also says that, should we request it, the Armageddon platoon is on standby to move up here, including Warriors.'

'Can't see those clanky old things being much help. If anything, they'll just stir up the locals and attract all sorts of trouble. But we could use a few more pax from the Basra brigade for cordon work,' said Barnes.

'We could ask for a platoon of infantry. Any paras down there at the moment?' asked the Boss.

'Think it's the Rifles. Couldn't hurt having a couple of sections up here.'

'Hold on,' said the Boss, 'says at the bottom they're sending up the SQMS.'

Stan wandered over with two cups of tea.

'Boss?'

'Yes, Stan.'

'What's the Bobby then? We staying here or PUFOing?' he asked.

'Staying put, for the moment, Stan. Depends how this hostage situation pans out.'

'Surely the Yanks will deal with that?' asked Stan.

The Boss shrugged. 'I'm sure they will. But I'm just getting the feeling that our lot in Basra are on to something and that they're not sharing it all with the Americans. I sense a bit of a "let's show 'em" one-upmanship pissing-contest brewing.'

'Boss?' Cookie wandered over with another signal. The Boss read it quickly.

'They've released a video onto the internet,' said the Boss. 'Shows two American hostages. One of them they've put in an orange boiler suit. That'll piss off the Yanks.'

'Proof-of-life video,' remarked Barnes. 'Looks like they're opting for the ransom route. Sensible, if you ask me.'

'So, if we rescue the hostages, do we get the hundred grand?' asked Stan.

'What do you think, Stan?'

'That Bob Hope's playing golf?'

'Correctomundo, mate.'

21

Easter Saturday, 10 April 2004
Jaysh al Mahdi Safe House
Somewhere in Central Ad Diwaniyah
1210 Local

Cunningham was roused out of his torpor by Poklewski getting up and hobbling over to the bucket. She turned her back, dropped her combats and squatted over it. Cunningham found himself staring at her white buttocks and noticed some nasty-looking bruising and contusions. She once again removed her trousers and then put on her underwear that had been in the pocket. Then she pulled them back up again and Cunningham quickly looked away. She returned back to the place where she had been sitting.

They once more sat in silence, Cunningham watching the fly as it circled around the bucket, his mind drifting between thoughts of home and recreating the scene of the missed turn. He played the sequence in his mind differently, where he hadn't missed the turn or where they had avoided the on-coming vehicles. He indulged a flight of fantasy whereby he had shot up the vehicles with his M16 before racing to the underpass and turning west to re-join the convoy. He was lauded a hero and credited with rescuing a vulnerable female. In this new version of events, his weapon had fired correctly and didn't jam because of his failure to clean it the night before. Maybe he'd also got a Purple Heart but nothing life changing or too unglamorous. Hell, maybe he would be put up for a Bronze Star. They would get back to Scania and SGT Andersson would want to be told about the escapade, how he'd remained so calm under such duress, picking off the vehicle drivers one by one with a single shot through the windshield, whilst Poklewski drove headlong at their attackers in an unflinching game of chicken. He would, of course, make sure she got some credit for her small but essential part in the escape. At the White House reception, he would make it known that without Poklewski behind the wheel he would not have been able to pull it off.

The fantasy was interrupted by a loud shouting and knocking that sounded as if it was coming from upstairs. There was a momentary silence and then the sound of a gun firing. This was followed by more shots, this time the rapid fire of one or more AK47s. More shouting ensued and the sound of the commotion came down the stairs into the basement. Outside the door, the bellowing continued, sounding like instructions being blasted out in what appeared to be Arabic. The key rasped in the door and it opened. Cunningham looked up and saw Blue Sneakers standing there. Behind him were two figures in black with olive-green military belts and ammunition pouches. Both had AK47s in their shoulders. Their faces were covered and only their eyes showed. They pushed Blue Sneakers into the room and he sprawled head first onto the floor.

Cunningham and Poklewski got to their feet. Poklewski backed away from the gunmen making muted animal sounds of fear. Her eyes were wide with terror. More men entered the room and quickly surrounded both the Americans. Cunningham felt his arms being pulled behind his back and he let out a shout of pain as his shoulder was wrenched. He felt the plastic cable ties once again being used to bind his wrists. He knew better than to struggle, and let himself be man-handled towards the door. Poklewski had sunk to her knees and was pleading in terror. She wriggled ineffectively to get out of the grip of the two men who held her but they, too, wrenched her arms behind her back, cable-tied them together, and hoisted her to her feet.

The man who had pushed the guard onto the floor put his rifle into his shoulder and shot the sprawled guard in the back, twice. The noise in the small room was deafening and a high-pitched whine rang in Cunningham's ears. He looked on with horror as the shot man tried to move away from his assailant. The shooter then walked up to the wounded man, casually put the muzzle of the rifle to the back of his skull and pulled the trigger. The head jerked forward and a geyser of blood erupted out of the entry wound and flowed thickly on to the cellar floor. The round exited out of the man's mouth and embedded into the wall near the toilet bucket. The body slumped, and as he died, the corpse took on the appearance of all corpses – deflated and empty.

Cunningham and Poklewski were pushed out of the door and up the stairs. As they entered into the main room of the house, Cunningham had to screw his eyes up against the glare of the sun. He could hear the noise of the traffic outside, the constant blaring of horns and revving of engines. He smelled food as he was pushed past a table on which a half-eaten lunch was laid and he then saw that the woman who had bought their meals was also dead. She was sprawled on the floor and wasn't wearing her head covering. She was about twenty years of age. Her sightless eyes were still open but under her prostrate body, a congealing pool of blood had already formed. They were pushed past the body by their tied hands and towards the open front door and into the courtyard. Beside the door were two further bodies. By the cast iron door to the street stood a man, also in black, who held open the door and beckoned the group to hurry. They half ran, half stumbled out the door and onto the street where there was a three-car convoy parked but with the engines running. The back door was opened and Cunningham was pushed in and onto the back seat and one of the men then got in beside him. He pulled out a pistol and thrust it into Cunningham's face. The man who'd shot the guard in the basement got behind the wheel. He passed his rifle to a third man in the passenger seat. He looked over his shoulder to check the progress of the second group with Poklewski, that Cunningham assumed was getting into the car behind. The vehicle in front was a white Japanese SUV which sped off, and the two cars followed.

Cunningham tried to look around but the guard with the pistol pushed his head to below the level of the window, and he stared at his boots instead as the car drove fast and aggressively, the driver honking the horn every few seconds. His mind was racing but he was failing to make sense of this latest set of events. He started to convince himself that they were being rescued. OK, perhaps not by the Seals, but probably by an Iraqi Special Forces unit that was working closely with the Americans. They would have been shot otherwise. Now they just had to get out of the hostile town, find a US FOB and they would be home. Cunningham began to relax. The ordeal was over and he had survived. He suddenly felt exhausted.

22

Easter Saturday, 10 April 2004
Forward Operating Base Echo
Head Quarters Multi-National Division Central South
1325 Local

'Boss...'

'Yes, Cookie?'

'There's a Chinook coming up from Basra with some Green Army. ETA ten minutes.'

'Thanks, Cookie. I think Banjo is on it. Wolfie, drive us up to LZ, would you? Get the crates in the back.'

'Sure, Boss. Ron, move your arse.'

They got into the Rover and drove over to the helicopter landing zone just as the deep throbbing of the Chinook's twin rotors became audible. The Boss shielded his eyes from the sun and looked to see if he could spot the airframe. It was coming in fast and low from the south-east. Wolfie stopped the vehicle a hundred metres from the landing spot and both men turned away. As it approached, the large plane climbed and turned and then, facing into the gentle breeze, it flared and landed with a soft bounce. The pilots killed the engines and the rotors began to slow to the whine of the turbos shutting down. The blasting sandstorm of the rotor wash petered out and the two Brits turned and faced the aircraft.

'Don't really trust those fuckers, Boss,' said Wolfie.

'Why not?'

'Because them rotors are one day going to get out of sync and clash and everybody will die in a big ball of flame.'

'I think the Boeing engineers have probably thought of that, Wolf.'

'Yeah, I know, but still.'

They dismounted the Rover and as the back ramp of the aircraft slowly came down, the loadmaster appeared in his green overalls, the sun glinting on the black visor of his helmet as he talked into the intercom. He was still clipped onto the airframe by a strop and his green leather flying gloves held on to the side of the fuselage. As the ramp levelled onto the sand, he unclipped both the strop and the radio lead and walked backwards down the ramp. He raised his arms and indicated that the passengers should dismount and eight infantry men walked off the aircraft. They were in full equipment and bowed under the weight of their bergens. They walked towards the two men in the Land Rover. The loadmaster turned around and signalled again with his arms towards the fuselage, and a large four-wheeled vehicle drove down the ramp and out towards the Land Rover.

'Here he comes, the cunt,' said Wolfie, grinning broadly.

'I hope he's brought up some decent supplies,' muttered the Boss to himself.

'It's only fucking Banjo,' shouted Wolfie at the approaching figure. The driver dismounted from the big vehicle.

'Morning, SQMS, nice to see you. What brings you here?' said the Boss.

'Hello, Boss. Thought I would come up and see how you were all getting on.'

'And you thought it a good idea to bring a Supacat along, too? What's going on, Banjo?'

'I can explain everything, Boss,' said Banjo. 'We've got ourselves a bit of a task, which I can't explain now because of the company. But I managed to persuade the OC that I needed to come up to deliver the orders in person and to bring up some replen. Also brought up some fresh, some mail and all sorts. Don't say I don't look after you, Boss.' He had a boyish grin on his middle-aged face. 'I was fucking bored shitless in Basra Palace, truth be known, so I thought I'd come along for a cabbie. Scouse around?'

'He's back with the others. We've got ourselves a nice little basha spot.'

'The OC is very fucking anxious about some cargo you're returning,' said the SQMS. 'I think you know what I'm talking about.'

'I do indeed,' said the Boss. 'In fact, I've got a couple of boxes ready to go.'

'Excellent, Boss. The SSM himself is waiting to pick it up at the other end.'

One of the infantry men came forward with his hand out and the Boss shook it.

'Lieutenant Whistler. I've been told to report to the SF unit at Echo. We are the QRF from Basra Palace as part of Hather.'

'Hi, I'm Tom. Get your guys to stow their kit on the SRV. You and three hop into my Pinkie and put the rest in with the SQMS.'

'Roger that. By the way, I'm Pete.'

'Nice to meet you, Pete,' said the Boss.

The young officer turned and briefed his men to stow their equipment in the two vehicles.

'Pete, this is Wolfie. I take it you've met the Squadron Quartermaster, Staff Player?'

'Yes, on the flight up.'

'How long have you been at Basra?'

'We deployed a couple of weeks ago,' said Whistler.

'This your first tour?'

'Yes, sir,' said Whistler.

'No need to call me sir, Pete.'

'Yeah. Sorry.'

'We'll get you settled into some accommodation. We need to find Frank The Yank. He's the KBR guy that sorts out the rooms. Important man, if a civvy.'

'I'm in your hands...um...Tom.'

'First, I need to put these two boxes on the Chinook for the return flight to Basra.'

'Corporal Lomax,' shouted the young officer, 'get two men to help load these boxes onto the airframe.'

'Yes, sir. Porter and Curtis, drop your kit and get these here boxes onto the chopper.'

The Boss wandered over to the loadmaster who was standing on the back of his ramp.

'Need you to take these two boxes back to Basra.'

'What's in them?' the loadmaster asked.

'That's classified. Please just take them back to Basra Palace.'

'If I don't know what's in them, they don't get to go on my plane,' was the adamant reply.

'They need to go back. It's important.'

'As I said, what's in them?'

Wolfie interrupted the conversation. 'Listen, you fat fucking wanker. If the major says he wants to put two boxes on your fucking Chinook, you say "yes sir, of course". Now stop being a cunt or by this time next week you'll be servicing drones at Benbecula Gunnery Range in Scotland.'

'Is he a major? He's not wearing rank,' said the loadmaster.

'Yes, he is, and he happens to be a personal friend of Brigadier Page. So, my advice to you, sunshine, is to stop playing the goat and do as we ask.'

'Sorry, sir, my apologies. Didn't realise. Not supposed to take unmanifested cargo...'

'Don't worry, loadie. We all make mistakes. All forgotten now. These are for Troops Hereford, Basra Palace. There will be someone at the airport to take them off you. He won't be wearing rank either, but just a quick word in your shell-like, he's a sergeant major with a low tolerance threshold. Good man.'

The two crates were stored at the front of the aircraft and tied down to the deck with red strops. The soldiers turned back to the vehicles.

'Major?' the Boss said.

'Nobody takes captains seriously, Boss.'

'You can say that again,' the Boss replied. 'Banjo,' he shouted, 'follow Wolfie and me. We are about ten minutes away from the troop. Wolfie, let's get back to the lads.'

'Hold on tight, everybody,' said Wolfie, and drove off towards the troop vehicles. As they arrived, Barnes stood staring with his hands on his hips. He couldn't hide the grin on his face.

'Wotcha, Scouse,' Banjo said.

'It's Conan the Storeman,' said Barnes. 'Banjo, you complete dick-head. What the fuck are you doing here? Haven't you got socks to be counting back there?'

'Fucking bored shiteless, Scouse. It was doing me head in,' he replied. 'I've got a few goodies for the lads, brought the mail. Persuaded the OC that you needed the Menacity and that I should be the one to bring it up.'

'How did you persuade Crab Air?' asked Barnes.

'They seem to be much more wilco out here than they normally are back home. Even the non-SF flight boys seem willing to please. Except for that loadmaster. Not seen him before.'

'Nice one. You remember Yip Romaro? He was that Delta Force guy that did a tour with us about ten years ago. Went on the jungle trip?'

'Yeah, sort of, John.'

'Well, he's here as well.'

'I remember him being quite a good hand,' Banjo said.

'Yeah, he is. You'll probably meet him tonight. Don't know what he's up to right now but he was leading the convoy protection when they got hit in the town.'

'Read about that this morning on the int report. Sounded a bit tasty.'

'John,' interrupted the Boss, 'this is Lieutenant Whistler from the Armageddon platoon in Basra.'

'Nice to meet you, sir,' said Barnes.

'Pete, get your lads sorted. Put the bergens and kit over there. You can remove your helmets and body armour whilst on base. There's a bit of incoming but it's usually at night. First things first, we will go off and try to book you into a CHU. The boys have got a choice of tented accommodation or they can basha up here with us and the vehicles. The good thing about here is that it's quite quiet and we're in the lee of the blast wall. They're unlikely to be able to get a mortar round in here because the trajectory is all wrong. The officers' accommodation is quite Gucci. It's where I'm billeted. Plus, there's the added advantage of your own shower and water-cooled shitter. Don't unpack yet, though. Your stay here may be shorter than we think.'

'Cpl Lomax, get the section to put backpacks over there. Helmets and body armour can be removed.'

'OK, sir,' shouted back the corporal.

'We need to find Frank,' said the Boss. Best place to ask is at Puzzle Palace. Place is actually run by the Poles but there's all sorts here from Mongolians to Norwegians. Follow me.'

'Who's Frank?' asked Whistler.

'He's the Sherman who shops at the tailor that caters for the fuller figure, "Mr Fat Bastards",' said Ginge.

The Boss walked towards the main building hoping to find Magdalena in her office. He remembered the way and was grateful for the cool air conditioning out of the sun, and wondered why all military buildings smelled the same: a mixture of floor polish, cigarette smoke and food. He knocked on the intelligence officer's door and poked his head round.

He saw Stanislav talking to the other Polish Intelligence NCO but no Magdalena.

'Hi, Stanislav, this is Pete up from Basra. Is Magdalena around?'

'Hi, Tom, hi, Peter. I don't know where Major Duda is right now. Perhaps she is in the food hall having lunch.'

'Oh...OK. Do you know where Frank hangs out?' asked the Boss. 'Peter here would like to be given a CHU for his stay.'

'The KBR office is down the hall on the left.'

The Boss nodded and said, 'Many thanks.'

As he was walking towards the KBR office, he spotted Magdalena. He felt a twang of delight remembering the previous night. She had been at the back of his mind all day and he was really hoping she felt the same.

'Peter, that's the KBR office. Ask for Frank.'

'Tom, sorry for asking. What does KBR mean?'

'Kellog Brown Root. American private contractors that are running this war.'

'Amazing...'

'Before you go, meet Magdalena Duda.'

'Hi, Pete Whistler. Nice to meet you.' He shook Magdalena's hand.

'I'm just taking Peter off to get a CHU I'll pop into your office once we're done?'

'My door is always open to you, Tom,' she said, her eyes twinkling. 'On another matter, Stanislav asked if some of you would like to accompany him on a routine patrol in Diwaniyah.'

'I think that would be useful and instructive,' replied the Boss. 'How many can he accommodate?'

'It will be a routine patrol into the town in support of the Iraqi police. Normally we send two vehicles, but we could perhaps take three this time.'

'Do you think it may be a bit mob handed? But it would be good to get a feel for the ground now that we've seen it from the air.'

'I think we can use two Scorpions and Stanislav will be in the ZWD. The Iraqi police will be in their own vehicles. Usually Toyotas,' replied Magdalena. 'Your men can sit in the Scorpions and maybe you can sit in with Stanislav. He often does our CIMIC patrols with the police.'

'Great,' said the Boss. 'When are they due to leave?'

'Scheduled to leave the gates for the RV with the IP at 1530 from the main gate.'

The Boss replied, 'We will be there.'

23

Easter Saturday, 10 April 2004
Badr Safe House
Somewhere in Ramadan District Ad Diwaniyah
1330 Local

The three-vehicle convoy turned sharply through double iron gates, which were shut behind it by two armed men. The guard with the pistol released Cunningham's neck but he was reluctant to take this as a sign that he could raise his head in case he attracted more violence. The car stopped quickly and he was pushed into the back of the front seat by the momentum. He remained looking down but was hauled up by his wrists and dragged out of the vehicle. He stumbled and fell out the door, and sat on the floor with his hands behind his back. He looked around and saw that Poklewski was being pulled out of the second car. The SUV was also in what seemed to be the sizeable compound of a large building. The fourth car was a new black Mercedes S-Class saloon. His hopes were raised that this was some sort of handover, maybe because the ransom had been paid rather than because they had been rescued. But he had doubts that a rescue would involve such rough treatment.

The idea of it being a rescue was, however, dashed, when once again, a black hood was put over his head. He was pushed forward toward the building, looking down between the hood and his body at his boots. He could hear the soft tinkle of running water and below his feet were paving stones rather than sand. He assumed this house belonged to a much richer family than the one from which he had just come. He heard Arabic voices and a door opening and he was pushed inside the building. There was the smell of cooking and he could sense a number of eyes on him, though he heard no voices. He had a sinking feeling of déjà vu as he was led along a corridor and then down rough steps into a basement. He heard Poklewski being led directly behind him and shortly after, he was pushed through another door. His escorts let go of his cuffs and he stood silently in the room. He heard Poklewski breathing next to him. Short little pants as if she was trying to keep the rising panic in check. He could see her boots, still undone, next to his about a metre distance. He heard the door slam shut and what sounded like a bolt being slid into place. Then, silence.

He stood still for five minutes, listening. He could hear nothing except the breathing of Poklewski.

'Hey, Alice?' There was no response other than a sob.

'Hey, Alice. Listen to me. I think someone's paid a ransom and we've been taken to a release point,' he whispered. He arched his head back to try to see more between the gap his hood made and could see her standing next to him. Her head was bowed and she was shaking and sobbing.

'They haven't killed us, have they?' he continued. 'They want us alive, whoever they are.'

'But they murdered the others. Why did they murder the others and not let us go?' she whispered, her voice quavering with emotion and anxiety.

'I dunno. I guess there's some internal feud going on with the Hajis. I'm going to sit down next to the wall.'

He walked towards the far wall, opposite the door, and slid down until he was sitting with his back against it. He could feel the cool plaster on his hands behind his back.

'LT, where are you?' Poklewski's voice had a ring of panic as if she had been left behind.

'I'm over here, by the wall. Look down between your hood and follow my voice. That's it...stop there. Turn around...feel the wall? I'm sitting on your right.'

He heard her slide down the wall and once again they were sitting side by side in an anonymous basement in a town they had never heard of.

24

Easter Saturday, 10 April 2004
Forward Operating Base Echo
Head Quarters Multi-National Division Central South
1500 Local

Back in the vehicle park, the Boss met up with Barnes and Whistler to explain the CIMIC patrol. They decided that most of the troop would go but Cookie would remain behind on radio stag. They would detail men from the Rifles platoon to help with the vehicle guard.

'Pete,' said the Boss, 'can I have two of your riflemen to help keep an eye out on the vehicles?'

'Sure,' replied Lt Whistler. 'Cpl Lomax, can we have two volunteers for guard?'

'Yes, sir,' replied the corporal.

'Right, you lot,' the corporal barked out, impressively loud, 'double in. Hurry up, double in.' When they had all gathered, he continued, 'I need two volunteers.'

'What for?' replied one of the men.

'Thank you, Curtis, you will do. Anyone else?'

The soldiers remained impassive. 'Who here has got a motorcycle licence?' the corporal asked.

'I have, Corporal,' said a soldier raising his hand, hopefully.

'Excellent. You can be the other, Walton. Your mother would be proud of you. The rest of you can have some down time. Explore the camp. Do NOT fucking get up to any mischief. You got that, Parker?'

The SQMS then stepped forward. He dipped his hand into his pocket and pulled out a self-rolled cigarette. He proceeded to light it with some ration issue matches.

'You got another of those then, Banjo?' asked Stan.

'Where are yours, Stan? Never share your rations, mate.'

'Come on, Banj. Not had a puff for a couple of weeks now.'

'The SQMS is famous for being able to roll a cigarette in his pocket with his left hand, whilst wearing boxing gloves in order not to share,' said Barnes.

The SQMS took out a plastic envelope of Old Holborn rolling tobacco and lobbed it at Stan.

'There you go, mate. Fill your boots. Ignore the haters.'

He also had a small, black bin liner full of mail. 'Okey dokey, Christmas has come early.' He delved his hand into the bag and pulled out an envelope and read the address.

'Cooke?'

'Yes, Jim,' Cookie answered with delight.

'Give that to Bruce.'

'Boss? Two for you, you must be very popular.'

The Boss took the two envelopes. 'Banjo, this is a mess bill and a payslip, for fuck's sake.'

'Beginning of the month,' the SQMS replied. 'What do you expect? Fan mail? Better than nothing at all, Boss.' Then he added, 'Here's a bluey for Staff Sergeant John Barnes, MBE, QGM,' and flicked the letter at Barnes.

Once the mail had been distributed, the SQMS retrieved another white, plastic bag from the bottom of the bin liner. 'Right, here comes the good stuff...' He put his hand in and pulled out a pink envelope. '"To an SAS soldier, Iraq".' He sniffed the envelope. 'This one is worth having. Who wants it?'

'Go on then, Banjo,' said Wolfie.

The SQMS flicked the envelope over to Wolfie.

'Good god, it honks,' said Wolfie.

'Get it open, man,' said ManBat as Wolfie tore at the envelope. 'Any pics?'

'Oh yes!' He took out two photographs of a topless young lady

'Give us a butchers, Wolf.'

'Hold on, mate, for fuck's sake,' said Wolfie. 'Oh man, she's got a swede like a blind cobbler's thumb.'

'But check out the rack.'

The SQMS put his hand into the plastic bag again. 'This is like fucking Santa Clause at the Squadron Christmas family day...ok. "To an SAS officer, Op Telic Iraq, BFPO 641".'

'That'll be me, then,' said the Boss.

The SQMS flicked the small parcel over to the Boss and he opened it. 'Bloody hell, it's a knitted balaclava. *From all the residents at Sycamore View Care Home, Bournemouth. We hope you stay safe and warm. Shelagh.*'

'You fucking missed out there, Boss.' said Ginge.

'Come on, Banjo, give us another go,' said the Boss.

'Did Rommel get another go?' replied the SQMS. 'Did he fuck. He fucking shat out like you, Boss. Here we go... "To an SAS Trooper on missions in Iraq, C/O the military, Hereford".'

'Go on then, Banjo,' offered Ron. The SQMS handed over the package.

'Wahey... photo!' he yelled in delight.

'She's a right minger, Ron,' said Bat. 'Porkier than that bird you were chatting up last night.'

'How did that work out for you, Ron?' asked Wolfie.

'She was so fat he had to roll her in the sand outside and aimed for the wet patch.'

'Right, quieten down and look in,' shouted Barnes. 'We are going on a CIMIC patrol with the Poles. Leave here in full belt kit 1520 for a 1530 departure. Cookie, you get to stay behind and keep radio watch. We will be in three vehicles driven by the Poles with our friend Lieutenant Stanislav whatshisface. Just to get a feel for the ground should we be required to do anything in the next forty-eight hours or so. It is now 1515, so get a shift on.'

The group dispersed to get rifles, helmets and belt kit, and then wandered over in a gaggle to the main dispatch area by the front gate. The Scorpion 3s and the ZWD command vehicle were waiting. The Scorpions had a belt fed machine gun mounted just behind the enclosed driver's cab but the back was open. Both vehicles had vertical metal wire cutters to deal with any wires laid across the road at head height to decapitate the top gunners. The Boss got in beside Stanislav and Barnes climbed into the cab of one of the Scorpions. The rest of the troop each took a seat in the open back of the Scorpions.

A Humvee pulled up beside the Scorpion and the Boss looked over to see Gubby and Yip grinning at them.

'You didn't think you Brits would get away with sneaking off without us, did you, Sir?' said Yip.

The small convoy went past the guard who raised the barrier, and then around the concrete crash barriers onto the perimeter road, where they turned north-east towards the town. As they approached the main road, they saw the Iraqi police SUV with Kassim, the police officer from yesterday in the front. He led off onto the road into Diwaniyah. There were the usual columns of hooting cars and small dirty trucks pumping out black exhaust. Numerous people, both men and women, walked towards the town or stopped under the brightly coloured awnings of the makeshift ramshackle shops that lined the road. There were long, two-storey buildings behind concrete walls, some of which had been painted in primitive patterns with lurid colours. Litter and detritus was everywhere, with streams of sewage running in the streets emitting a strong stench, along with the smell of exhaust fumes. The Boss wondered to himself whether the combination of ten years of sanctions and the invasion last year had made people lose any pride in their surroundings. What was clear to everybody was that the failure to implement visible and tangible benefits, power, water and security being the most important, was now fuelling the insurgency. The more the allies focused on the insurgency, the worse the economy became, which in turn, diverted attention away from rebuilding and forcing the coalition troops to concentrate on just staying alive.

As they approached the outskirts of the town, Stanislav pointed out the spot where the Humvee had been stopped and the hostages taken.

'So, if they had just gone straight on, they would have driven past the gate of Echo?' asked the Boss.

'I'm afraid that is true,' he replied. 'But they didn't know where they were and probably hadn't been briefed about Echo. It wasn't part of the contingency plan. I think the Americans are very restricted on how they operate. The blowing of the bridges and the ambushes would have pushed them off course and a new course wouldn't have been inputted into their systems.'

'Nothing beats knowing where you are on a map you can hold in your hand,' said the Boss.

'Further up this road is the junction where the ambush took place yesterday. The burned-out tanker is still smoking, I am being told.'

As they reached the junction, they turned right past the waste ground that had sheltered the insurgents. The Polish top gunners were alert to any renewed hostilities but they travelled east undisturbed towards the river that split the town in two. The police then turned north along the western bank of the river and the Boss observed that the town was much like all the other towns he had seen in his tour. Teeming with people and traffic, it was a chaotic yet functioning urban system that somehow seemed to work. He noticed the Ferris wheel and the high telecoms mast by the river crossing and made a mental note of them as useful landmarks. They crossed over the river on a box bridge, and the town seemed to become tighter and more claustrophobic. The streets were narrower and driving was impeded by pedestrians in the street blocking the passage of the vehicles. The Boss felt little sense of menace from the crowds that, other than the children who held out their hands to the troops in the hope of sweets or coins, ignored the small convoy.

Kassim called in on the radio in the Boss's vehicle. There had been a murder in the poor neighbourhood of Al Jaza'ir. They diverted off the patrol route to accompany the police to the scene. After ten minutes, they turned into a narrow street. The houses were packed tightly together and the crime scene was marked by a small crowd of on-lookers. There was much shouting and gesticulating as Kassim and his driver dismounted from their Landcruiser.

'Should we get the vehicles into some sort of all-round defence and use the top gunners as a deterrent?' asked the Boss.

'We don't normally have to worry about the Iraqi people here,' said Stanislav, 'but I feel that the situation is changed a bit since yesterday.'

Barnes had dismounted from the other vehicle and ordered the British troops to get inside the gated compound.

Kassim came over to Stanislav and the Boss. 'The people are angry that we are not protecting them. I have told them that we are here protecting them now.'

They walked into the house past two dead bodies by the door. Both had been shot. Inside the main room, a lunch was laid and a further body lay on the floor, also shot. The Boss had drawn his Sig Sauer as he poked around the room. He was mindful of the scene-of-crime protocol but also curious as to what had happened. This was not a random murder; it was a pre-meditated slaughter.

He moved down the stairs and into the basement where there was a fourth body. This corpse had been shot both in the back and in the base of the skull. The empty cases on the ground suggested it had been an AK47. There was also a round in the wall and a bucket with what looked like piss in it. The Boss also noticed a single cut cable tie.

'Stanislav, Kassim...' he yelled up the stairs.

Both men, accompanied by Barnes, appeared at the door.

'Jesus, Boss, I thought you were in some sort of trouble then,' Barnes said.

'Look at this. I don't think this is a murder as such but more a rescue. Someone was held here in this room and now they've been taken. Who owns the house, Kassim?'

'We have established that this house was owned by a local businessman who lived with his son, daughter and son-in-law,' Kassim replied. 'The family is not known to us.'

The second policeman spoke to Kassim in Arabic.

'He apparently owned an internet café.' There was more rapid speaking. 'It is a few streets away on the main commercial road out towards the river.'

'We need to get there pronto and claim the computers,' said the Boss.

'Why would we want to do that?' asked Barnes.

'Because, Einstein, we know that they use internet cafés to communicate,' replied the Boss.

'Oh yeah, all that wiggly amp stuff from yesterday.'

Kassim ordered up an Iraqi police cordon whilst he drove the police Landcruiser, followed by the four other vehicles to the address of the internet café. When they got there, they found a single room lit by strip lights that housed six old computers. Outside was a tangle of telecommunication cabling and a small satellite dish. The Boss ordered a rough cordon to prevent anyone from entering the room. A small crowd of curious bystanders had appeared and were watching the troops as they went about unplugging and removing the computers into the back of the two Polish Scorpions. Again, the Boss's intuition that this was not a hostile crowd proved correct and they were not hampered. Most people had already heard that the owner and his son-in-law, who ran the little business, had been murdered.

The Boss asked Stanislav to alert Brian Mendoza's SigInt platoon they were bringing in some computer equipment that needed analysing.

'Man, there's going to be some rough porno on these machines,' said Bat.

As they were loading the machines into the back of the Scorpion, Kassim appeared and told them they had to be put in the back of the Landcruiser, informing them this was an IP enquiry and that they were there as military aid to the civil powers, that the investigation was not to be jeopardised by breaking with standard operating procedures and convention.

'He is right, I'm afraid,' said Stanislav.

'He may be right, but he's not taking the computers,' argued the Boss. 'There are two kidnapped coalition soldiers and that makes it a military matter.'

'Damn straight,' said Yip. 'This is a matter for the US Military Authorities.'

'But, my friend, this is an Iraqi police murder investigation.'

'Ain't no more, Kassim. I'm commandeering this equipment for the US military,' said Yip.

'You cannot do that.'

'Watch me, buddy,' Yip replied, making a small yet significant movement with his rifle. Kassim looked at him and then shrugged.

'You may have to answer to General Oothman. He will not be pleased with this transgression. He talks with Mr Bremer most days. There will be trouble for you.'

'We will release them to you once we've scanned the hard disks,' said the Boss, hoping to defuse the situation. 'We probably have better equipment to see what's on them and therefore help you with your investigation.'

'The Iraqi police do not want help. Why do you think you know everything? Why do you tell us always what we should be doing in our own country?'

Despite Kassim definitely being unhappy, Yip and the Boss weren't going to give way. Both knew they would probably be out of the region in a couple of days and threats from Iraqi generals didn't really worry them too much. Stanislav, as a lieutenant, felt that he could always shelter behind the Boss's higher rank. He also knew that

Mendoza only needed a few hours with the machines to get access and copy their hard disks. After that, everything could be returned with profuse apologies by Major Duda.

Yip and the Boss took Stanislav to one side and made it clear that they now had to go back to Echo. The IP could either follow them back or go back to the murder house. There was no question of the patrol continuing. He reluctantly agreed and ordered his drivers to mount up. The British soldiers, who had taken up fire positions around the vehicles, got back in, and the crowd parted as they drove off across the bridge and back down the way they had come.

They went through the barriers as two clattering Hind D helicopters were landing on the LZ.

'I never thought I would be on the same side as those things,' the Boss said to Stanislav. 'All the old Soviet kit is now seen as blue forces. Quite hard for the old hands to acknowledge sometimes.'

'Sometimes,' Stanislav replied, 'I think they are more blast and noise than threat to the enemy. They are good for morale and it helps having them overhead when patrolling in the town, but give me an Apache any day to, as you say, save my ass.'

'Don't want to be on the wrong end of one of those boys, that's for sure,' the Boss said.

'We can drive almost straight to LT Mendoza's office and offload the computers.'

They found the Signals Intelligence Platoon commander in his office in the main unit. The Boss explained how they had recovered the computers from the café and asked him to see if they contained anything useful. His team worked in a small, cramped office filled with electronic equipment, none of which the Boss recognised. Heavy coax cables were fed through the window to a pair of large satellite dishes on the ground outside and the walls were covered with maps and tables. A few of the men had headphones and were listening in to radio chatter or scanning to see if they could intercept the walkie talkies.

LT Mendoza said he could get a couple of men onto the

computers quickly and didn't think it would take him long to crack any passwords that might be protecting the data.

'We can access a normal hard drive in a matter of minutes. These are Seagate drives and we can isolate them from the password protection quite easily. We can then copy the data and return the computers. Should be ready for collection by, what's the time now...say, six this evening,' he explained.

'Perfect,' said the Boss. 'I now need to find Major Duda and tell her that she might be getting an irate Iraqi general on the telephone. All Sergeant Major Romaro's fault.'

The Boss wandered down the corridor to the major's office and, having knocked, poked his head in.

'Come in, Tom,' she said. 'You have been here less than a day and already you are making trouble for me.'

'I can explain...'

'I have had the general commanding the Iraqi Eighth Army on the telephone demanding to know why an unknown junior English officer had forcibly removed evidence from one of his investigations. He is demanding the return of the kit or he will go to Bremer. He probably has already notified Bremer of his displeasure, in fact.' She paused and looked half quizzically and half resignedly at the Boss.

'We can return...'

'I have spent most of my spare time here trying to keep the Iraqis and especially General Oothman on our side. I thought I had won his trust. And now this.'

The Boss couldn't really tell whether she was genuinely annoyed or just going through the motions. Then again, knowing what was on the computers may lead them to the hostages whilst a little pissing contest with an Iraqi general would be forgotten in the next week or so. Either way, he wouldn't be around to face the consequences.

'OK, Magdalena. Sorry to cause you a bit of trouble, but you will have to trust me on this. We can send the computers back by six this evening. It's not as if they are going to do anything with them. It's just dented pride.'

'In which case, you owe me big time, English Captain.' She was smiling now and the Boss knew that he had won the case.

'I'm sure I can make up for it this evening by buying you a drink. I would offer to take you out to dinner but, you know, snake and pygmy pie in the cookhouse is hardly a romantic treat.'

'I will let you buy me some Chardonnay, then,' she said.

'Ok. It's a date. I now need to go and check the boys are ok. Can I leave the returning of the computers to the IP in your capable hands?'

'I will do that for you. I can send over Stanislav.'

25

Easter Saturday, 10 April 2004
Ramadi District
Ad Diwaniyah
1630 Local

Clocktower climbed the stairs to his flat and unlocked the sturdy iron door with triple locks. He went inside and put his keys down on a small table by the door, keeping hold of his Glock. He called out a greeting to his wife, who was in the living room watching TV with his daughter. He could hear the shrill animated music of a cartoon.

He went to the kitchen, opened the boiler cupboard, lifted a loose floor board, and pulled out a safe from the floor behind the boiler. He punched in the numbers and opened the door and pulled out a pink Samsung flip phone. The manilla envelope he had been given this morning was in there still unopened, resting on a pile of dirty dollar bills.

He closed the safe door and pushed it behind the boiler. He closed the cupboard and then picked out a large tin of rice and a baking tray. He poured the rice onto the baking tray until he located the sim card, which he then put into the phone. He turned it on and pressed redial.

Letting the phone ring four times, he hung up. He then put the phone into the rice tin and poured in the rice and put the tin back in the cupboard. Composing himself, he went into the living room to find out how is wife and daughter's day had been.

AT 1659 HE retrieved the phone from the rice tin. He then rolled a handkerchief into his mouth and called the number again and was instantly answered. He said nothing until he heard the lady's voice.

'Hello?'

'The tourist is leaving tonight and will go home tomorrow. He has bought the present for his family.'

'OK, that's very interesting. Do you know where he bought the present?'

'He will pick up the present tonight and go home tomorrow.' With that, Clocktower hung up. Still using the phone, he used the keypad to send out an eight-figure grid reference. He then texted that he would be at the location too. The phone pinged back.

It was unlikely but not impossible that people who wished him harm might be listening in. The muffled voice might sow doubt, but the main thing was to keep the conversation to below a minute. This would prevent the phone being traced through the tower network but, perhaps more importantly, he didn't want his prize information falling into the wrong hands. In his view, the wrong hands meant the Americans. If they could decipher his very basic code they would spring the hostages and he would have no chance of getting any reward. It absolutely had to be kept between him and the British. Furthermore, there was every chance they would ignore his final text and he would end up dead. The risk was high. Very high. But the reward was greater. Enough dollars to start a new life in the West as a legitimate refugee with residential status. That was worth the world to him.

26

Easter Saturday, 10 April 2004
Badr Safe House
Somewhere in Ramadan District Ad Diwaniyah
1750 Local

C unningham was finding it difficult to keep track of time. He calculated he had been in the latest basement with Poklewski for between three and six hours. Nobody had come in and he was getting very thirsty. The room was hot and stuffy and the absence of any windows made the atmosphere close and uncomfortable. He tried shifting his body weight to ease the pain in his shoulder and his cable-tied wrists but soon realised nothing he could do would relieve the pressure. He had an idea that he might be able to chew through Poklewski's cable ties but he had found the plastic too hard. His teeth were not strong enough and anyway, what would they do with their hands once their captors returned? They would just probably get another punishment beating. Poklewski was very reluctant to antagonise them, which was hardly surprising after what she had been through. At least this time they had stayed together. And at least she was talking to him again. It was a small comfort to him that maybe they were forming into a team.

His mind, once again, turned to what he was going to do about toilet facilities. At least the others had given him a bucket. There was no bucket here, and although his persistent headache and lack of water during the time he'd been held here indicated that he was badly dehydrated, at some stage he would have to urinate in his combat trousers. He was no longer worried about the shame as such, more about the discomfort and threat to health it might pose in the long term. He no longer cared about the stink or the dirt, in fact, he was quite proud that it might be distasteful to his captors. He found that his change of attitude now gave him strength. OK, they might kill him at any moment, probably would, but he was resigned to his fate. All the fear of the last twenty-four hours, the last three months even, had left him. There was a sense of calm in his head and he noticed that he could think more clearly now. Events had slowed down and the panic had totally left him.

'Hey, Alice, what are you going to do once we're released?'

'Dunno, LT. I'm sure as hell going to leave this place at the first opportunity.'

'I think they'll transfer you out to Germany or even back to the States. We'll get the papers in as soon as we get back to Navistar. There ain't no way they'll keep you in country after what you've been through. Besides, you'll need a whole lot of sick leave or whatever.' He found the words came with difficulty. He knew the physical scars would take some time to heal but the mental damage would last forever. Her life had been permanently and irrevocably changed for the worse.

They lapsed back into silence. They could hear no traffic outside nor any sound from the rest of the house. The size of the courtyard suggested it had been a large house in an expensive neighbourhood, set back from a quiet road. Not like the hustle around the small house where they had first been taken.

He was shaken out of his dozing by the bolt shifting and the door opening. He struggled to his feet as three armed men came in. They carried in with them a saucepan that was full of water, and left it by the door. Then they backed out.

He shouted after them. The usual stuff about being taken to the US forces at once, rewards, the need to be untied, the retribution they were risking by not freeing them. But the door was closed and the bolt slid back with a rasp and a clang.

He looked at the water in the saucepan and then knelt down like a dog and drank a bit.

'Hey, Alice, come and get something to drink.' He looked over at her and noticed that she'd wet herself. 'Come on, you need to drink. It'll make you feel a little better.'

She stood up and hobbled over and also got down on her knees and drank some water, her blond hair getting wet as she leaned forward, her arms rigid behind her back. She knelt upright, her eyes closed, her wet hair dripping slowly down the front of her t-shirt.

The water reinvigorated Cunningham. He began once again to speculate how he could get out of the situation he now found himself in. The basement was probably, in fact, an empty storeroom. It was windowless and like the last one, had a single light bulb in the ceiling that had been on since their arrival. Other than going through the walls, the door was the only means of entry and exit. But with his hands bound, he had no choice but to wait for circumstances to change.

27

Easter Saturday, 10 April 2004
Forward Operating Base Echo
Head Quarters Multi-National Division Central South
1800 Local

'Wotcha, Yip. Remember Jim, don't you?' Barnes had watched the American sergeant major amble across the vehicle park towards the British encampment.

'Yeah...sort of. Yip Romaro. I was pulling security on the convoy that started this whole mess. Nice to meet you.'

'Likewise, Yip, Jim Player. I think I was away a lot of the time you were with the Squadron. Did a stint at 23 around that time.'

'I remember. You were called Banjo,' said Yip.

'Still am, by some,' replied Banjo. 'Oi, Bruce, you getting a brew on or what? For fuck's sake. Jesus, Yip, the young soldiers of today. I imagine you want a cuppa?'

'OK, Banjo, relax, mate,' shouted back ManBat. 'Man of your age needs to watch his blood pressure.'

'I would love one. The captain about?' asked Yip.

'He'll be over shortly. I think he's giving the Polish int major a bit of his woeful chat,' said Barnes.

'That's how rumours start, Scouse.'

'It's no longer a rumour. Word has it that he got his leg over last night. Those mortar rounds you heard? That was the, shall we say, climax of his evening,' said Scouse.

'Well, I must say, even I felt the earth move. She's a handsome woman and after a year out here I can see where he's coming from. Anyway, looks like he's coming over now.'

They watched as Stanislav's vehicle came over with the Boss standing above the cab at the top gunner's position. As the vehicle came to a halt he gave the roof a slap, shouted his thanks and vaulted out.

'They're returning the computers to the IP. Mendoza hasn't told me what's on them yet, though,' he announced to the group.

'He's told me, though,' said Yip. 'All but one are clean. Well, clean is not quite the right word. Apparently, riddled with viruses and the hard drive caches were stuffed with porno images.'

'Cache as in weapons' cache?' asked Barnes.

'Sort of. It's a temporary storage facility for stuff you have been looking at,' said Yip. 'If you want to know more than that, you'll have to ask Mendoza. Above my paygrade. Anyway, one of the machines had an email account they've managed to hack.'

'Anything good?' asked the Boss. 'And why didn't he tell me this. I've just been to see him to pick up the machines.'

'LT Mendoza won't release what he considers US confidential information to a foreign military.'

'Fuck. Me. Sideways,' said the Boss. 'I thought we were all on the same side.'

'Luckily for you he told me. Actually, to be fair, he knew I would tell you,' said Yip. 'What it indicated was that the initial capture was done by the local JAM militia. The dead guy was just holding them until they could be transferred. We think to Najaf. There was a bit about the ambush. It was hoped that a convoy would come down

Jackson after the blowing of the bridges around Scania. They reckoned they could hit the convoy and be back in out of sight by the time we reacted at Echo.'

'Well, they were right there,' said Barnes.

'The secondary ambush was organised from Najaf. It was just an opportunity ambush. Hit and run. The old bloke who owned the house was pushed out during the day,' continued Yip.

'Yeah, we saw them leave. Though to complete the picture, he was in on it too. He handed over the IED to the ambush group.'

'There was some correspondence also about taking the reward. The Diwaniyah lot quite fancied the moolah but someone higher up, probably in Najaf, said the hostages had to be moved out of town to somewhere more secure. They felt we would be on to them quickly. I think they were going to move them tonight.'

'So, who did the hit?' asked the Boss.

'Mendoza thinks it was a Badr group. And I'm inclined to agree with him. We have no previous knowledge of group rivalry within JAM, it's too far south for Al Qaeda. The Fedayeen are a spent force. Mendoza said there's still a chance that it was more a criminal than an insurgent event. Someone powerful knew where they were, fancied the reward and was prepared to kill a family to get it.'

'Sounds unlikely to me,' said Barnes.

'Me too,' said the Boss. 'It would take some balls to start fucking with the militia in a town that's as tightly run as this one.'

'We've matched the room with the proof-of-life video that was released earlier. Definitely the same room,' confirmed Yip. 'So, the problem is, who's got them now and why, which is exactly the place we were at this time yesterday.'

'What are Delta up to?' asked the Boss.

'Boss, I don't know, and you know that if I did know, I wouldn't be able to tell you anyway,' said Yip. 'You can be sure they're taking an interest in this and everything we know, they already know. LT Mendoza will be passing all info up to Balad. The Pentagon is briefing the White House. Rumsfeld is liaising direct with Balad. He's missing out the NSA in the middle. Doesn't trust them, I'm told.'

'Fair enough,' the Boss said. 'Although, you got to ask yourself if US Military Intelligence is functioning totally efficiently.'

'There's a number of emperors guarding their empires. Must be the same with you Brits?'

'I guess so,' said the Boss with a shrug.

'Ok, well I'm off to get some chow. Gubby's picking me up at 1815.'

'That's probably him coming over there,' replied the Boss. 'We'll see you up at the cookhouse then.'

As the American got in his Humvee and drove off towards the main building cluster, Barnes handed the Boss a sheet of signal paper.

'This came in. Thought you might want to see it first.'

The Boss took the paper and read it. It was from Hereford via Basra Palace and had been encoded. Cookie had decoded it clearly and written it out in pencil.

'Fuck me. This changes everything,' the Boss said.

'Certainly does, Boss.'

'Who else knows?'

'Just you and me. Oh, and Banjo, because he's a nosey cunt. But he's quite a senior nosey cunt,' said Barnes.

'We can't let on to the Yanks just yet. Cookie, burn this could you? John, is everybody ready to move? This may accelerate.'

'Packed and ready. Wagon's got a full tank. Even the Supacat is loaded. Mr Whistler has got his section on five minutes notice to move, too. They're having their main evening meal. We can put most of them in the Supacat and maybe sit a few in the DPVs.'

'In which case, time for a quick scoff.'

28

Easter Saturday, 10 April 2004
Badr Safe House
Somewhere in Ramadan District Ad Diwaniyah
2030 Local

Cunningham was beginning to get really thirsty. Like Poklewski, he had now wet himself too and found the relief very gratifying. He still maintained his weird pride in being dirty for his captors, after having relieved himself. He didn't give a damn about the smell or the shame. If they were going to force this on the two of them then they could suffer, in a small way, the consequences. He had not yet got to the point where you could no longer resist the urge to defecate but when it came, then he would have no option and would gladly soil himself. Sure, he would have to live in his own excrement but a small sense of satisfaction told them they would have to put up with the stink, too.

Poklewski had become less monosyllabic and he, in turn, had

stopped trying to keep up with the bright-siding. He had also, in the last few hours, come to accept his situation. He knew he was probably being kept for some sort of execution but that his executioner would be someone of note in the ranks of whichever organisation had captured them. They wouldn't just let any old Haji kill them. He hoped it would be quick – a bullet to the head would do the trick. He also rather hoped he would be first and that he would have the strength and resilience to die without fuss and panic. He didn't know if he could, but he was now steeling himself for the inevitable. The total panic he had experienced when he thought he would be executed on camera earlier on that day had somehow hardened him to his fate. He looked across at Poklewski. She sat, with her back to the wall and her hands still bound behind her back. Her head was on her chest and she was either dozing or doing some sort of quiet reflection of her situation. He wondered if she blamed him for their predicament.

He was jogged out of his musings by the sound of footsteps and voices outside the door, and his heart leapt a tiny bit. Maybe they were coming to release them. Or just some food and water would be good. In fact, he now thought of himself as bored, so just any change of environment would be good. He looked at the door as the bolt slid and it opened. There were five armed men. They shouted at them both and indicated with rifle gesticulations that they should get to their feet. Cunningham remained sitting but Poklewski struggled to her feet by flipping over on to all fours before rising. He noticed her hands behind her back were discoloured from the interruption to the circulation. One of the men came over to him and give him a resounding kick in the thigh and yelled in his face. His rifle barrel was going up and down, trying to make Cunningham rise. Then a second kick came in.

'OK, buddy, I'm getting up. I am an officer in the United States Military. Your behaviour constitutes a violation...'

He got no further as more yelling and a slap to the face silenced him. He stood there smarting, hoping that the eye watering from the blow would not be taken for crying. He was beyond crying now.

His tormentor took out a black hessian hood and a roll of black masking tape. Cunningham was gagged with the tape and then hooded, and for extra good measure, the gap between his chin and the hood, which he had previously used to see, was closed as the hood was taped to his throat. He stood still in his darkness and listened to the tape being used on Poklewski. He then felt a hand grab his jacket from the front and pull him forward. He stumbled but stayed on his feet as he was pulled toward the door. The slight change in temperature told him he'd left their cell and then he pitched forward on to his knees as he tripped on the first step of the staircase. He was hauled to his feet by his combat jacket and guided up the stairs. Another hand had bunched his jacket at the back to guide him upwards. He counted the steps. There were a dozen until his foot made to go up the final one that wasn't there, and he again pitched forward but was kept upright by his two wardens. He was stopped after a few paces at the top of the stairs. There was a commotion, voices all talking in Arabic at once and he sensed there was nobody in overall charge. The hand at the front of his jacket kept him still. He then heard *Go*, and was again pushed forward. He had a slight trip over what he presumed was a door lintel and then felt he was outside in the night. The air was cool but humid, as if it had just rained. He heard a door open, a car door perhaps, and then he was bundled into a space. He lay on his side not moving. Then he felt Poklewski being pushed on top of him. He shuffled to one side to make room for her. He considered they must be in the trunk of an SUV, and he could feel her beside him, breathing fast and shallow.

A heavily accented voice said, 'No talk,' and then he heard the trunk door being closed. He shuffled upright but his head was constrained by a surface above him. He felt her beside him and he moved his knee to make contact. She pushed back against him and he felt comforted. He wondered if he could have done all of this on his own. If he could have coped without totally breaking down.

The ignition brought the vehicle to life and he felt it moving off. He could hear the voices of the passengers in the front but their conversation was muted, almost whispering. He smelled tobacco and assumed they were all smoking as they drove, and he began to wonder where to but found that he didn't really care. He just hoped at the next stop they would release his hands, which were now throbbing with pins and needles. He decided that constant speculation was not helping. He began to think he would now try to escape. Jeez, they were going to kill him anyway, at least being shot trying would avoid the whole being on the internet thing. He would save his family the trauma of having to watch or knowing others had watched his death – no, his murder, on a screen. Suicide by cop, they called it back home. He knew God would forgive him if he chose to go that way.

He lost track of how long they had been in the SUV. The start of the journey had been one of halts and turns as if they were navigating the streets of the town, but now they seemed to be going along in a straight line. The engine note suggested they were going at a fast cruising speed. There was a good chance they would be stopped at a roadblock. Both the coalition forces and the Iraqi police manned roadblocks or VCPs at night to enforce curfews and to prevent the shipment of weapons or the planting of roadside IEDs.

The automobile began to slow to a halt and he heard a conversation in Arabic, presumably through one of the windows. He held his breath in case they wanted to look in the trunk. As the car moved off he felt a crushing disappointment. He sensed the slow speed and then the swerve left and right as it went through the chicane of a roadblock, and then it sped off once again in a straight line. It could have been driving for another hour or so before it again slowed down and made a turn. *To the right*, he thought. He made a mental note. An hour's drive; one VCP; and then turn to the right. He repeated to himself three or four times. The vehicle was now bouncing on an uneven track, moving slowly over the rough ground, and the two of them were finding it hard not to roll around. They carried on down the track for at least ten minutes before the SUV finally stopped. He heard the passengers get out. More voices, this time louder, congratulatory, almost celebratory. It must have been a risky move out of the town. Cunningham now assumed they were at their final destination and that it was out in the country, away from coalition forces. Away from being rescued. The voices receded and he was left with Poklewski in the dark.

'Hey, Poklewski?'

'LT?'

'I think we've been taken out of the town. Maybe to a farm or an isolated house.'

'What's going to happen to us, LT?' There was fear in her voice. A trembling in her body as she lay sprawled next to him.

'I dunno. Let's hope that out here they can undo our hands. Mine hurt like hell.'

'Mine too. Or they did. I can't feel them now. Are they going to kill us?'

'Nah, they're going to trade us for a reward and then our guys are going to kill *them*.'

'LT, you always look on the good side. It's nice. It helps.'

Cunningham felt a little proud and a little elated that she didn't think him as some kind of dork.

'Positive mental attitude, Alice. That will keep us alive.'

'I'll try, LT.'

'Here they come...'

The back door to the SUV opened and the hands were once again on his combats. He was dragged out of the vehicle, falling to the ground, and then lifted up on to his feet. He was pushed and pulled forward and felt sand or gravel under his boots. As he was taken into a building, he used this as his chance.

'Water,' he mumbled through the tape. 'And toilet.'

'You. Silence.' He was pushed forward again and into a room. *Obviously no basement*, he thought. This was his third cell in twenty-four hours, or forty-eight, or a hundred and forty-eight. He had no idea.

He stood in silence. Then he felt the tape being ripped from his throat and the hood was taken off his head. He looked around and saw five men, all with head coverings so that he could only see their eyes. All were armed and all had olive-green belts and ammunition pouches. Next, the tape was ripped from his mouth and he took in a great gulp of air.

'I need...'

'Silence.'

Cunningham stopped talking. One of the five approached him with a large knife and he instinctively backed off. His pulse was racing and he felt the urge to vomit. His wild eyes must have alerted the man, as he raised his hand in a calming gesture and pointed his knife at the ground. The hands spun him round and he felt the knife sawing at the thick cable ties before his arms were released. The rush of blood was agony and he could do little but stand there and shake his hands to try to recirculate them. He saw that Poklewski was also having her hands unshackled. She put her hands under her armpits and began to twist from side to side as the blood made its agonising way into her fingers.

The man re-sheathed his knife onto his belt and then told them to get undressed. Both he and Poklewski stood still, dumbly. The command was shouted, louder this time, and the rifles were gesticulated. Cunningham began to unbutton his combat jacket to remove it. He dropped to it to the ground. The rifle muzzle indicated the trousers next and the boots. He sat down and undid his boots and then stood up and removed his trousers. He was now just in his socks and underwear. The rifle muzzle indicated the socks too, so he removed them as well. He looked over to Poklewski, who was standing next to him in just her bra and pants. Her body was covered in purple and yellow bruising. Her white bra contrasting with the vivid mottling of her body. Absurdly, he thought, that the one act of kindness they had received from the woman that had taken away Poklewski's underwear and returned them washed and ironed, had made a real difference to Poklewski's dignity right now.

They stood semi-naked in the room whilst their garments were picked up and searched. The cable tie was taken out of Cunningham's trouser pocket and thrown on the floor. The clothes and both pairs of boots were taken out by one of the men. He reappeared with two orange jumpsuits and two pairs of leather flip flops.

'Wear,' he commanded.

Cunningham stepped into the orange jump suit and stood gormlessly looking at his captors. He was judging that this was not the time to be a pain in the ass. That time, he hoped, would come soon.

A large plastic container of water was brought in, as well as a bucket.

'What about food?' demanded Cunningham, but the men ignored him and closed the door.

From the picture on the side, it had once contained orange juice or some orange flavoured drink.

'Hey, Poklewski, have some water.' He handed her the five-litre container. She drank from it for what seemed like a long time and then handed it to him. He put it to his lips and drank. The warm water tasted faintly of oranges and plastic.

The door opened again and they indicated to Poklewski to accompany them. She immediately became hysterical and shouted and screamed. She backed into a corner but the men grabbed her by her arms and dragged her through the door. One of the men came close to Cunningham with his weapon raised, pointing straight at his head. He could see the man's one open eye through the rifle sights. He could also see down the cavernous muzzle and he froze. The man backed slowly out of the room, not lowering his rifle until the door slammed shut.

Cunningham stood still for a while after they had left and he could no longer hear Poklewski's screams. He thanked the Lord that he was a man but then had the thought that he could easily be next. He had heard that American POWs had been sexually abused in captivity. He stood wondering what would be next. He wandered aimlessly over to the water and took another draft and then relieved himself in the bucket. He contemplated defecating but didn't feel the urge. He thought to himself that he hadn't had a crap since the morning of the convoy. When had that been? Two days ago? Maybe three? He was pretty sure it was night as they wouldn't have risked such a trip out of town during the day. Maybe he had been gone four days. He began thinking that his folks would now have been told he was missing presumed dead or captured. He put the thought out of his mind and once again, sat facing the door with his back to the wall.

29

Easter Saturday, 10 April 2004
Forward Operating Base Echo
Head Quarters Multi-National Division Central South
2030 Local

Yip was thinking about wandering over from the Chow Hall to the MWR to attend the leaving get together for the remainder of the convoy that had so disastrously finished at Diwaniyah. They were due to be transported tomorrow first thing back to Navistar in Northern Kuwait. There, they would be debriefed so that any lessons could be learned, and then reformed into a new unit. The injured and dead would be replaced by new bodies coming in from the States. It was a pretty tough introduction to military transportation, the "sustainer push" of the planners, for the mainly part-time soldiers of the National Guard. He felt that they had performed their tasks well. Despite the casualties, there could have been many more fatalities and worse, prisoners taken. If it hadn't been for the Brits being where they were, it would have been a total disaster. As it was, many of the loads had had to be destroyed beside the road as the trucks were no longer serviceable. As for the US dollars, Yip was beginning to wonder if he'd been rash in signing it over to the Brits at the height of the ambush. His main concern, at the time, had been to get his convoy to safety, not worry about money that didn't belong to the United States in the first place. Presumably, the Brits still had it on their vehicles. There were never less than two troopers guarding them night and day. He thought he might just wander over to them and get it back.

'Um...Sergeant Major?' It was LT Mendoza. He seemed anxious and his stutter was worse than normal.

'Yes, sir, that's me.'

'You might be interested in something that we're working on. The int picture is building on the hostages. But everything I'm getting from Balad is saying *STRICTLY US EYES ONLY*. So I can't share it with Major Duda, really. Nor the Brits.' He looked pleadingly at Yip, constantly blinking.

'Sure, sir. You got a moment now? We can talk it over.'

'I was hoping you would say that. Come to my section office.' He led the way back through the now quiet staff rooms, past the Polish intelligence section, which was closed, and to his own office. The SigInt platoon were all there working at their screens or twiddling electronic dials on what Yip assumed to be scanning and listening devices. The men, mostly wearing headphones, barely looked up as they entered.

Yip sat on the edge of the desk as Mendoza went over to a white-board on which he'd drawn out a diagram of inter-connecting nodes.

'What we have seen is a large uptick in unidentified radio chatter. When we decrypted the computers you brought in, we found that a JAM cell had planned the ambush on the convoy. It seems it had been co-ordinated with the blowing of the bridges over the Euphrates on Friday. Al Sadr issued a call to arms publicly but also the cellular structure of the JAM regional active service units had been informed that they should hit American targets. The Haji group that hit the convoy, and we're certain there are more than one such group in

Diwaniyah, was local to this area here...' He pointed to the large-scale map of the town. 'This is where you found the bodies and here is where the café is. All very local. But that JAM cell has now gone quiet. We are presuming that with the raid on the café, they've switched to another means or are just lying low. It's probable they don't know who hit them any more than we did. They may even think it's a Special Black Ops hit by us.'

'What's your point, sir?' asked Yip.

'Well, just as the JAM cell went black, we began picking up burst transmissions from somewhere else.'

'What do you mean "somewhere else"? LT, this is not floating my boat at the moment. What are you trying to tell me?'

'Well, sir, and this is just my thinking, these radio bursts are from sophisticated military communications equipment. My contact at Balad has also picked them up.'

'LT?'

'Yes, Mr R...Romaro,' he stuttered, his eyes blinking.

'Get to the goddamn point, will you?'

'Yes, sir, sure, sir. I think it might be Iranian.'

'You telling me you think the Iranians are holding them hostage? Does Balad think this?'

'Er, no, sir, I mean, Sergeant Major.'

'Do you mean no, you don't think the Iranians are holding them, or no, Balad doesn't agree with you.'

'Er...the former. But it might mean that whoever has them is being directed by the Iranians. Balad have a Rivet Joint flying the border with Iran and there's definitely some correlation with frequency activity from the Quds Force of the Revolutionary Guard.'

'So, you think whoever has them is being directed by Tehran and that the hostages may be renditioned across the border?'

'Exactly, Sergeant Major,' replied Mendoza.

'What happens then? Why would Iran want American hostages?' Yip asked.

'Because, Sergeant Major, we're transporting insurgent fighters to Bagram in Afghanistan or Guantanamo. You know that proof-of-life video? They were wearing orange jumpsuits. They're mimicking the coalition forces. Iran will use them as propaganda. Maybe even execute them for war crimes or give them life sentences for espionage. There are also very strong rumours of prisoner abuse at an American-run prison up in Baghdad.'

'The rumours about Abu Ghraib? If they are true, then there's going to be a very, very difficult period coming up for our mission in this country.'

'I just thought you should know because they were... sorry... *are* your soldiers,' said Mendoza. 'I think that JSOC know where they are being held and that they are going to launch a hostage release operation.'

'Appreciate it, LT. Thank you.'

Yip decided to forego the MWR for the moment and go pay a visit to the Brits. He couldn't share the information that Mendoza had told him but he felt he should keep them informed of the general situation. He also decided that he should raise the question of the US dollars. It should really be returned to the US authorities if they were going to remain in camp for the while. He didn't know where or how they had secured the bundles of notes but splitting up a pallet between their vehicles wouldn't take up much room. Still, it was unsecured and they should at least formalise the handover and until then, keep it locked away, safely. The Brits would understand.

He walked over to the vehicle compound where they'd set up their encampment. The evening was overcast and heavy with moisture. He reckoned they might change their mind about the CHUs if it began to rain.

At first, Yip thought he had got lost but quickly realised the British vehicles were no longer there and had left. Not even said goodbye. Typical.

He wandered back to the MWR where drivers and escorts of the convoy were reliving their day of combat. He had just sat down with SGT Andersson when Gubby came in.

'Sergeant Major, sir. You are wanted outside. Looks official.'

30

Easter Saturday, 10 April 2004
Badr Safe House
East of Fajr, Dhi-Qar
2100 Local

They came for Cunningham about half an hour after they'd taken Poklewski away. Three men with rifles came into the room and gestured for him to follow. They didn't tie his hands or hood him. He was led into a bigger room next to where he had been held. He was initially struck by the bright lighting and a large black flag pinned to the far wall. It depicted a hand holding an assault rifle flanked by laurel leaves and Arabic writing. In front of the flag was a trestle table with a white tablecloth. On it was a big bowl of fruit, a plate of pastries, cans of Coca-Cola, and a packet of Camel cigarettes. There were three white, plastic chairs arranged with their backs to the flag.

A guard indicated for him to sit with his back to the flag in the centre chair. As he did so, he noticed there was a video camera on a tripod and four other men behind it facing the table. The bright lighting came from two professional looking electric photographer's lights. All the men were in black paramilitary dress, except for two. One was wearing green military fatigues with his maroon beret folded and held in one of his epaulettes. The other was in a silver, three-piece lounge suit, white shirt but no tie. He wore orange lace up leather shoes and Cunningham noticed desert sand in the welts. The man was unshaven and smoking.

Cunningham sat down and looked at the man in the silver suit.

'Welcome, my friend. Might you please tell me your name?' The voice, though heavily accented, was mellifluous and fluent. Cunningham looked at him, wondering what he should do or say. His basic training had said that, on capture, any information freely given to the enemy should only include name, rank, number, and date of birth.

'First Lieutenant Eugene Cunningham of the 751st Medium Truck Company, the 105 Transport Battalion of the United States Army,' he replied, looking directly into the camera, speaking out as confidentially as he was able.

'Welcome Lieutenant Cunningham,' silver suit man replied. 'Would you like something to eat or drink? We have some delicious fruit or maybe some coconut kleicha? We make the best in the world, you know, despite ten years of illegal sanctions.'

'I'm good, thanks,' Cunningham replied.

'Oh, come now, Lieutenant. I am sure you are hungry and thirsty after your ordeal. Your fellow American, Alice, very much enjoyed some Coca-Cola and fruit. Perhaps you would like a cigarette?'

'Don't smoke. What have you done with her?'

'Maybe we can tempt you with some traditional mint tea?' persisted the man. Cunningham said nothing. He was beginning to wonder where this was all going.

'So, Lieutenant, tell me, what did you come to Iraq for? Was it to kill Iraqis?'

The question took him by surprise. 'No, sir. I've told you, I'm from a Transportation Battalion serving as part of the Operation Iraqi Freedom deployment.'

'The War here is illegal, wouldn't you say?'

'No, sir, I would not.' Cunningham kept looking at the camera and tried to speak out boldly.

'You have killed mainly women and children, bombed the hospitals and imprisoned thousands of innocent civilians in your concentration camps. There you torture and murder them. The pictures will emerge very soon onto the internet for the world to witness your war crimes.'

'My job,' replied Cunningham, 'is to deliver equipment for the Iraqi people. We are here to help the people of this country. I'm not here to kill anybody and those that are killed are killed in self-defence. The US Army does not kill civilians. That's what your government does.'

'So, you admit that the Americans have killed civilians?'

'Well, sure. Some have been killed in the crossfire but the American military does not target civilians. It is very carefully stipulated in standing orders. We have to positively identify targets before we can engage. We follow orders.'

'Would you say the Americans are winning this war?'

'Yes, sir.'

His interrogator stubbed out his cigarette in an ash tray at his feet and immediately took out a silver case, extracted another cigarette and lit it with a heavy gold lighter. He took a drag, looked at the tip and then exhaled.

'Has your government asked you to spy on the Iraqi people?' he asked.

Cunningham was again taken aback by the question. 'No, sir. I am not a spy.'

'You have been arrested by the Iraqi authorities and they are formalising charges of murder and espionage.'

'I was captured after my convoy was ambushed by insurgents.'

'No, Lieutenant Cunningham. You were arrested after your military unit opened fire on civilians in the town of Ad Diwaniyah.'

'That's bull dung. And you know it.'

The man continued: 'Your co-defendant, Private Alice Poklewski, has admitted to charges of murder, espionage and conspiracy. Her co-operation will perhaps save her from the death penalty...'

'She did no such thing. You've forced a confession out of her. She was beaten, tortured and raped. She would say anything to you animals that you wanted to hear.' Cunningham was shouting now. 'Where is she? What have you done to her?'

'Hush, my friend,' instructed the man. 'She freely admitted to her crimes. She was ordered by your generals to do these things against the Iraqis. We know that you are both working also for the Israelis.' He pronounced this *Iss-Ra-Yealies*.

'I have no connection with the Israelis and I deny any involvement with murder or any other trumped-up charge you might care to throw at me.'

The man was looking at him, smoking. 'She explained to us that she was forced to be your concubine and that she had no option but to obey orders. She is now grateful to be safe and she is being well looked after. Tell me, Lieutenant, do you think that your war is illegal?'

'You are wrong there, this war was sanctioned by the UN,' Cunningham replied.

'But there was no vote for war. Not even the French would support the American call for war. The Americans have tried to command their lackeys to vote with them but even they refused. You are not here for the UN. You are not wearing blue helmets. Your tanks are not painted white. The UN does not allow for helicopter gunships shooting into towns.'

Cunningham stared at him. There was an awkward pause in the conversation while the man continued to smoke impassively.

'You are here for the oil and to do the Israelis' bidding in a crusade against Islam and the Prophet Mohammad, praised be his name.'

'No, sir, that's not true,' was all Cunningham could think to say.

'The evidence is incontrovertible, my friend. Where are your weapons of mass destruction? There are none. It is well known. Even Mr Blix denied any such weapons. Yet the Americans gave us an ultimatum to disarm or face invasion. Tell me, Lieutenant, how do you disarm if you have no weapons?'

Cunningham looked at the man. He was too tired for this conversation. He hadn't kept up with the pre-invasion news in the UN Security Council and he didn't really know the answers to his interrogator's questions. He had an urge to agree with him. What did he care? He just wanted to go home.

'Would you say the Americans think of themselves as honourable people?'

'For sure. That's who we are. That's what we do.'

'So, you agree with me and the rest of the world that this war is illegal. The UN have already declared it illegal. Millions of concerned citizens around the world are protesting at the American war crimes. They know the American government wages war by killing civilians. You did so in Vietnam.'

'I don't know. I'm just a trucking officer in the National Guard. I wasn't in Vietnam. I am not a spy. I am not a murderer.'

'But you freely admit that this war is illegal. The UN did not sanction the invasion of Iraq. There was not even a vote for them to lose. That is a fact, my friend.'

'If you say so. I don't follow politics. I'm just a transportation officer.' He was speaking quietly now and no longer looking at the camera.

'I can understand your frustration at your criminal government and in the great Satan, Bush and his little devil friend, Bliar,' the man said, mispronouncing "Blair". 'The people of America will one day rise up and overthrow their tyrant leaders.'

Cunningham remained silent. He reached out and took a pastry from the plate and then helped himself to a can of Coke. The sugar rush made him feel extraordinarily hungry.

'Please. Help yourself. You are our guest in our house. The Americans are running death squads in the towns that kill any civilians they encounter. Can you tell me what you know about these?'

'That is total bull. There aren't any. That's just made-up crap.'

'There is very compelling evidence that the Americans are paying the leaders of these death squads.'

'I don't believe there is any evidence at all,' replied Cunningham. He leaned forward and picked out a small brownish banana and began to peel it. If there was food available, he reasoned, he might as well eat it.

Silver suit man stood up and said, 'We are working with the authorities to release you back to the Americans. It is very complicated. But meanwhile, you must rest.' He then turned on his heels and left, the man in the green uniform following him. Cunningham reached out and took two oranges before his guards indicated for him to stand up. He was led back to the other room where he found Poklewski sitting against the wall and facing the door.

31

Easter Day, 11 April 2004
Dhi-Qar Province
0130 Local

The small group of vehicles was parked up in a palm grove in all-round defence. They had turned south out of Echo down route 8 to avoid the town and then driven east along route 17 without headlights for two and a half hours. They'd then turned off the main route down a track and headed south until they found a secluded spot amongst the palms. The Boss had used the Rifles Section for a defensive cordon, with Corporal Lomax and one rifleman covering the route in with a GPMG at the point where the track forked. The rest of Whistler's men were positioned around the vehicles. They lay facing out from the main group on listening watch. It had been raining for two hours and they were soaked through and chilled.

A two-man team of Ginge and Stan had gone forward to locate the farmhouse and had reported back that they now had eyes on the target. The building was in a compound approximately four to five kilometres from the vehicles. There were three four-by-fours parked outside in the yard, including an Iraqi police Land Cruiser. The lights were on in the house but nobody had entered or left the building since their arrival. After an hour of observation, Ginge and Stan had very slowly circled the compound to check for other entrances or to see if there was activity they had missed. So far, all seemed quiet. Ginge reported back that about five hundred metres from the target was another farm compound, but it seemed either deserted or its occupants were all asleep. Occasionally, they heard a dog bark, but it was too far away to be of concern.

First light was about 0430 local. The Boss had agreed with Barnes that they would assault the house at 0415. They would move the remainder of the troop up at 0200 leaving them just under two hours to travel the five kilometres. The vehicles would remain static, with Corporal Lomax and three others from the Rifles, and Cookie watching the comms with Basra. Banjo would lead the vehicles in via the track once the assault had been launched. The Boss had been very surprised to be given the order to rescue the American hostages. He knew that two of the British Army's most senior officers in Iraq were ex-Regiment men, but even so. But the hostage situation was now located in the Northern quarter of the British sector of South East Iraq, so it was in the British TAOR. They'd also been told that at least one Iranian national was likely to be in the farmhouse and that the hostages were to be moved the next morning across the border into Iran. If they crossed the border, then it would be impossible to retrieve them and a long and tedious diplomatic spat would ensue. The Americans could remain in an Iranian prison for years or even be executed on trumped up charges. The immediacy of the situation demanded an immediate action response.

Their orders, which had arrived via a secure message to Cookie, had been to rescue the hostages. This was important because it did not imply, very purposefully, that the orders were to kill the insurgents. However, in executing these orders, they all knew they had the option to neutralise any threat to life of either themselves, the hostages, or any unconnected party that happened to be in the vicinity. So, if a fire fight started, they would respond with the maximum firepower at their disposal. Nevertheless, the difference between a hostage release and a good old fire fight was immense. Targets had to be identified, threat assessed and either left or dealt with in milliseconds. Everyone knew the last thing they could do was shoot a hostage. It was a high stakes gamble by Hereford and by Basra Palace. The Boss mused that only DSF and the colonel and some high ups in the British contingent had been told. Some very high ranking and stellar careers could be ruined if he fucked this up. Not least, his own. But there was no time to cordon off the access roads to the border and any interception of the hostage movement might risk the lives of the Americans and would involve shooting up an Iraqi police vehicle.

Basra had told him that an Iraqi policeman, codenamed "Clocktower", was not to be harmed under any circumstances. He would be wearing his uniform and have his maroon beret in his epaulettes. The Boss assumed the Land Cruiser was his and that the orders came from Box. They had obviously infiltrated or were trying to infiltrate a Badr Group or perhaps even an Iranian cell located in Iraq. *It always works like this*, he mused. The best intelligence comes from traitors within the enemy itself. Northern Ireland had a very deep and well-placed number of sources both within PIRA and INLA. They had agents in the Yugoslav war and were now running agents in Afghanistan, Pakistan, Iran, Syria and only God knew where else. Some sources were flaky, like Curveball, who'd been run by the Germans. It was Curveball that had made up everything the American and especially the British Governments had wanted to hear about Weapons of Mass Destruction. And it was now beginning to look like a crock of shit. They were meant to be on mobile platforms but nobody had ever found anything like that. Curveball was now living as an asylum seeker in Germany, safe from the hell he had helped unleash on his country. He knew on good authority that the British SIS and the German Federal Intelligence Service had warned he was not wholly reliable, but the American and worse, the British Government, had given him credence. It was all in that stupid dossier, allegedly written by the drunk bully of a journalist that the Prime Minister kept on a short leash as an attack dog. Fuck, the Prime Minister had even written the foreword, warning the country that it was potentially forty-five minutes from imminent destruction. What a complete bell end.

The Boss walked over to the poncho strung between two of the Rovers, to get out of the rain, which had again intensified. Rain was good. It helped mask noise and it kept people indoors. Nobody was going to go outside for a stogie and a quick walk in a rainstorm like this. Nevertheless, he was still chilly and his thin desert cams offered little warmth. The rest of the troop were standing around trying to keep warm, waiting for the move forward to the target. They had removed all equipment save for weapon and ammunition, taping every buckle and strap down - Barnes had made each one perform a couple of star jumps on the spot to eliminate any rattling equipment. They would move forward using the NVGs attached to their helmets and meet with the forward OP group. The farmhouse compound was small and the dwelling itself probably only had four rooms, perhaps five. There was only one door in, so they would go straight through and then one fire team would go left and one right. The Menacity had a "Barclaycard", which he had issued to Ginge. With it came some solid shot made from wax, infused with powdered lead. It would take off door hinges which Ginge would then use to gain access to any room.

The Boss looked at his watch and then motioned to Barnes that it was time to get going to the FRV. He'd mapped out the bearing and would use both his Silva compass and his GPS to ensure he got to the RV on time. Wolf would be lead scout and take on the onus of map reading with the Boss behind, checking the bearing, and then ManBat pace counting. Lt Whistler would sit in the middle of the patrol with four of his men and Barnes would follow up the rear after Ron to make sure that nobody was trailing them from behind. Progress would be slow and they would stop every two or three hundred metres to check bearings and listen for any signs of compromise.

They lined up and did a final check of equipment and a quick radio check with Cookie on the radio. Wolfie set off at a slow pace, picking his steps carefully, and the rest of the Troop followed in single file. Going through the palm groves was easy, as the farmers had cleared the ground scrub. The rain was coming down hard and there were puddles of standing water between the trees. Despite the slow movement, the activity and the nervousness of the move warmed everybody up. In front of him, Wolfie stopped and went down on one knee. The Boss also dropped to his knee and faced out to the right. The rest of the patrol alternated arcs each way. Then the Boss threaded his way through to Wolfie to make sure that nothing untoward was occurring to the front.

'Just having a listen, Boss,' whispered Wolf. They could hear the dog barking again in the distance. 'Reckon we've come about three hundred metres.'

'Happy with the bearing?'

'Yeah, I think about another k of this palm grove and then it will thin out. We cross the ditch and then it'll be a simple tab into the RV.'

The Boss stood up, as did the rest of the team, and prepared to move off. Rifles were in their shoulders and they were constantly scanning into the gloom, trying to look through the trees rather than at them. The rain eased off as they approached the ditch, which was now full of black water. Wolf stopped and scanned through his night sights. He located a small plank over the ditch which would spare everybody wading through the water. The patrol crossed the obstacle one at a time with all-round defence until the whole troop was across. Wolf and the Boss checked the bearing again using the silva compass. The farm compound should be approximately six hundred metres to their front. The FRV was a hundred metres short of the farm. The last leg in would be taken extra slowly with multiple stops to listen.

Just short of the FRV, Boss indicated for the patrol to go firm and then he and Wolf moved forward to try to locate Stan and Ginge. They were well ahead of schedule, so it was possible the OP were not yet in position at the RV. The low, dark silhouette of the compound walls was visible on the light of the horizon. The rain had cleared now and the stars were out, giving an eerie glow to the landscape. Wolf and Barnes stopped still as the dog started barking again. It was closer this time but still far enough away not to be a worry. The Boss heard a low whistle, much like a bird tweet, and knew that Ginge could see him standing. He replied with his own small whistle and then spotted the two troopers lying about twenty metres to the side. The Boss went back for the rest of the troop and led them into the final leg before the advance to the target.

'Thank fuck you lot turned up, I'm freezing my knackers off here,' whispered Ginge in his lilting Scottish accent. 'There's been no movement for the last few hours. They'll be kipping like good 'uns in their warm little scratchers.'

'Any indication that they're holding the hostages?' whispered the Boss. Assaulting the house had a high inherent risk of starting a fire fight and if they killed Iraqis inside and there were no hostages, some very awkward questions might be asked.

'Can't be certain, Boss. There was some sort of bright light in one of the rooms so they may have been filming something, but I can't be certain what.'

The Boss looked at his watch: 0337. They would remain here until 0400 and then move forward to the compound. Whistler and his men would secure the outside of the perimeter, ensuring that nobody came on to the objective. Once they entered the courtyard, they would be prepared to go noisy if they were fired upon or otherwise compromised. If it went to plan, they would first make their appearance known when Ginge blew first the top and then the bottom hinges off the front door. If the door didn't fall open at that stage, the Barclaycard would be used to blow out the lock, but they weren't anticipating much security on such a lowly dwelling that looked as if it might have been abandoned for the last few years. The Boss assumed that the farmer lived in the other building three or four hundred metres away, with his noisy guard dog.

They moved off in single file with Ginge leading. The sky was just beginning to show the first glow of dawn and the Boss saw that he had the shotgun over one shoulder. They stopped and got down on one knee again, probably for the final time. The Boss signalled to Whistler that he should begin to move his men into all-round protection of the compound entrance once the assault party moved forward. He looked at his watch again: 0403. He decided, for the final leg, he would dispense with his NVGs and use the ambient light from the approaching dawn until they entered the building. The smaller file slowly moved towards the entrance to the courtyard. The Boss could make out the four-wheel drive cars parked outside, including the police car. As they moved through the gate, Ginge took the shotgun off his shoulder and went firm on one knee. The Boss indicated to Bat and Wolf to check the vehicles to make sure nobody was asleep in them. With weapons raised, they very slowly approached the cars from the rear at a crouch. One by one, they looked in through the rear window and then gave the thumbs up to indicate they were empty.

Once the vehicles had been cleared, the team lined up next to the door, the two fire teams either side of Ginge. Using his fingers, Ginge located the hinges in the dark and once satisfied, gave the thumbs up. The two troopers behind him, both with flash bang grenades, also gave the thumbs up. This was the moment and once again, the Boss felt his heart pounding, his mouth dry and the familiar taste of fear in his throat. He dropped his NVGs back over his eyes and flicked off the safety.

The first blast from the shotgun shattered the silence. The second followed quickly and the door fell in. He'd forgotten to put in his ear defenders and the sudden detonation left him with a ringing in his ears. The two flash bangs were rolled in and detonated instantly – a rapid series of intensely loud bangs and blindingly bright flashes. The assault team went through the door, trained not to be silhouetted against the frame, which is where any defender would instinctively fire.

Fourth to enter through the front door, the Boss noticed what was probably the main room behind an interior door, and a man sat slumped in a white plastic chair asleep, as though he was supposed to be guarding the room. The entry startled him awake but the flash bangs had momentarily delayed his reactions. He made a grab for his rifle but slumped forward as two double taps hit him in the chest. He fell out of his chair and lay inert on the floor. Ginge kicked the discarded AK away and tried the door quickly before blasting both hinges out. Ron went through and turned left into the room, quickly followed by the Boss, who went right. Ginge moved on to the next door with the second fire team.

Inside the room, the Boss, rifle raised to his shoulder, saw two people in orange jump suits sitting with their backs to the wall.

'Get down! Get down! Lie on the floor. Put your hands where I can see them. Don't move. Don't move!' he yelled above the firing coming from another room. Both complied and rolled into a face down lying position. Covered by Ron, he kicked apart the first and then the second person's legs. Both lay still, not daring to move at all.

There was gun fire from yet another room. First, a burst of automatic fire and then four or five single shots. He could hear the team shouting to dominate the situation.

The Boss approached the first prostrate body and shouted, 'Keep still! Don't talk!' and knelt on their back. He ran his hands up the legs, into the groin, up the back, round the neck, and then down each of the arms.

'Clear!' he screamed at Ron, who moved his rifle to the next body. The Boss approached the other person and went through the same routine.

'Stay down. Keep still.' She was a female and she got the same search treatment. He noticed her wince as his hands went into her groin area and then he stood up.

'Turn over! Turn over!' he yelled. She didn't move. 'Turn fucking over.' He prodded her with his foot and she rolled on to her back. She avoided any sort of eye contact. He systematically searched her front, noticing that she was visibly trembling and had her eyes closed.

'Stay down. Don't move.' He then went over to the other body and yelled for him to turn over. He rolled on to his back and looked up at the Boss.

'I am Lieutenant Cunningham of the....'

'Shut up. Keep quiet.' The power of the Boss's voice silenced the American. He, too, was searched.

'Clear!' shouted the Boss. He stepped away from the figures on the ground. 'Get up. Get up. Stand up!' he shouted. The man slowly got to his feet, clearly stiff from the night of sitting asleep against the wall. He seemed disorientated and the Boss realised that he was struggling to see in the dark. The female remained on the ground, her eyes closed.

'Get up...' shouted the Boss in her face. But she just lay there, so he reached down to the front of her orange boiler suit and hauled her onto her feet. The Boss then grabbed her by the collar and walked her through the door and out towards the courtyard. At the entrance, he saw Banjo, so he handed her over to him and Whistler's cordon and went back into the other room. He saw Ron outside the door.

'Ron, grab the flag in there for the Squadron Interest Room, will you?'

'Sure, Boss.'

In the opposite room, there were five men lying beside rudimentary cots, all in their underwear. He could see all had been shot, save one who had opted to sleep in his uniform. The Boss saw the maroon beret folded through the epaulette and gave a small thank you that he hadn't been taken out in the confusion. There was one body, bleeding heavily from a number of abdominal wounds, who was moaning softly. It was clear he would not survive.

'Where's Ginge and Stan?' he asked.

'Third room. Next door,' replied Wolf, not taking his eyes off the bodies lying on the floor.

The Boss moved to the final room. The door was still intact, so Ginge would have found it unlocked. Inside, another man lay on the floor with Stan shouting at him to be still whilst he was searched. There was a coat hanger with a white shirt and silver-grey suit hanging from the window. Stan hauled him to his feet and ran him out of the building to the courtyard.

Outside, it was rapidly getting lighter. The Boss turned off and tipped up his NVGs.

'Banjo, get some help for the hostages. Put the detainees together under Mr Whistler and get him to detail a couple of his boys to search the bodies.'

'Wilco, Boss. You should know, we are about to have company,' said the SQMS.

'What do you mean? What sort of company?' said the Boss, before he turned away and vomited.

'You ok?' asked Banjo.

'Yeah, fine. Sometimes happens after an op like that. It's nothing.'

'You should report to the MO when we get back, Boss. That's not normal and Barnie has told me he's worried about your health. Seriously, Boss. These things can happen to anyone. You need to speak to someone when you get back.'

The Boss took a swig of water, spat it out, and then took another swig.

'What were you saying about "company"?'

'The cut off commander has reported there are four large, four-wheel drives heading this way. He thinks they're American but couldn't be sure. They went down the other fork in the track where he was positioned. About three minutes ago.'

'OK...get Cookie to gather them all in and drive down the track as soon as possible. They need to be aware there may be friendly forces in the area but are not to engage unless fired upon and they are certain about the PID.'

'OK, Boss.'

The Iraqi prisoners were being marched out of the building, cuffed hands behind their backs and made to sit on the ground facing the wall of the building. Two of the Rifles platoon stood over them with their SA80s in the shoulder. They had already been hooded.

'Get those hoods off,' the Boss shouted at the two guards. 'No hoods. Where's Barnie?'

'He's with Stan attending the wounded man,' replied Wolf. 'What's with the hoods, Boss?'

'New rules. No hooding detainees.'

'Really?' replied Banjo. 'Since when? Why?'

'Human rights abuse, apparently. Even though we did it in training.'

The Boss heard the faint but unmistakeable thump of a helicopter rotor. 'Banjo, did you call in the helis?'

'No, Boss.'

'Get the air markers out, I think we've attracted the interest of the Americans.'

The helicopter was now visible: an American Apache. It was joined in the air by a Chinook. The gunship circled around the other farmhouse whilst the Chinook remained high out of effective range of small arms and RPG. The Boss checked that the air markers and the flags were prominent, but nevertheless felt nervous.

'Ron, get Barnie out here, will you?'

Rocket ran back into the house and reappeared with Barnes and Stan. Stan was wearing latex gloves covered in blood.

'Couldn't save him, Boss.'

'Never mind, Stan. Go and check the hostages, will you? John, we've got American company. It looks like they might hit the other farmhouse.'

The Boss got out his binos, checked the rims and scanned the farmhouse. His view was partially blocked by some trees but as he watched, he saw four GMC Suburbans drive through the gate at speed and then slow to a stop. All were black and had blacked out windows. As he watched, the doors were flung open and a team of black-clad soldiers rushed the door. He heard the distant voices shouting, along with some detonations, which he assumed were the doors being blown. Then there was a couple of shots. The Americans threw a cordon around the house as the assault progressed out of sight inside. The Apache was now hovering and he noticed that the Chinook was coming in. He saw yellow smoke just outside the courtyard and the large helicopter flared just as it touched the ground. The back ramp was already down and further soldiers deployed. The final two to deplane were what looked like a senior officer and the familiar outline of Yip Romaro.

'This could be awkward for you, Boss,' murmured Barnes, not taking his eyes from his binos.

'Why me?'

'As you are fond of telling me, you have the pips on your shoulder. I'm just a humble NCO doing as I'm told.'

32

Easter Day, 11 April 2004
Dhi-Qar Province
0430 Local

Cunningham sat on the ground with his hands on his head, waiting for someone to tell him what to do. The rescue had been extremely fast and he was beginning to realise that although he and Poklewski were safe, it seemed his rescuers were, in fact, British. He looked around and saw that two of his captors were bound and hooded, sitting on the ground facing the wall of the farmhouse. His shoulder still ached from the beating he had received and his headache throbbed away in his skull.

A large man approached. He was older than the other soldiers around, probably late thirties. Maybe the same age as SM Romaro.

'You can take your hands off your head now, sir, ma'am. My name's Jim and we are part of the UKSF deployment from Basra. There's going to be a lot of questions coming at you in the next few hours and days, so what about a brew and banjo for now?'

Cunningham looked at him. "Scuse me?' He hadn't really understood the question. 'My name is Lieutenant Eugene Cunningham...'

'Yes. We know who you are. You are safe now, Eugene. Relax. We'll get you returned to your unit very soon. For now, though, would you like something to eat and drink?'

Cunningham looked at Poklewski, who was still sitting and staring at the ground. He looked at the British soldier and saw that he was being offered a black plastic mug. He took it and sipped. It was hot, very strong, milky, sweet tea, and it tasted good. Realising he was shaking, he clasped the mug in both his hands. The man bent down to Poklewski and looked into her eyes.

'Ma'am?' he said softly and offered her a second mug. She looked at him and started sobbing, her body heaving with the effort.

The British soldier looked somewhat taken aback. 'I know it was made by a crap hat, but it won't be that bad. No need to cry. Could be worse. Could have been made by the Boss.' He looked at her offering a little smile and she returned his gesture with a slight smile of her own through the tears. He put out a hand and gently lifted her to her feet, then gave her the mug. She also held it in both hands but remained motionless.

He wandered back to his vehicle and came back with two sandwiches made with white bread.

'Here you go. NATO standard-issue egg banjo. Food of the gods and breakfast of champions. And I make the best in the whole fucking army. That's why they call me "Banjo". Get on the outside of that.'

Cunningham took the sandwich and cautiously peered inside. There seemed to be a fried egg. He bit into it and, like the tea, found he was starving. The egg burst and the yolk ran down his chin and down his hands.

'You must be the officer then?' the British soldier asked.

'Yes, I'm LT Eugene Cun...'

'I know who you are, sir. Just messing with you.' He was smiling and Cunningham felt the tears welling up before they began running down his cheeks. It was embarrassing but he couldn't help himself. After the bad treatment he had received, for however long the time had been, a small act of kindness was bound to break him up.

'Do you mind if I ask you how long I've been in captivity?'

'It's early Sunday morning. I believe you were captured in the afternoon last Friday? So about thirty-six hours.'

'Sheesh, felt like about a week.'

'Yeah, captivity does that to you, I'm told,' said the Brit.

'Do you have corpsman? Got a very bad headache,' Cunningham said.

'Let me see what I can do,' the Brit replied, and wandered back to his large strange-looking vehicle.

Since being captured, Cunningham had been fantasising about various acts of revenge on his captors, but he now felt deflated. The two Iraqis facing the wall looked defeated. He thought he would have been over there to give them a beating or a kicking but he had no desire now. He recognised the man in the silver suit and the one in the green uniform with the beret, who were both sitting crossed legged, hands on heads, facing the wall. The two British soldiers standing over them, cradling their rifles, were having a conversation without taking their eyes off their prisoners.

He could hear the rotors of a helo over the ringing in his ears and looked up to see a Chinook coming in to land. Someone had popped some smoke on the LZ and the back ramp was already down. He expected this was the moment he would be handed over to his own countrymen, although they were still some distance away. He assumed that was the most suitable spot to put down the large bird. He watched as a team rushed from the body of the aircraft and realised they were assaulting a second farmhouse. He wondered if there were other hostages that were now being rescued in a joint operation. Perhaps most of the convoy had been captured and had been separated. Now that he was safe, he felt pride in surviving his ordeal; he was no longer the FNG. He sipped his tea and then wandered over to one of the soldiers.

'Hey, soldier, d'ya know what's going down over there?'

The soldier looked at him from under the rim of his helmet and replied, 'Not a fucking scooby, mate.'

He was approached by a swarthy British soldier. 'Good morning, sir. I'm the medic. Is there something I can do for you?'

'I have a really frickin bad headache, sir, and my shoulder hurts like hell,' he replied.

'No need to call me sir, I work for a living. Call me Stan. What I'm going to do for you is ask you to drink this little cocktail for me. It's rehydrate powders as you're almost certainly badly dehydrated and also suffering from shock. It's not too bad. Sort of an orangy flavour.'

Stan pulled two packets of powder from a bag and poured them into two almost full bottles of water. He gave the bottles a vigorous shake.

'Also, I want you to take two of these little pills, which are Ibuprofen, and two of these which are paracetamol. They should numb both your headache and the shoulder pain, although you should seek medical help as soon as you get back. I'm sure they'll be checking you over carefully as soon as they can. You don't have any allergies, do you?'

'No, sir. Could you also attend to Poklewski? She's my driver. She's been treated pretty bad by these sons of bitches.'

'What do you mean by that, sir?' asked Stan.

'I dunno. I mean, she sort of said that they interfered with her. You know. Sexually.'

'She'll be evacuated to a military hospital as soon as we get the choppers in. It's best she's seen there by a proper team. In the meantime, I'll give her the same as you and a little magic pill as well.'

The corpsman called Stan walked over to Poklewski and offered her the bottle of orange water. She took it and drank it down. He then asked her about her allergies and gave her the same four pills he'd given to Cunningham, before he fished into his backpack and produced two more pills.

'Diazepam.' He looked at her. 'It will relax and calm you for the ride back. We're going to get you to a hospital very shortly, ma'am.'

Poklewski looked at the Brit and gave a smile. 'Thank you.' She then started crying.

'You sit there, love. You're safe now. Nobody's going to hurt you. These guys here will be looking after you until we can get you back home safely.' He smiled a toothy grin and gave her a wink.

Cunningham returned his gaze to the other farmhouse. The operation seemed to be over and two elderly Iraqis were being held outside. He saw they were an elderly couple, a man and a woman, and assumed they were husband and wife. The troops were swarming about the outside of the house and it was clear there were no hostages. One of the grunts came out with a rifle and handed it over to another of the figures outside.

He looked over to the Brit officer who was standing with his hands in his pockets, his rifle tucked between his arms and his body, resting on his ammunition pouches. The two older men were chatting and laughing as if they hadn't a care in the world and Cunningham felt that he, too, could now adopt that kind of ease with the senior NCOs. The Brit officer occasionally picked up his binos that were hanging around his neck and scanned the activity around the other building. He seemed to be waiting for the group of Americans to come over. Cunningham looked over to the farmhouse and saw that two of the black Suburbans were, indeed, bouncing their way down the track towards them.

The British officer and the other two men stood waiting as the large automobiles skidded to a halt in the wet sand. The passenger door and rear doors opened and three Americans stepped out. One seemed to be a senior officer and another one a younger officer dressed in black combat fatigues with a lot of non-issue equipment hanging from his person. The third he recognised as the sergeant major from the convoy, Yip Romaro.

'Morning, Yip,' the Brit Officer said, his hands still in his pockets and a black mug of tea at his feet, the merest hint of a grin on his face.

The senior American officer announced himself. 'I am Colonel Larry Petermans of 1st Special Forces Operational Detachment,

Delta. I'm the senior officer commanding this operation. Are you the officer commanding this unit?'

'I am, actually,' said the Brit Officer. 'Tom.' He stuck out a hand which the American ignored.

'I need you to gather all your assets and hand over any American or Iraqi personnel to my command.'

'Sure, no probs,' the Brit replied. 'Did you find what you were looking for in the other building?'

'Negatory, soldier. I am not at liberty to discuss on-going US military operations with unauthorised foreign personnel.'

'Sir,' said SM Romaro, 'this is the commander of the UKSF detachment I was telling you about. They have secured the release of detained US combat personnel. Isn't that right, Captain?'

'Broadly speaking, yes,' confirmed the Brit Officer.

'This zone is now under command of the US JSOC and you and your men are required to comply with US military law,' continued the colonel. 'You take your orders from me now, son.'

'This "zone" is actually in the Multi-National Division, South East, and is under command of Major General Andrew Stewart, formerly of the 13/18th Royal Hussars. And I take my orders from him,' said the Boss. Cunningham was astonished at his confidence and lack of deference. He had never witnessed such disregard for rank and wondered how the American Special Forces colonel would handle it. Not well, as it turned out.

'Soldier, may I remind you...'

'I'm a captain,' said the Boss.

'You don't appear to be wearing any rank, Captain.'

'It's an old tradition in my unit,' he replied. 'Puts the men at ease.'

'Who is your commanding officer, son? He may wanna hear about this, swear to God.'

'Lambo? You can find him sitting next to General McChrystal. Send them both my best wishes.'

The older British NCO, who had been grinning like a child throughout this encounter, let out an audible snigger, turned away, and took a sip from his black mug. The other NCO stepped in.

'Sir, we have secured your personnel. One male and one female. They are safe and appear unharmed but I think they may require medical attention when they get back to base. We have one possibly Iranian prisoner who we can release to you and we have one Iraqi policeman, who I am not authorised to release. I will need written orders from 20 Armoured Brigade, Basra Airport to do so. I hope you will understand, sir.'

The American colonel ordered the American captain to organise the hand-over of both the released hostages and the prisoner and turned on his heel and went back to his Suburban. The car sped off leaving the American captain and SM Romaro.

'Jesus, Boss,' said one of the Brit NCOs, 'do you have some sort of career-ending death wish? Fuck me.'

'Sorry, I'm just fed up with this tic tock Yank bollocks, no offence, Yip,' he replied. 'Why can't he just thank us for what we did and have a cup of tea, or whatever that clown drinks. Besides, I've got written orders not to hand people over to the Yanks, so I figured I'd get away with it.'

The American officer approached Cunningham and shook his hand. 'Welcome back, Eugene. I'm glad you and Poklewski are ok. I guess we do owe the Limeys a thank you...'

'Don't mention it,' said the Brit officer. 'Why did you assault that house?'

'You want the official reason, or the real reason?' the American asked.

'The real reason is you got the wrong house. I'm presuming there's an official excuse for it?'

'Yeah, we were monitoring radio traffic, mobile phones and the like. We were zeroing in on the right area and we had a UAV airborne. The cloud cover and then the rain last night meant we had to ground it. We thought this building was abandoned because we didn't pick up any human activity around it on the heat detectors over the period before the UAV was grounded. We've known this area was a possible safe house for somebody. We didn't know who or quite where, though,' the American explained.

'And who did you shoot?' asked the Brit.

'Someone shot a dog.'

'That's a shame. Did you find anything?'

'Yeah, a small weapons cache,' replied the American.

'Is that a cache of weapons for dwarves or just a couple of old rifles?' asked the Brit NCO.

'Funny. No. If I'm being totally candid with you, it was a farmer and his wife and he had an old military rifle.'

'You got it?'

'Yeah. It's in the back of the SUV.' He went to the automobile and pulled out an old vintage rifle with a wooden stock.

'Oh my,' said The Boss, trying to get a better look at it. 'Give us a butchers.' The American handed over the rifle.

'This...er...sorry, I don't know your name...' said the Brit.

'Captain Brent Schapker.'

'This, Brent, is a Short Magazine Lee Enfield Mark III.'

'If you say so, Tom.'

'I do and it is. Do you know what I think? I think it was left here from the siege of Kut in 1917. There must have been tens of thousands of these in Iraq. Tell you what, Brent, this will still be more accurate than that crappy old Colt of yours.' The Boss cocked the weapon and ejected a bullet. He looked at the base. 'Yup...bingo...1917 round made by Kynoch. This is a military antique and it's still got the original ammunition.'

'He had about five hundred rounds in boxes of twenty. Well, anyway, it's got to be handed in and it will be destroyed. Unless you want to hand in your own crappy Colt and keep this,' said the American,

'Ha. Touché. It's a shame, though, as you Americans seem to destroy much of what you come across in the world.'

'Come on, Boss,' one of the Brit NCOs said, 'no need to give him a hard time. Not his fault.'

'Yeah. Sorry, Brent. Impolite of me. If you get some of your vehicles over here, we can hand over the prisoner. But we keep the one in green. I think he may be one of ours.'

'Eugene,' said the American officer, 'we're going to get you and Poklewski back to the 86th Combat Support Hospital in Baghdad. Once you've been given the all clear, you'll be shipped back to Camp Virginia in all likelihood. If you have serious medical problems, you will be airlifted to Ramstein, Germany. You two guys are heroes. Everyone is gonna want to hear your story.'

Cunningham looked at him. 'I don't think I'm a hero, sir.'

'Call me Brent, please.'

'I don't think I'm a hero, Brent. I took a wrong turn and got captured. That's about it. What happened to the rest of the convoy?'

SM Romaro stepped forward. 'We managed to get most of the vehicles out of the kill zone. Lost a couple of tankers. I'm afraid Sneddon and Luckenbach didn't make it. Luckenbach was killed in the first contact and Sneddon died during the dust-off flight.'

'They are the heroes, then,' said Cunningham.

'Excuse me, Sergeant Major. Did you say Blake Luckenbach is dead?' Poklewski asked.

'Yes, ma'am. I'm afraid so. He was shot in the head in the first contact. Died instantly. Chen was badly wounded when she triggered a roadside IED. I think she may have lost her arm. She'll be on the way to Ramstein now. I'm sorry.'

Cunningham watched as Poklewski turned away from the group and went and sat down again on the step of the farmhouse door. She buried her head in her hands. He wandered over to see if he could comfort her, not having a clue what he was going to say.

He looked up as two of the British soldiers came out of the farmhouse. Between them they were carrying the slumped body of one of his captors. They laid the man down away from Poklewski and shouted to the rest of the squad that the Iraqi was still alive. One of the soldiers was pressing a first field dressing on to the wounded man's chest.

Poklewski stood up and went over to the man. Cunningham also went over, feeling somewhat awkward. He stood beside her and looked at the wounded man who was staring wild eyed at the soldiers around him.

'GRENADE!'

The Brit soldiers were already diving away from the Iraqi. Cunningham looked as the Iraqi opened the palm of his hand and the lever of a hand grenade flipped into the air with a metallic click. He was mesmerised as the lever spun through the air and the grenade rolled away from the wounded man's hand, coming to a fizzing stop at Poklewski's feet. She screamed and turned away and he instinctively threw himself at her. He knocked her off her feet and both were falling through the air as the grenade detonated.

The blast caught him mainly in the back. Thousands of small metal shards shredded his flesh and he was killed almost instantly.

As the smoke cleared, one of the prostrate soldiers unslung his rifle and shot the Iraqi three times. The body jerked as each bullet struck. There was a loud shout of *Medic!* from somewhere and Stan grabbed his kit and ran over to the scene. Cunningham was lying still, his orange jumpsuit stained by a growing map of blood on his back. Poklewski was struggling to get out from under his body, screaming and shrieking.

The Boss and Barnes ran over to scene closely followed by the Brent. Barnes checked the Iraqi for any life. Stan was desperately trying to find a pulse on Cunningham and then turned him on his back.

He started CPR by thumping the dead man's chest. Wolfie joined him and, kneeling at by the head of the wounded man, began mouth-to-mouth resuscitation.

'Brent...' shouted the Boss 'do you have any medical resources with you?'

'Yeah, we do. Load him into the Suburban. We got medical facilities and a doctor in the Chinook.'

'Boss, I think he's a goner. There's no pulse.'

The Boss surveyed the scene. Poklewski was being bundled away towards the British vehicles, and the rest of the men were formed into an outward facing all round defence. The American vehicle was driving towards them.

'Keep trying Stan. We owe him that,' the Boss instructed.

The body was loaded into the open boot of the Suburban and Stan and Wolfie, climbed in. Stan kept up his compressions as the vehicle bounced and lurched its way back to the Americans. The Boss watched the short journey to the Chinook where the Americans were already preparing a stretcher.

Barnes broke the silence. 'Come on Boss. Let's go and have a brew.'

'Yeah...'

'There's no blame.'

'We should have searched the bodies.'

'It was the Rifles platoon. They weren't to know. It must have been the guard on the chair by the door. He would have had the grenade in his hand when they searched his body. They were involved in trying to save his life once they realised he was still alive.'

'John, you are right, of course. You usually are. But it doesn't make it easier. We had it in the bag and then we fucked it up.'

'We didn't fuck anything up, Boss. It was a text-book hostage release. Shit just happens.'

Banjo had two black mugs of tea ready for them. He put an avuncular arm around the Boss' shoulders.

'Nothing to be done about that Boss. Let's drive over to the Yanks, hand over the girl and collect Stan and Wolfie. Then we can fuck off home.'

33

Tuesday, 4 May 2004
Ramadi District
Ad Diwaniyah
2330 Local

Kassim Abdullah finished his sweet, mint tea and was preparing for bed. He was still in uniform, his government issue Glock 9mm in its holster at his right hip. With the increase in sectarian violence he never had it out of reach. The Mahdi had now begun to police the streets themselves and were enforcing a strict Sharia compliance. The real police were becoming targets and the Badr forces were, in turn, assassinating dozens of people a week in tit for tat killings. His department, the Serious Crime Unit, was among the most savage. He'd had enough.

He checked in on his wife, who had retired to bed early, and then he went to the kitchen. He opened the cupboard that housed the water boiler and extracted a small safe from behind the tank. He punched in the six-digit number and opened the thick door. He took out a wad of US dollars from his trouser pocket and put them into the safe. He estimated he now had sixty thousand US dollars, half of which had been paid to him by the British Military Government in Basra and half of which he had extorted from local businesses. When he reached a hundred thousand dollars, he would escape to Jordan with his wife and seek asylum at the British Embassy. He'd been promised protection from the British Government and he now considered his hometown of Diwaniyah too dangerous. Elements within both the Iraqi Badr movement and their sworn enemies, JAM, would both kill him instantly if they knew he was working for the British. As would the Iranians. He could no longer live with the stress and the pressure. He had to get out. He'd already been interrogated by the Badr about his capture by the British; why he was the only survivor; what had happened to the Iranian; how had they known where the safe house was. It was an unpleasant experience and he was sure he hadn't totally convinced them. It was only because he'd managed to give them the DVD of the interrogation that they didn't kill him there and then.

He closed the safe door and replaced it behind the boiler. Maybe another month. Perhaps two, at the most. He would have to increase his demands for protection money from the local shop keepers and traders.

He heard the dog from downstairs starting to bark. It was an annoying dirty creature, kept chained up in the courtyard mainly for security. He stopped to listen, but within seconds could hear nothing.

He turned to the bathroom, when he was startled by a large explosion, and turned to see a number of black clad men burst into his house through the front door. He instinctively reached for his Glock but was hit by six bullets in the chest. It was instantaneous. The hysterical and terrified screams of his wife failed to register in his already dying brain. He collapsed on the bathroom floor, the Glock still in the holster.

34

Thursday, 6 May 2004
DIS MOD Main Building
Whitehall London

'Morning all,' said the man in a charcoal grey suit as he entered the open plan office on the top floor of the Ministry of Defence. The suit had seen better days and was now straining under pressure from an expanding waist. 'Who wants a cup of coffee?' He put his hand through a mop of thick, dark brown, straight hair.

'Yes please,' said the younger man, David, sitting at a desk and listening to something through headphones.

'Well, take your fucking headphones off and go and make one. And whilst you're at it, a NATO standard no sugar for me. Bloody Nora, when was it that the junior officers stopped making the coffee?' He blew a couple of soft harrumphing raspberries through his lips and quizzically raised an eyebrow at the youngest member of the team. He was greeted with a raised middle finger.

'Swivel. And most of us are civilians. Actually, got some bad news from south of the River, Eric,' David said.

'Go on...' said Eric.

'Do you want to go and make your coffee first?'

'No. Tell me now.'

'The Americans have topped Clocktower.'

'You're fucking joking...'

'Nope. Last night. Standard house raid. Apparently, he raised his Glock when they went to question him about something or other.'

'Fucking Yanks. Every time. Just as we're getting something useful. I suppose he was dobbed in by one of theirs as working for the Iranians.'

'Well, he *was* working for the Iranians.'

'He was working for us. For Vauxhall. For me.' Eric's voice had risen in volume and pitch as his frustration came to the surface. 'It's taken me a year to get him close to the Quds. He was the bloke that got us an EFP. He fucking led us to the hostage release done by Hereford that we all had to pretend was the Americans. But no, Langley had to eliminate him.'

Eric stood there, thinking, his reading glasses perched on the end of his nose. His hand went back into the mop of hair.

David frowned as he watched Eric brush through his dark locks. 'Eric, do you dye your hair?'

'No, I do not. Is your suit made of plastic? Actually, I met him once. Years back. His real name was Kassim Abdullah al-Britanni and he did the Troop Leaders' course at Bovington.'

'Really? We trained him up?'

'Yup. Well, actually, he was fucking useless, if truth be known. They were fighting the Iranians then. His father was some minor diplomat in London. That's why they called him "al-Britanni". I don't think he wanted to be a soldier at all but a year being trained by us both fast tracked him up the ranks and kept him out of the bloodbath on the border.'

'You know, I'm still pretty sure the American head shed genuinely believes it was them that released the hostages,' David suggested.

'Course they do. As Winston Churchill said, "It's amazing what you can achieve if you let others take the credit".'

'Harry S Truman said that.'

'Said what?' asked Eric, absent-mindedly looking at a morning briefing paper.

'He said, "It is amazing what you can accomplish if you do not care who gets the credit".'

'Listen, whippersnapper, if I say it's fucking Churchill, you just have to say, "yes, Eric", OK?'

'You're such a dinosaur. If you are making coffee, white without. Thanks.'

'Fucking youth of today. Anyway, how did you know it was Truman?'

'I've got it written here on a card. You've used it before, so I checked it out.'

Eric blew more harrumphs as he headed off towards the kettle.

'Also, Eric?'

'Yes?'

'Vauxhall have sent you a package. I've put it on your desk.'

'Hold on, let me make my fucking coffee. Right, why's there no fucking milk? 'Kin civvies.'

Eric returned to his desk with the two coffees and gave one to David. He picked up the slim package from the internal mail service, slit it open and extracted a DVD. Turning it over with a puzzled expression, he slid it into his computer and it began to auto play. The scene showed a brightly lit room with a young man sitting at a table containing food spread out on several plates. He seemed to be drinking Coke and was wearing the orange boiler suit they all associated with allied prisoners captured by the insurgents. Eric pressed pause and turned up the volume.

'You might all want to watch this,' he said loudly, pausing the video. The rest of the office staff gathered around his desk.

He pressed play again. There was loud Middle Eastern music and garish video captions in Arabic. Then the music stopped abruptly.

The prisoner was looking away from the camera and a voice was suddenly heard, coming from someone else who was obviously in the room, too:

. . .

'WELCOME, MY FRIEND,' the voice said. '*Might you please tell me your name?*' Arabic subtitles appeared at the bottom of the screen.

'*First Lieutenant Eugene Cunningham of the 751ˢᵗ Medium Truck Company, the 105 Transport Battalion of the United States Army,*' came the prisoner's reply. He was now looking directly into the camera and the team of onlookers could see his face was bruised and swollen with one eye partially closed.

'Welcome, Lieutenant Cunningham,' said the unseen voice. '*Would you like something to eat or drink? We have some delicious fruit or maybe some coconut kleicha? We make the best in the world, you know, despite ten years of illegal sanctions.*'

'I'm good, thanks,' the prisoner replied, briefly scanning over the food in front of him.

'*Perhaps you would like a cigarette? Or maybe we can tempt you with some traditional mint tea?*' the voice said, but this time the prisoner didn't respond.

'*So, Lieutenant, tell me, what did you come to Iraq for? Was it to kill Iraqis?*'

'Yes, sir,' the prisoner said with a deadpan expression.

'*The War here is illegal, wouldn't you say?*'

There was no response from the prisoner as he continued to look directly into the camera.

The voice continued: '*You have killed mainly women and children, bombed the hospitals and imprisoned thousands of innocent civilians in your concentration camps. There you torture and murder them. The pictures will emerge very soon onto the internet for the world to witness your war crimes.*'

The prisoner shuffled on the chair slightly as he replied very clearly, '*My job is to deliver equipment for the Iraqi people. We are here to help the people of this country.*'

There was a very subtle pause before the voice said, '*But you admit that the Americans have killed civilians?*'

'*Well, sure. Some have been killed in the crossfire but the American*

Military very carefully stipulate in standing orders that we have to identify targets before we can engage. We follow orders.'

'*Has your government asked you to spy on the Iraqi people?*' asked the voice.

Eric noticed the prisoner's expression suddenly change, as though the question he'd been asked offended him. '*No, sir. I am not a spy.'*

'*You have been arrested by the Iraqi authorities and they are formalising charges of murder and espionage.*' Another slight pause, then '*Lieutenant Cunningham, you were arrested after your military unit opened fire on civilians in the town of Ad Diwaniyah.'*

'Yes, sir,' said the prisoner, and again Eric's eyes narrowed.

The voice continued: '*Your co-defendant, Private Alice Poklewski, has admitted to charges of murder, espionage and conspiracy. Her co-operation will perhaps save her from the death penalty. She freely admitted to her crimes. She was ordered by your generals to do these things against the Iraqis. We know that you are both working also for the Israelis.*' The unusual pronunciation of "Israelis" didn't escape any of the office staff's hearing.

There was another pause and the prisoner was now looking at the food in front of him.

'*She explained to us that she was forced to be your concubine and that she had no option but to obey orders. She is now grateful to be safe and she is being well looked after. Tell me, Lieutenant, do you think that your war is illegal?*'

'*You are wrong there, this war was sanctioned by the UN,*' the prisoner replied, turning his head slightly from a stream of smoke that seemed to drift into view, most likely from a cigarette.

'*But there was no vote for war. Not even the French would support the American call for Crusade. The Americans have tried to command their lackeys to vote with them but even they refused. You are not here for the UN. You are not wearing blue helmets. Your tanks are not painted white. The UN does not allow for helicopter gunships shooting into towns.'*

There was silence from the prisoner as the smoke suddenly disappeared from view.

'The evidence is incontrovertible, my friend. Where are your weapons of mass destruction? There are none. It is well known. Even Mr Blix denied any such weapons. Yet the Americans gave us an ultimatum to disarm or face invasion. Tell me, Lieutenant, how do you disarm if you have no weapons?'

'I don't know,' the prisoner replied after a few beats. 'I'm just a trucking officer in the National Guard.'

'So you agree with me and the rest of the world that this war is illegal. The UN have already declared it illegal. Millions of concerned citizens around the world are protesting at the American war crimes. They know the American government wages war by killing civilians. You did so in Vietnam.'

'I wasn't in Vietnam.' The prisoner's deadpan expression materialised again.

'But you freely admit that this war is illegal. The UN did not sanction the invasion of Iraq. There was not even a vote for them to lose. That is a fact, my friend.'

'Yes, sir. If you say so,' the prisoner responded, his voice slightly quieter than before.

'I can understand your frustration at your criminal government and in the great Satan, Bush and his little Devil friend, Bliar.' Eric's eyebrows shot up at the unfortunate mispronunciation of "Blair". The voice added, 'The people of America will one day rise up and overthrow their tyrant leaders.'

The prisoner then leaned forward and helped himself to some food and a can of Coke.

'Please. Help yourself,' the voice said. 'You are our guest in our house. The Americans are running death squads in the towns that kill any civilians they encounter. Can you tell me what you know about these?'

'For sure. That's who we are. That's what we do.' Eric looked at David and mouthed *What the fuck?*

'There is very compelling evidence that the Americans are paying the leaders of these death squads.'

But the prisoner seemed unconcerned now as he helped himself to a banana. And with that last clip, the video ended, playing more music and displaying further graphics.

'IT'S GOOD. But it's fake,' said David.

'Course it's fake,' Eric agreed. 'Doesn't matter if it's fake, though. It's circulating and it'll go viral on the net. People will believe this crap.' He looked inside the envelope that had contained the DVD. 'Apparently, this was sent to the government by the Daily Mirror. They're looking for a comment. It was bought by one of their reporters in a street market in Bradford. Fucking hell.'

'Let's not forget, either,' David pointed out, 'that the Mirror published the pissing photographs last Friday.'

'They were fucking fakes, too,' said Eric.

'I know that. Just saying someone needs to get on to the Mirror and stop them making the same mistake again.'

'MOD should do that. Whether it'll work, God knows. I some- times wonder who's fucking side our press are on. What else have we got then?'

Eric looked at his morning summary from the Foreign Office.

'Here we bloody well go again.' He held up the piece of paper, and his glasses, which were still perched halfway down his nose, made him have to tip his head back to read.

'"US General admits at least 3 prisoners killed by U.S. personnel in Iraq. (US newspaper USA Today) - US Army officials acknowledged that three detainees have been killed, including one who was trying to escape, and 10 other cases of prisoner deaths are under investigation. The killings were uncovered by army criminal investigators who had been asked to look at 35 cases, including the deaths of 25 prisoners in Iraq and Afghanistan since December 2002". It gets better: "US forces killed three civilians in Bagh- dad. (Iraqi newspaper Al-Mashriq) - US forces killed three Iraqis by mistake in Al-Taji district to the north of Baghdad. It was reported that the victims were in a car when one of the passengers tried to light a cigarette using a pistol-like lighter, the US soldiers thought it was a real gun and started shooting". And, of course: "Demonstration in front of the Abu

Ghuraib prison. (Iraqi newspaper Al- Mashriq) - Hundreds of Iraqis staged demonstrations called for by the Muslim Ulema Council in front of Abu Ghuraib prison, protesting the mistreatment and humiliation of the Iraqi detainees by the US forces".'

Eric put the paper down and laughed out loud. 'It really is truly amazing. Who have we got to replace Clocktower? Is Highwire ready yet, do you think?'

35

Monday, 14 June 2004
Agricultural and Industrial Credit Bank
Northern Nicosia
Turkish Republic of Northern Cyprus.
1430 Local

The man stepped through the smoked glass doors and into the cold air-conditioned interior of the bank. It was as reported and he saw no visible CCTV. He was towing behind him by its handle a cabin-baggage suitcase on wheels as he approached the bored-looking teller behind the glass partition.

'I would like to make a cash deposit into my account, please,' he informed her.

The lady looked up with a false smile. 'How much would you like to deposit?'

'Four million, one hundred and fifty thousand US dollars, please,' said the man.

'Do you have the money with you, sir?'

'Yes, I do. In this case.'

'And you say it is in cash?'

'Yes, it is. In US dollars. Hundred-dollar bills.'

'Come with me, please.' She got up from her seat and went to a door that led out into the public part of the bank. She then rang a silent bell and waited by a second door. It was opened by a man in a suit and she went in, beckoning the man to follow. They went into a small office with a table, three office chairs and a computer. The teller left them and went back to the front of the bank.

'Have a seat please. You say you have an account with us?'

'Yes, I do.' The man opened his wallet and took out a bank debit card. 'The account name, number, and SWIFT code is on there.'

'Can you tell me where this money has come from, sir?'

'I run a real estate business. We've sold a villa to a Russian client who wanted to pay in cash.'

'We have to make checks on the money. Standard procedure to ensure the serial numbers are not listed and the currency is not counterfeit. I can see that you opened this account in London about ten weeks ago.'

'Correct,' the man said.

'May I see the money?'

'Yes.' He pulled the wheeled suitcase up onto the table and unzipped it. He showed the contents to the banker who reached inside and took three bundles. Each was an inch thick and contained one hundred, one-hundred-dollar notes, making a total of ten thousand US dollars each. He examined the wrapping and then extracted a note from each of the three. He then examined the watermark carefully before opening a programme on the computer and typing in the serial numbers.

'The name of your company is Alphaboat 4 and it's a GBL2 registered in Mauritius?'

'Correct,' said the man.

'Please come with me. We need to count the money.' The banker rose from his chair and led the man out of the small room to an open plan office where six or seven people were working at their computers. He opened the case and cut the paper wrappers from each of the bundles and loaded them into an automatic counting and weighing machine. The machine flicked rapidly through the notes and then re-banded them with a paper wrapper. At the end of the procedure, the red LED said *USD4150000*. He placed the bundles neatly in a plastic tray and logged into a computer on a spare desk.

'The serial numbers are not listed here as stolen. Would you like us to take the transfer fee from the overall amount or will you be paying separately?'

'Please take it from the aggregate amount.'

'Certainly, sir.' He pressed a button and the large printer in the room whined and spat out two sheets of paper.

'Please sign here and here. All I need now is to see your passport.'

The man took out a British passport from his breast pocket and showed it.

'I will need to take a photocopy,' the banker said, taking the passport from the man's hand.

'Sure.'

He then went over to the printer again and photocopied the passport. He clipped this to the signed form and put it in the plastic tray with the cash.

'I think we are now complete. The money will show in your account in three days' time. This copy is for you.' He handed the man the second signed copy of the transfer form.

'Thank you,' the man said and rose from his seat, taking the empty suitcase with him. He was shown out of the room and then back into the public part of the bank. The original teller didn't look up. He stepped out of the doors into the searing Cypriot sun and walked across the road and down a side street where he got into the passenger side of a Toyota Corolla that had Southern Cyprus plates and an international car hire company's sticker in the back window.

He settled into the passenger's seat and looked at the driver.

'Well...there's no going back now.'

'I hope you fucking know what you're doing, Boss. We've crossed the Rubinon to the dark side.'

'Trust me. I'm a Rupert. And it's the Rubicon.'

GLOSSARY OF ACRONYMS AND SLANG

50: Browning belt fed machine gun, half inch calibre also 'fifty cal' (US)

ACORN: Military Intelligence Officer (UK)

AK47: Automatic Assault Rifle. 7.62 short calibre (Sov)

AlphaCharlie: Ass Chewing. Slang for verbal reprimand (US)

Anaconda: US Supply depot north of Baghdad

ASR: Alternate Supply Route

AvGas: Aeroplane Fuel

AWACS: Boeing RC135 Airborne Early Warning and Control planes

Barclaycard: Franchi SPAS12 12 gauge gas operated shotgun. 'Opens any door' (UK)

Basha: Military slang for field bivouac (UK)

Belt Kit: Webbing belt that carried essential water, magazine, first aid and 24 hours rations. (UK)

Bergen: Military slang Backpack (UK)

BFPO: British Forces Post Office (UK)

BFT: Blue Force Tracker. GPS tracking for vehicles (US)

BIAP: Baghdad International Airport

BLR: Beyond Local Repair (UK)

BMP: Soviet tracked armoured personnel carrier (SOV)

Bobtail: Tractor not pulling a trailer (US)

Box 800: Slang for Secret Intelligence Service/MI6 (UK)

Bradley: Tracked Armoured vehicle (US)

BUP: Battle Update Briefing held daily on most bases (US)

CAS: Close Air Support normally a plane or helicopter providing fire (US)

Casevac: Medical Evacuation of a casualty (UK)

CENTCOM: Central Command (US)

CHU: Containerised Housing Unit. Accommodation made from containers

CIMIC: Civilian Military Co-Operation. Part of the Iraqi reconstruction effort

Claymore: Remote Operated anti-personnel mine

Click: Kilometre

CLS: Combat Life Saver. Designated medic (US)

Colt Canada: L119A1 assault rifle. 5.56 calibre (formerly Diemaco AR15s) (UK)

Compo: Military slang for field rations (UK)

CPA: Coalition Provisional Authority, based in the Green Zone Baghdad

Crab Air: Royal Air Force (UK)

D30: Old Soviet Artillery Gun

DFAC: Dining Facility on base (US)

Dhobi: Military slang for laundry (UK)

DIS: Defence Intelligence Staff. London based Intelligence analysts for MOD

DPV: Desert Patrol Vehicle – modified Landrovers. (UK)

DShK: Soviet Heavy Machine Gun. 12.7mm calibre, belt fed (Sov)

Dzik: Armoured Personnel Carrier (POL)

EFP: Explosively Formed Penetrator or anti-tank bomb

Expectant: Casualty that is probably going to die

Fedayeen: Iraqi Paramilitary Group loyal to Saddam Hussein

FGA: Fighter Ground Attack

FNG: The Fucking New Guy (US)

FOB: Forward Operating Base (US)

Fobbit: Military slang for someone who never leaves an FOB (US)

FRV: Final Rendezvous

GAU8: 20mm gatling gun mounted on an air frame

GBL: Global Business Licence issued to foreign companies based in Mauritius

Gonk: Slang for sleeping (UK)

GPMG: General Purpose Machine Gun. Belt fed 7.62 calibre. (UK)

Green Army: Non special forces soldiers (UK)

Green Slime: Military slang for the Intelligence Corps (UK)

Grunt: Military slang for an infantryman (US)

GSW: Gunshot Wound

Haji: Military slang for an Iraqi (US)

IED: Improvised Explosive Device – Home-made bomb

IP: Iraqi Police

ISCI: Islamic Supreme Council of Iraq

ISG: Iraq Survey Group. Group with Overall Responsibility for Interrogation (UK)

JFIT: Joint Forward Interrogation Team

JSOC: Joint Special Operations Command

KBR: Kellog Root Brown. Private military contractor part of Halliburton

Khams: Iraqi extended families or tribes

KIA: Killed in Action

Kiowa: Bell OH58A Kiowa four seat observation helicopter

Link: Belted machine gun ammunition

LN: Local National i.e. Iraqi (US)

LocStat: Location Status or position on the ground

LZ: Helicopter Landing Zone

M1: Abrams Main Battle Tank (US)

M1078: General Purpose medium sized truck (US)

M16: Standard issue assault rifle. 5.56 calibre. Aka Armalite (US)

M19: Automatic belt fed grenade launcher (US)

M203: Underslung Grenade Launcher for a rifle. Usually an M16 (US)

M242: Chain gun 25mm calibre (US)

M915: Tractor. The Workhorse of the convoy system (US)

M998: High Mobility Multipurpose Wheeled Vehicle or 'Humvee' (US)

MBE: Member of the Order of the British Empire. Honorary medal (UK)

Medivac: Medical Evacuation of a casualty (US)

Menacity: Supacat HMT400 Surveillance and Recon Vehicle Offensive Action

Minimi: Belt fed machine gun 5.56mm calibre

MO: Medical Officer or doctor (UK)

MOD: Ministry of Defence (UK)

MRE: Meals Ready to Eat.

MSR: Main Supply Route (US)

MSS: Mission Support Site (US)

MTS: Movement Tracking System. GPS and communications for vehicles (US)

MWR: Morale, Welfare and Recreation. Leisure centre on base (US)

NCO: Non Commissioned Officer

NLAW: Next Generation Anti-Tank Weapon. Hand held (UK)

NVG: Night Vision Goggles (UK)

OIF: Operation Iraqi Freedom (US)

OP: Observation Post

Pad: Slang for a married soldier (UK)

PID: Positive Identification of a target prior to shooting

PIG: Obsolete Armoured Personnel Carrier (UK)

PRC 319: Secure manpack radio (UK)

PUFO(ing): Military slang to go home. 'Pack Up and Fuck Off'

QGM: Queen's Gallantry Medal. Medal for bravery (UK)

QM: Quarter Master (UK)

QRF: Quick Reaction Force

REMF: Rear Echelon Muthafucker. Slang for non-combat troops (US)

Reveille: Time to get up (UK)

Rivet Joint: Airborne Intelligence gathering plane made by Boeing (US)

RMP: Royal Military Police (UK)

RON: Rest Overnight

Route Irish: Road between BIAP and CPA

RPG: Rocket Propelled Grenade (SOV)

RPK: Light belt fed machine gun 7.62 calibre (SOV)

RTB: Return to Base

Rupert: Slang for an officer (UK)

SAPI: Small Arms Protective Insert. Body armour plates (US)

SAW: Squad Automatic Weapon 5.56 mm calibre (US)

Scooby Doo: Military (rhyming) slang for clue (UK)

Semtex: Plastic Explosive

SF: Special Forces

Shemagh: Male headscarf common in the middle east

Sherman: Military slang. Sherman tank, yank. (UK)

Sig Sauer: Automatic pistol. 9mm calibre

SigInt: Intelligence gleaned from eavesdropping on radio traffic

SOP: Standard Operating Procedure

Stag: Guard Duty for security (UK)

Stryker: 8 Wheeled Armoured Personnel Carrier (UK)

Swede: Military slang. Head or face (UK)
T55: Soviet Main Battle Tank (SOV)
TacBe: ARI-23237 Personal Tactical Beacon (UK/US)
TAOR: Tactical Area of Responsibility
TCN: Third Country National (US)
TCP: Tactical Control Point. Military presence on a road
Terps: Military slang for an Interpreter (US)
TOC: Tactical Operations Centre (US)
UAV: Unmanned Aerial Vehicle or drone (US)
UGL: Underslung Grenade Launcher (UK)
UH60: Sikorsky Black Hawk helicopter (US)
Ulu: 'Upstream' in Malay. Military slang for wilderness (UK)
VBIED: Vehicle Borne Improvised Explosive Device
Warrior: Tracked Infantry Fighting Vehicle (UK)
WMD: Weapons of Mass Destruction
Zero: Radio callsign for the unit commander (UK)

ABOUT THE AUTHOR

'Scott Leigh' was an officer in the British Army for 10 years. He was commissioned into a Challenger Regiment before passing Selection for Special Forces. He spent a number of years spent as a Troop Commander with the Special Air Service and a tour commander with BRIXMIS.

Since leaving the Army he has established a successful business career and is a director of a number of companies that operate in this country and in frontier markets in tropical Africa.

He is married with two children and divides his time between Oxfordshire and London.

Printed in Great Britain
by Amazon

5c7e31fa-183a-4944-8a80-8ceb076668beR01